COWBOY CLASSIFIEDS

Cowboy
SEEKING
SOMEONE
TO LOVE

JANICE WHITEAKER

CHAPTER ONE

CAMILLE TURNED SIDEWAYS to avoid banging her knuckles on the frame of the door.

Again.

She carried the heavy box marked with bold black letters into the open-concept kitchen Nora designed for the home she and Brooks built on their spot at Red Cedar Ranch.

The two-story house was stunning. All clean lines and light and airy spaces.

Which wasn't a surprise. Nora was amazingly skilled at making a house into a home everyone wanted to call their own.

"I told you to leave that box for one of the boys." Maryann gave her a stern look.

"It's not that heavy." Camille slowly squatted down toward the floor, squeezing every muscle she owned to make sure the box gently slid onto the hand-scraped laminate Nora put through the whole space.

"It's absolutely that heavy." Maryann lifted a brow. "And I know damn well at least one of my boys was out there."

One of them definitely was.

The same one Camille did her best to ignore every time their paths accidentally crossed.

Which seemed to happen daily.

She worked the folded flaps of the box open. "It's really not that bad."

Maryann stared down into the box, her hands slowly coming to her hips.

Nora suddenly slid between them, cutting off Maryann's view of the cast iron skillets stacked inside the box. "Would you and Bill have time to go pick up the pizza I ordered?"

Maryann sighed. "We'd be happy to, dear." She patted Nora on the shoulder as she turned. "Call me if you need us to get anything else."

Nora kept her body between Camille and Maryann. "I think I have everything else. Thank you so much." She stayed put until Maryann was gone, the front door clicking closed behind the Pace family's matriarch.

"Thank you." Camille stood up, a pan in each hand.

Nora snagged them away, turning to slide the skillets onto the open shelving of the wide island centered in the large kitchen. "She's not wrong."

"It's not that big of a deal." Camille grabbed two more pans, passing them to Nora.

"It's starting to be a big deal." Nora gave her the same lifted-brow look Maryann had given her minutes earlier. "We've talked about this."

They had.

At length.

"It's not as easy as everyone seems to think it is." The whole situation was complicated as hell.

They were family.

She was an employee.

There was a difference.

Clara, Mae, and Nora were Maryann's daughters-in-law.

Camille was the woman who ran The Inn.

No matter what anyone else thought, there was a line between them, and it should probably stay there.

Otherwise complicated could turn to disastrous.

Camille passed over the last pan before grabbing the empty box and going to work collapsing it down so it could be stacked into the back of the trailer with the rest of the boxes they'd emptied over the last two days.

It was the third move-in they'd done this year.

First was Brody and Clara. Then Mae and Boone. Now Nora and Brooks.

Three out of four of the Pace boys were happily paired off and it was only a matter of time before the fourth followed suit.

"That was the last box from the trailer." Camille headed for the front door.

"Don't you dare." Nora pointed right at her. "If you disappear I will hunt you down, hogtie you and drag your happy ass back here."

"I should get back to The Inn. Make sure everything's okay." It was her job.

Her place.

"I'm not kidding, Camille." The look on Nora's face paled anything Maryann had managed to shoot her way. "We will come for you." She rounded the peninsula separating the kitchen from the large family room at the front of the house. "You're staying for the party, just like everyone else is." She snagged the box from Camille's hands. "You helped just as much as everyone else did. Maybe even more."

"It's my jo—"

"I swear to God if you say 'it's my job' one more time I might lose my shit."

Camille clamped her lips together.

Because somewhere along the way Nora went from a city girl with self-doubt to a woman she wouldn't cross.

It made her a little jealous.

No. Not jealous. She was happy for Nora. Happy that her friend finally found where she belonged in the world.

Envious.

Camille was envious of Nora's confidence in her new life.

Among other things.

"Now." Nora huffed out a breath, plastering on a smile. "Let's just relax and enjoy the rest of the day."

It looked like she might be stuck. Caught between the fine line of friendship and boundaries she tried hard not to overstep. "Okay."

Camille stuck her hands in the pockets of her cut-off jean shorts, rocking back on her heels. "Your house looks really good."

"Thank you." Nora reached out to grab the front of Camille's yellow t-shirt. "I really like your shirt."

"Thank you." Camille smiled a little. "I thought of you when I got it."

Yellow was Nora's favorite color and it was tastefully spread around the house in throw pillows, area rugs, and towels.

"Do you want something to drink?" Nora backed into the kitchen where she'd been working on wiping down the counters in preparation for tonight's move-in celebration.

"I'm okay." She fully intended to find a way to sneak out of here. It felt wrong to butt into what was clearly a family festivity.

Nora opened the door to the fridge. "Are you sure? I've got lemonade—"

Mae came in through the back door, one of Clara and Brody's three-month-old twins tucked into one arm. "Does anyone see the diaper bag?"

Nora snorted out a laugh from where she was still perusing the refrigerator. "Auntie Mae strikes again."

"Why do they always crap their pants the second I pick them up?" Mae wandered around the kitchen, eyes scanning the space. "I'm going to get a complex about it if they don't quit."

"You just make them comfortable." Camille smiled at the bright blue eyes staring at her from the crook of Mae's arm. "Isn't that right, Ella Bella?"

"I think she just likes to watch me gag while I try to change her." Mae moved to the living room as she continued her search. "I think these two are going to be just as much trouble as the other two." She straightened, shooting a grin Nora and Camille's way. "Makes me proud."

Nora carried a pitcher of lemonade to the butcher block counter. "They do have a reputation to uphold around here."

The Pace boys, now the Pace men, had caused their fair share of stirs in Moss Creek over the years. "Their dad and uncles are pretty well-known."

A slow smile spread across Nora's face. "I wasn't talking about the Pace men."

No. She probably wasn't.

It was one of the main reasons Camille would never really fit in around here, even if she wanted to.

One of these things wasn't like the others.

And she was the thing.

Clara, Mae, and Nora were all the kind of women who stood up for themselves. Stood up for the people they loved.

She'd never done either of those things.

Camille backed toward the front door, taking advantage of the poop-induced distraction. "I'm going to go check on Calvin."

Mae looked up from where she sat on the sectional that was delivered to the space the day before, doing her best to work Ella out of the singlet snapped over her diaper. "You better not disappear."

"I already told her we'd hogtie her and bring her back so we could force-feed her pizza and fun." Nora cringed as Mae opened Ella's diaper. "Holy hell. How does she turn milk into that?"

Mae gagged, leaning back to suck in a quick breath before going in with a handful of wipes.

Camille seized the opportunity and quietly backed out the front door.

"Hey."

Clara's bright voice sent her spinning in place.

Brody's wife smiled up at her from the base of the stairs leading to the front porch. "Where ya goin'?"

"I was going to check on Calvin." Camille glanced down at the baby in Clara's arms, unable to resist smiling at the little girl's angelic face. "Mae has Ella inside."

"Oh good." Without warning Clara came up the stairs and dumped Ella's twin sister, Faith, into Camille's arms. "Can you hold this one so I can pee?" She didn't wait for an answer, just ducked inside the house.

Leaving Camille standing on the porch with a baby.

A baby that made it all but impossible to sneak away.

She sighed, starting to bounce a little as she swayed from side to side. "What am I supposed to do now?"

Faith stared up at her with the same bright blue eyes her daddy and sisters had.

And uncles for that matter.

They were a Pace family trait it seemed no one escaped.

"Well." Camille looked around for anyone she could pass Faith off to, but her options were slimmer than slim.

They were none.

"Shit." She had work to do. A job the Paces paid her to perform.

And no one would really realize she wasn't there. They were all just being nice. And no matter how many times she explained they didn't have to be, they continued on because clearly the Paces were polite to a fault.

"Let's go find someone else to hold you." Camille made her way down the steps and around to the back of the house. "Where's your daddy?" She expected everyone else to be behind the house since they weren't out front.

Unfortunately, that's not what she found.

"Hey, Mom." Calvin waved, grinning wide as he ran her way, smile holding as all his attention went to the baby chewing on her already soggy fists. "Hey, Faithy."

"Have you seen Brody?" Camille resisted the urge to look around.

Nothing good would come of that.

"He went with Uncle Brooks and Uncle Boone to go get the stuff for the party we're having." Calvin hooked one of his fingers in Faith's small fist. "Are you having fun with Aunt Camille?"

It took everything she had not to react.

Not to do anything that might steal her son's joy.

He'd had so little of it in his life.

Mostly because of her.

Calvin's eyes snapped up to hers. "Wanna watch us practice football?"

This was the hardest part of being here.

She knew her place.

Knew her purpose on Red Cedar Ranch.

But her son seemed to have fallen into a spot she didn't know how to pull him from.

He believed he was one of them. A member of the family kind enough not to tell him any differently.

Keeping Calvin from overstepping without breaking his heart was a battle she constantly fought.

And would never win.

"Only for a minute." Camille reached out to swipe at her son's sandy blond hair. "Then I need to get back to The Inn."

"No you don't." Calvin said it matter-of-factly. "Mimi said you were taking the night off."

"Cal. You're up, Buddy."

The deep voice calling to Calvin tested her willpower.

Her commitment to maintaining some sense of respectability.

Reasonability.

"Gotta go." Calvin turned and raced away, stopping beside Wyatt, the soft boyishness of his face turning serious as he faced Brett.

Brett immediately sent the football Calvin's way, putting it exactly where her son stood, making it easy to catch, even for a boy who'd never touched a ball in his life.

Brett clapped, beaming. "Great catch." He held both hands out.

Like he thought Calvin might be able to get the ball back to him.

Camille cringed when her son leaned back, one arm stretching as he tried to return the football.

Not tried.

Did.

Calvin shot the ball right into Brett's outstretched hands.

Brett caught it like it wasn't a complete miracle the ball made it to its destination. "Perfect." His attention turned to Wyatt as he sent the ball Wyatt's way.

Camille blinked a few times, trying to wrap her mind around what she just saw.

It had to be a fluke.

Luck.

Calvin hadn't played any sports outside of gym class at school. The reasons for that were numerous and painful.

But ultimately that was her fault too.

She held her breath as Brett tossed the ball Calvin's way. Once again, her son caught the perfect throw.

And once again he returned the favor.

"Let's take a little break." Brett rested one hand on his back, arching his spine. "I'm an old man. I get worn out easy."

Calvin cackled, grabbing his belly as he laughed. "You're not old."

Her son was right.

Brett was the opposite of old.

He was the youngest of the Pace boys. Barely twenty-five.

Practically a baby.

A baby that was coming right for her.

Camille took a step back. There was no way to avoid it.

There were certain things she needed to remember in this new life she had.

One. She was an employee. Not a friend. Not a member of the family.

An employee.

Two. This one was the most important. Brett Pace was not and never would be interested in her.

She was too old.

Too divorced.

Too broken to offer any of what a man like him would want.

No. Not a man.

She could not start thinking of him as a man. He was a baby.

Too young.

Brett wanted someone his own age.

Someone with no kids.

No baggage.

"What do you have there?" Brett's eyes fixed on Camille's face, locking her feet in place as he continued to advance on her.

"Clara needed me to hold Faith so she could go to the bathroom."

Brett's steps slowed as he got closer, his eyes finally moving to where Faith stared up at him. "You hit the jackpot, little girl."

"Do you want to hold her?" Camille didn't wait for an answer. She immediately started trying to pass Faith off to her uncle. Unfortunately it required a single step in Brett's already close direction.

And that single step went right into a dip in the freshly-worked ground.

A dip she wasn't prepared to navigate.

The change in elevation immediately threw off her balance, sending her tipping to one side.

"I got ya." Brett wrapped both arms around her, pinning Faith between them as he held her tight, his blue eyes steady as they held hers.

And damn it if she didn't stare up into them like one of the women she read about nearly every night.

It was a terrible thing to have happen.

She worked so hard to stay away from this man.

Ignore the things he made her want to think she deserved to feel.

To know.

Camille planted her feet, fighting for a steadiness she definitely didn't feel. "I'm okay."

14

But Brett didn't let her go. His arms stayed right where they were as he somehow managed to come even closer. "You sure? Don't want you to get hurt here." He gave her a slow smile that warmed every part of her body. Including the parts she was pretty sure might be DOA. "I don't know where Nora keeps the Band-Aids."

The reminder of their first real interaction was unnecessary.

The moment was one that replayed in her mind daily.

It was the beginning of her problematic situation with Brett.

He'd been so gentle. So sweet. Cleaned up and bandaged a cut she had on her finger before dealing with the mess from the broken dish that caused the injury.

It was also the day she found out he was the one on the other end of the walkie talkie Calvin was never without.

Which would also be a problem if she let herself think about it too long.

One more reason she could not allow herself to think about Brett Pace.

The baby.

"I'm fine." Camille meant to step away from him.

Meant to stop looking up into the set of eyes so blue they could blend in with the sky.

Meant to remind herself this man was not looking for an instant family.

A used woman.

And she was about as used as it got.

It's all Junior had ever done. Used her.

She cleaned his house. Cooked his food.

Made his excuses.

Given him any money she managed to make.

And it was never enough to keep him from dishing out his drunken rage by the fistful.

The thought of him was enough to turn any warmth in her to ice.

At least she finally had the reminder she needed.

Camille dropped her eyes and backed away. "I should go find Clara." She turned away, moving faster, upset and embarrassment warring over which would get to make her look more foolish.

Nora came out the back door right as Camille rushed toward the house. She smiled, but her expression was uncertain. "Everything okay?"

"I just forgot something." Camille didn't waste time passing Faith Nora's way. "I'll be right back."

It was a lie. They both knew it.

She'd told it a million times.

Camille hurried up the side of the house, ignoring the pinch in her ankle as Brett called after her.

She couldn't go back. Not now.

So she walked faster, her steps turning to what might be called a run as she rushed to her car, falling inside and backing out as fast as she could.

But she made one more mistake as she pulled away.

She looked in the rearview mirror.

And what she saw there sent her stomach to her feet.

Brett stood in front of Nora and Brooks' new house, arms crossed over his wide chest as he watched her go.

Watched her run from him.

From the inappropriate emotions she couldn't seem to stop.

But Brett didn't look mad at her hasty and possibly rude retreat.

He looked...

Determined. Focused.

Intense in a way she wasn't used to.

Brett was always so relaxed. So easygoing.

And the man watching her kick up rock didn't look either of those.

Camille gripped the wheel of the new used car she'd bought with her own money.

Money she earned because of the kindness of the Pace family.

And she needed to show them how much she appreciated all they'd done for her.

That was why she was going back to The Inn.

It was her job.

It was what was keeping her son fed and housed and safe.

It was what had to be her top priority.

She let out a little breath as she pulled into her parking spot at The Inn, relaxing in spite of the chaos waiting for her inside.

The Inn had taken off and they were fully booked most of the time.

It was doing so well they'd been able to hire a full-time chef for the meals, which meant she could focus on housekeeping and scheduling which was a full-time job all by itself.

Maybe more than.

Mariah was in the kitchen when Camille went in, standing over a pan of sizzling pork chops. Her red brows came together as she frowned Camille's way. "What are you doing back already?"

"We got everything moved in." Camille hooked her car keys inside the utility closet just off the kitchen before making her way back to where her friend was preparing dinner for the weekend's guests. "So I came back to see what needed done here."

Mariah didn't appear any less confused by the explanation. "I thought you were gone for the night."

Camille opened one of the dishwashers and went to work loading in the few items from the sink. "Why would you think that?"

"Because Maryann told me you would be." Mariah wiped her hands on the apron across her front. "I can get those."

"Don't worry about it." Camille finished racking up the cups and utensils before grabbing a dishrag and going to work on the counters. "It's my job."

She had to keep saying it.

Keep repeating the fact until there was no disputing it.

Because forgetting her place here wasn't an option.

CHAPTER TWO

BRETT TURNED FROM watching Camille drive away to find a line of Pace women staring him down.

Nora had her arms crossed as she glared his way. "Good job. She was gonna stay until you screwed it all up."

"I really thought we had her with the baby." Clara shifted Faith in her arms. "Next time we should get her to hold both of them."

"Next time someone needs to stay the hell away from her." Mae's scowl was the deepest and it was focused solely on him. "You spooked her."

"She almost fell. What did you want me to do? Let her hit the ground with Faith?" Brett glanced back at the trail of dusty air still lingering from Camille's retreat.

"You wouldn't have been able to touch her if you hadn't already been so close."

Nora's accurate assessment of the situation sent him spinning back toward them. "You shouldn't spy on people."

"You shouldn't push people who aren't ready." Mae came right back at him.

It had been a year.

More than.

A year of waiting. Watching Camille find her metaphorical footing. Watching her get her bearings in the new life she had.

He was proud as hell of her, but it was becoming more than a little clear she wasn't looking too far ahead of the path she was on.

Wasn't seeing all the possibilities that really lay in front of her.

"I didn't push her." Brett stalked past his sisters-in-law on his way to the backyard. "I caught her."

He found Calvin and Wyatt in the backyard, still working on the skills they'd been practicing all spring. "How's it going, boys?"

"Did my mom leave?" Calvin's disappointment was obvious.

"I think she had to run back to The Inn, Buddy." Brett hated the way Cal's face fell.

Because while Camille might not realize she was one of them, her son most definitely did.

Calvin knew he was part of this family. Knew he was loved. Taken care of.

Protected.

Unfortunately his mother was struggling to see things for what they were.

"Will she come back?" The question carried a hopeful edge that stuck in Brett's gut.

"I don't know." He patted Calvin's shoulder. "I'm sure she will if she can."

Cal nodded, his eyes dropping to the ground.

This was the hardest part of all of it. Watching a little boy who knew his momma was hurting and that there was nothing he could do to help her.

The sound of a horn honking dragged Brett's attention from Cal. "Sounds like Mimi and Pop are back." He snagged the football from Wyatt. "They're gonna need some extra hands."

"Okay." Both boys immediately took off, running toward the front of the new house Brooks built for the woman he loved.

Brett glanced up at the two-story ready to be filled with kids and noise and chaos.

All the things he'd wanted for as long as he could remember.

He pulled his baseball cap off, raking one hand through his hair. "Hell."

It looked like he was gonna have to keep wanting.

Keep waiting.

Brett kicked at the dirt as he followed the boys toward the front, tossing the ball off as he went. By the time he got there, both boys were loaded up with pizza boxes. His brothers had pulled in right behind his parents and Brody, Boone, and Brooks were each carrying in the large trays their mother used for side-dishes and desserts. Brett went to the back of Brody's truck and pulled out a vat of macaroni salad before falling in line with his brothers.

Nora was inside, lining the trays down the wide surface of the center island. It could easily hold the massive amounts of food it took to feed their family and the wide walkways around it left plenty of room for buffet-style serving. She'd clearly thought the kitchen out, making sure it was perfect for the way they lived.

His mother came in with a few bags of chips in her arms. Her gaze immediately snapped around the space. "Where's Camille?"

Every eye in the room came his way.

"She went back to The Inn." Brett pulled back the clear film from the pasta he carried in.

His mother propped one hand on her hip. "What did you do?"

"She almost fell. I made sure she didn't." How in the hell was he the one in trouble for this? "Then she left."

His mother huffed out a breath. "You spooked her."

Mae pointed at Maryann. "That's what I said."

"She's not a horse." Brett went to the next tray of food and lifted the wrap covering it, tucking it at the backside of the mac and cheese. "Why am I the one who spooked her?" He lifted his brows at the women standing together on the opposite side of the island. "You three aren't exactly subtle."

His mother pointed to the front door. "Go get her."

Brett moved to the tray of baked beans, folding back the foil wrapped tight across the top.

"Did you hear me?" His mother's tone was sharp.

He glanced up to see who she was talking to, only to find his mother's lifted brow stare was directed straight at him. "You want *me* to go get her?"

"You're the one who ran her off."

"Then I'm the last person who should go get her." He'd been here before. Gotten a little too close too fast.

Paid the price because of it.

Camille wouldn't even look his way for three weeks after he bandaged her cut finger. He wasn't going back to that.

The best thing he could do was let her be. Give her a little space.

"Just go tell her you're sorry for whatever you did." Maryann leaned close as Calvin and Wyatt came in from washing their hands in the bathroom. "Fix it."

He'd tried.

They all had.

"If she doesn't want to be here we can't make her." That was what it really came down to.

Camille was a grown woman. If she didn't want to be a part of their family then she should be allowed to make that choice.

Unfortunately his mother definitely didn't share that opinion. "Go get her."

Brett wiped one hand down his face. "Fine." He fished out the keys to his truck. "But don't blame me when this makes it all worse."

There was no good answer to any of this.

His mother had the best of intentions. She wanted to give Camille the unconditional love she deserved. Wanted Camille to see she had a whole line of people ready to support her. Take care of her.

Keep her safe.

But so far any attempt they'd made had fallen on deaf ears.

Which made him think maybe Camille wasn't all that interested in their particular brand of love and support.

It wasn't for everyone.

And maybe Camille was one of those people.

He climbed into his truck and drove the same gravel path Camille had taken not long ago. A familiar twinge of excitement pulled at his gut.

He felt it every morning when he went to The Inn. Went to where she was.

He'd taken on every job that put him there. The horseback tours offered to their guests. Taking care of the pool and the grounds around it.

Whatever could keep him close to Camille and Cal. Just in case they needed something.

But there was no reason to be excited now. Chances were good he was leaving empty-handed which meant he was better off not going back.

Facing the wrath of the women in his life.

The Inn was loud and busy when he pulled up. People were everywhere. Splashing in the pool. Rocking on the porch. Wandering the grounds.

The new cook stepped out the front door as he parked, going straight to the heavy bell anchored to one of the posts and whipping the clapper from one side to the other.

The dinner bell was one of the most popular features at The Inn. For some reason visitors loved it. Made them feel like they were on a real ranch.

Which they were.

Just one that had never had a dinner bell before.

Everyone knew when food was served. If they showed up, they got it.

If they didn't, then they went hungry.

Which is probably what he'd end up doing since going back without Camille wasn't an option.

Brett slowly climbed the stairs to The Inn, tipping his head at Mariah as he passed. "Evenin'."

She gave him a wide grin. "Looking for someone?"

He paused, letting the people on the porch through the door first. "Sounds like you might already know the answer to that."

He'd seen Camille and Mariah alone in the kitchen more than a few times, side by side on the stools, talking for hours so it didn't surprise him that The Inn's resident chef might already be clued in.

"I kicked her out of the kitchen, but she just went and started doing laundry." Mariah sighed. "She won't stop working."

"I noticed that." Brett pulled off his hat, holding it against his chest as he went inside. "Guess I'll go see what I can do."

It was the main reason he was willing to do this at all.

Camille was going to work herself to death if someone didn't stop her. Whether she was using it as a distraction or something else didn't matter at this point.

The woman needed a damn day off.

Brett passed through the kitchen where the scent of seared meat and freshly sautéed vegetables hung in the air. The visitors of The Inn were lined down the large table, ready for their third meal of the day. He nodded at the bachelorette party he'd taken out riding early that morning. "Evenin'."

A few of the women giggled, offering him waves and *hello*s.

Two years ago he would have been thrilled with all The Inn offered.

A never-ending procession of potential partners to choose from.

But now he was only focused on one specific thing the opening of The Inn brought.

And she was in the laundry room on the second floor.

Camille was easy to find.

All he had to do was follow the soft sound of her voice as she sang.

It was something she did as she worked. Might not even realize it.

The tune was always the same and just quiet enough he could never place it.

But it drew him in every damn time.

A literal siren, luring him to destruction.

Because he was going to have hell to pay when Camille didn't show back up at Nora and Brooks'.

And he'd bet everything he had that was exactly what was going to happen.

Camille would find every excuse to stay at The Inn and work.

The woman hadn't taken a single day off since she'd started and his mother was getting testy about it. Honestly, he understood where she was coming from.

It wasn't right and it wasn't fair, but it was turning out to be difficult as hell to make a person take a break.

Especially when that person was sneakily hard-headed.

The singing stopped, melody abruptly clipped short.

Camille's head slowly came into view as she leaned to peer down the hall. Her eyes widened when she saw him. "Do you need something?"

He needed lots of things.

None of them anything he'd admit to her.

Not yet.

But tonight Camille was going to hear a little of the truth she refused to see.

"I think you know why I'm here." He leaned against the open doorway as Camille turned back to the dryer she was unloading. "My mother wants me to bring you back to the party."

"I have work to do." Camille pulled out a sheet that seemed to keep coming.

"She doesn't care." Brett stepped into the small room as the giant swath of fabric filled Camille's arms. "There's always work to do on the ranch. Sometimes it just has to wait until tomorrow." He caught a corner peeking out from the pile and pulled, collecting the thick cotton as he searched for another corner. "A body can't work forever, Camille. Eventually it shuts down."

She tried to pull the sheet away from him, but it was too large for her yank to do anything but stretch it between them. "I'm fine."

"For now." Brett finally found a second corner and lined it up with the first, backing up as he let the fabric fall loose. "But eventually you're going to drop."

"You should go back to the party." Camille was trying to shut the discussion down, which was fine, but she also seemed to think he had the option of going back to the party without her.

And he was making sure she knew the truth.

Brett held tight as Camille tried to pull the sheet away. "Can't."

Her eyes jumped to his. "Why not?"

"Because I'm supposed to come back with you." He shook his head. "Won't go over well if I don't."

"I can't go back." Camille's eyes drifted across the sheet. "I need to get these folded."

"Right now?"

"If I don't then they'll wrinkle." Camille slowly pulled one of the corners on her side free. "And then I'll have to wash them again to get the wrinkles out."

"What next?" He held his end of the sheet as Camille lined up her corners.

"Next?" Camille's surprise was obvious.

"Once we're done with the sheets. What are we doing next?" Brett walked toward her, bringing his ends to hers, taking advantage of her shock and snagging the sheet away from her.

"You don't need to do anything."

"And you don't need to do everything." Brett finished folding the cotton into a neat stack before lining it on the shelf with the rest of the clean sheets. "But you keep tryin'."

Camille's lips pressed flat as she stared his way.

Brett stepped in front of the dryer, pulling out the next sheet and going to work folding it.

This was uncharted territory for her. He got that.

Her parents were both gone, and both her older sisters moved away the second they turned eighteen. She'd been on her own for years. No family. No friends.

She needed time to get used to having both. What it meant. How it worked.

And he'd give her all the time she needed.

But come hell or high water the woman was going to take a break now and then. Even if he was the one who had to pick up the slack to make it happen.

"Did you eat dinner yet?" Brett finished the second sheet and added it to the collection.

"I'm fine."

"Not what I asked." He pulled another item from the dryer, frowning as the gathered edges came into view. "Hell."

Camille almost smiled, managing to smother it down just after the dimple in her cheek peeked out at him. "I can do that one."

He passed it over before leaning against the industrial dryer. "Show me."

Camille hesitated a second, her eyes finding his and immediately dropping to the fabric. "You want to learn how to fold a fitted sheet?"

"I want to see if you can really fold one."

She scoffed. This time she did smile. "Would I really lie about that?"

"Maybe." Brett crossed one boot over the other. "If it got you out of having to go back to Nora's."

Camille's smile changed, softening in a way he didn't really understand. "It's not my place."

That was an interesting statement.

"And you think your place is here?"

"I know it is." Camille tucked one hand into a pocket of the sheet. "I'm pretty sure it's literally in my job title." She stacked another pocket on top of the first one, pulling it down and around the first.

"You know that's not how my mother works." Brett tried to follow along as she continued stacking the corners of the sheet onto that one hand. "She claims everyone she can."

Camille shook out the tucked together sheet. "Your mother is a nice person." She stepped around him, going to the small counter set on one side of the dryer and laying out the partially-folded sheet.

"Nice?" Brett edged closer to the woman he'd watched from a distance for over a year.

Biding his time.

Waiting her out.

"Nice." Camille folded the rounded edges of the sheet toward the center and suddenly the mess looked square. Two more folds and it looked just as perfectly folded as it's flat counterparts.

"I don't think nice is the right word." His mother's reasons for wanting Camille at the party had nothing to do with her being nice.

And everything to do with her desire to fix anything she could for the people she loved.

And his mother loved Camille.

"Fine." Camille added the sheet to the shelf. "Kind. Your mother is kind." She closed the door to the now empty dryer. "Thank you for helping." She gave him a tight smile. "I'll see you later."

Then she walked out of the room.

Like she thought their conversation was over.

Brett followed behind her.

She stopped just outside the utility closet, jumping a little when she saw he was still there. "What are you doing?"

"Helping." Brett opened the door to the storage room where they kept cleaning supplies, along with all the toiletries. "What's next?"

"I—" Camille shook her head. "No."

He lifted his brows. "Nothing's next?"

She pressed her lips together, slowly shaking her head. "Nope."

It was a ploy to get him to leave.

And he was going to use it against her. "So you're ready to go back to Nora's then."

"What?" The shake of Camille's head sped up. "No."

"Well," Brett risked moving a little closer, "we can stay here and keep working, or we can go back to the party." It almost looked like Camille held her breath as he risked another inch her direction. "But either way you're stuck with me for the evening."

CHAPTER THREE

SHIT.

She had to find a way out of this.

Away from Brett before she started noticing things. Dangerous things.

Like the way he smelled.

That the bit of hair peeking from the skin across his jaw held a hint of red.

The thin white line of a scar running just above one brow.

"You should go back to the party."

Brett shifted his feet, the wide expanse of his chest coming closer. "I don't disagree, but like I said, I can't go back alone."

"I have to stay here."

"Then we'll stay here."

Camille stared up at him. Partly because she couldn't believe this was happening.

And partly because she didn't really want it to stop.

"Come back to the party with me, Camille. It will make my mother happy. She'll feel less guilty about how much you work."

That jump-started the tiny bit of her brain that was still working. "She shouldn't feel guilty."

"You never stop working." Brett's big body seemed to take up most of the space around her.

Most of the space in her mind.

"She feels like she's taking advantage of you."

It was the most ridiculous thing she'd ever heard.

If anyone was taking advantage it was her.

She had a place to live. Food. Electricity. A pool.

There was no way to work enough to earn all the Paces gave her.

And that was before you added in everything they gave Calvin.

Some of that was immeasurable.

"She's definitely not taking advantage of me."

Brett's blue eyes moved over her face.

Lingering too long.

Seeing too much.

"What's it gonna be then? Are we going back to the party or are we staying here and working?"

Neither option was a good one.

But one meant spending more time alone with a man she couldn't get attached to.

Sooner or later Brett would find the woman he would build a home for.

The woman he would take care of.

The woman he would love.

And she would have to watch it all happen.

"I can go to the party for a little while." It was the lesser of two evils. At least at the party she would be able to stay away from him.

"Party it is." Brett backed away holding one arm toward the stairs. "After you."

The closeness of his body forced her to brush against him as she passed, the clean, fresh scent of his skin as unavoidable as the rest of him seemed to be.

Brett stayed close as she went down the stairs. She tried to go in the direction of the closet where her keys were dangling from their hook, but Brett blocked her path, tipping his head toward the front of The Inn. "Door's this way."

"I need my keys."

"I'll drive." Brett's hand rested on her back, wide and warm where it pressed into the thin fabric of her t-shirt as he urged her along. He opened the door, sending her out onto the porch first. "Then we won't have so many cars to move around when someone wants to leave."

"What if I want to leave before you're ready?" Camille glanced back toward the closet housing her keys as Brett pulled the door closed.

"I'm not much of a night owl." Brett shot her a smile that flipped her belly and warmed her skin. "I'll probably be the one ready to go home and get in bed."

Camille's eyes drifted down all on their own, falling victim to the smallest of suggestions.

Brett Pace in a bed was something she should never allow herself to imagine.

But right now there was no stopping it.

Luckily he seemed oblivious to the thoughts she was too weak to shut down.

It had been so long.

So long since she'd been touched.

Kissed.

Held.

It used to be easy to do without.

But recently the desire for connection was derailing all her good intentions.

Brett was too young and her past was too complicated.

Camille cleared her throat, hoping it might also clear her mind. "I think everyone around here goes to bed early."

"Not everyone." Brett pulled open the passenger's door of his truck. "Brooks would stay up all night if he could."

The fact was mildly interesting, but nothing she could really think about considering what she was facing down. "Why is your truck so tall?"

"It's not really that tall." Brett moved in at her side. "Just doesn't have running boards." He was very close.

Again.

"Thought about putting some on, but then decided against it." His voice seemed lower.

Softer.

"How does anyone get in it?" Camille eyed the floorboard. She might get her foot up in it, but anything that happened after that would be ungraceful as hell.

Not that she was trying to impress Brett Pace. That would be one of her more foolish decisions.

And she'd made some epically foolish decisions in her life.

Would pay for them forever.

So would her son.

"No one else really gets in my truck." Brett's gaze lingered on her face. "Just Duke."

Camille struggled not to smile at the mention of Brett's dog. "Why isn't he at the party?"

"Duke is a big fan of parties with kids." Brett took a little step back. "He likes to help them clean their plates." His handsome face twisted to a frown. "Then he barfs it all up."

"Poor Duke."

"He's not the one who has to clean it all up." Brett leaned in, stealing back the breathing room he'd given. "Can you imagine if he puked on Nora's brand-new floor?"

"It's laminate. It would wipe right off." There were worse things in the world than a little dog puke.

Like grown man shit.

She'd cleaned that up more times than she would ever admit.

It was one more reason she had to get herself together.

The life she had and the life Brett had could never line up.

"Not when it's hotdogs."

The laugh escaped all on its own, running free before there was any hope of stopping it.

"Yeah. Laugh it up." He tipped his head to the cab of his truck. "You ready to get in?"

"You still haven't told me how."

The words were barely out of her mouth when Brett's hands gripped her at the waist, holding tight as he lifted her off the ground.

She grabbed his shoulders out of reflex, fingers digging into the thick band of muscle there as he hefted her butt up into the seat.

His hands didn't linger, but the sear of their heat into her skin did.

Like a brand.

"Ready?"

Camille stared down at him.

How had this happened?

Not just this specific moment. All of them.

How had she accidentally ended up wishing her life had been different?

Not because of the man she put behind her. Camille didn't actually regret Junior the way most people would expect.

It was the man in front of her who was causing this problematic view of her past.

A past she both loved and hated.

Which fed a guilt she would never overcome.

"Let's go." The faster they got to Nora and Brooks' the sooner she could line people up between them. Replace the emotional barrier she lost somewhere along the way with a more physical one.

Brett closed the door, boxing her into the only bit of his world she should ever see.

Camille did her best not to look at any of it.

It was what she tried to do whenever she was faced with the temptation of a world she wasn't really a part of.

She was not one of them.

Never could be.

Brett easily swung up and into his seat, relaxing back as the giant tires crunched over the gravel.

It felt oddly comfortable to sit here with him.

And being comfortable around Brett was not a good thing.

"Thank you for including Calvin when you work with Wyatt on his football skills." She needed to be grateful for the kindness of this family. The way they allowed her son to be included.

Brett was quiet for a minute, eyes staring straight ahead. "I'm working with both boys."

"Well, thank you for letting Calvin feel like he's a part of it." It was overly nice of him to do that, and she'd avoided telling him. Mostly because she avoided him in general.

"He *is* a part of it." Brett shook his head. "Both boys want to play and we're tryin' to give them the best shot we can."

Football was big in Moss Creek.

Even Little League was competitive.

And costly.

Even if she'd known Calvin wanted to play, she never could have afforded it before.

"Do you think he might be able to make the team?" The tryouts for this year's team were long past, but if she started saving now then next year she could more than pay for the fees that went along with it.

"I'm not sure *might* is the word I would use." Brett glanced her way. "Cal's got a wicked arm on him. If I can get him moving a little faster he will be a hell of a player."

A familiar ache settled into her chest. "Oh."

She'd missed so much in the last decade, unable to see past the days as she faced them, and over the last year it had become painfully clear just how much she'd failed her son.

"There's a private camp coming up soon that I think he might really benefit from." Brett rested one arm on the console between them. "I'd be happy to take him if you're interested."

She'd been unable to give Calvin much. He'd always worn thrift store clothes. Packed his lunch because even the school lunches were too costly.

Especially when you were married to a man who refused to let anyone know just how little they had.

"When is it?" She shouldn't take any more from these people.

They'd already done so much.

But this wasn't for her.

And she could work harder. Do more.

Repay this kindness like she did all the rest.

"Starts in a week."

"Are there any openings left?" It was so late. They were probably already full.

One more way she would let her son down.

"I'm sure they can find room for him." Brett pulled to a slow stop, parking off to one side in the fresh gravel leading to Brooks and Nora's house. "Does that mean you're okay with him going?"

She'd been working hard to dig out of the hole Junior left her in. All the money from the sale of the house went to paying off the many mortgages stacked against it.

Almost everything she made went to paying down the credit cards she'd been stuck with when her ex-husband went to jail, leaving her the only one on the hook for anything with her name on it.

But she'd managed to replace the truck she'd been driving since high school and sock away a little nest-egg that might just be enough to cover the fee of this camp. "How much does it cost?"

"It's free." The answer came a little faster than she expected.

"Free?"

"Yup." Brett opened his door and climbed out.

Camille pushed open her own door, leaning out to peek down at the ground, trying to gauge just how far the drop was. "How can it be free?"

"Just is." Brett reached her side of the truck and stopped in the open door, holding his hands her way. "You comin' out?"

"Are you sure this is a good camp?"

"Positive."

"But good things usually aren't free."

Brett grinned up at her. "Some of the best things are free, actually."

"Like what?"

One sandy brow lifted. "You really want me to answer that?"

Yes. Desperately.

"No." Camille stretched one foot toward the ground, trying to slide her way down the side of the seat to safety.

Unfortunately, once gravity got her it didn't let go, and all her weight hit right on the ankle she'd bent earlier, and it immediately gave out.

Brett caught her as she started to go down, keeping her from hitting the ground.

Again.

"You okay?" The concern in his voice was evident.

It almost made her consider telling him the truth.

But the truth was more complicated than she could convey to another person.

Hell, she barely managed to wrap her own mind around it.

"I'm fine." Everyone assumed it was a lie.

It wasn't.

"Is that the same foot you stepped on funny earlier?"

"Nope." That one *was* a lie, and she was happy to tell it.

"You sure?"

"Yup." Camille stepped away, making sure she didn't limp at all on the ankle that might be more than a little irritated by the missteps she continued to make.

Brett stayed put, but the weight of his gaze rested squarely on her as she walked toward the house, fighting the gravel every step of the way.

The front door of the house opened, and Nora rushed out with Mae and Clara hot on her heels. "You came back."

All she could do was plaster on a smile and power through.

Luckily she'd gotten real good at that over the years.

Nora led her into the house. "Are you guys hungry?"

You guys?

Camille peeked out of the corner of her eyes to find Brett close beside her.

"Starving." He rested one hand on her back, urging her toward the line of food still laid out. "We worked up an appetite folding sheets at The Inn." He snagged a paper plate from the stack and passed it her way before grabbing one for himself. "Camille here can fold a fitted sheet into a perfect square."

"Witchcraft." Nora pulled out a can of cola from the fridge and passed it Camille's way. "I just wad them up and shove them in the closet."

"I had to learn." Camille scooped a little mac and cheese onto her plate. "Otherwise I ended up having to clean up a bunch of broken beer bottles from the—"

The room suddenly seemed very quiet.

Camille slowly looked up from the spoonful of coleslaw hovering over her plate.

Every set of eyes in the room was on her.

Filled with pain.

Pity.

Sadness.

Shit.

Only one person seemed unaffected by the memory that easily slid free.

"What kind of pizza do you like?" Brett continued down the line of food, flipping open the first box. "Looks like this one's Hawaiian."

For the first time Brett was the easiest person in the room to focus on. "That's fine." She held her plate out while he dropped a slice on.

"We're gonna go find someplace to sit." Brett's hand returned to her body, directing her toward the back door.

Folding chairs were set up all over the space just behind the house, spread around the fire pit dug into the ground.

"How about here?" He took the cola from her hand and tucked it into the netted cup holder on one of the green camp-style chairs.

"Thank you." Camille slowly eased down.

What happened in the kitchen was one more reason she shouldn't be here.

Most people didn't seem to be in the same place she was when it came to her ex-husband.

She'd spent a decade letting Junior control every aspect of her life.

Her time.

Her money.

Her emotions.

And she'd be damned if she gave him any more.

Camille stayed silent as she worked her way through the food, making sure to eat every bite of what she'd added to her plate.

Luckily it wasn't a whole lot. She'd managed to make everyone uncomfortable before her plate was even half-full.

"Ready for dessert?" Brett took her empty plate and stacked it on his.

"I'm okay."

"That's not really an option." He thumbed over one shoulder toward the house. "You can either come make your own, or I can make one for you." He wiggled his brows. "And I get real heavy-handed."

Camille looked around the yard, doing a quick headcount.

"House is empty." Brett's words were soft as he leaned closer. "I already checked."

"I'm not trying to avoid anyone."

"I know that." He tipped his head toward the door. "Come on. Let's go real quick."

If she had to go then now *would* be the best time.

Camille pushed up on the arms of the chair, making sure her irritated ankle was stable before following Brett into the house.

There, she was forced to choose between a line of brownies, cookies, and cobblers, all of which looked more than amazing. She settled on a small, frosted brownie

41

and a scoop of peach cobbler. "I'm not sure how you stay looking like you do with all this food around all the time."

Camille clamped her lips together, but it was too late.

Once again, her mouth got away from her.

Running wild before she could even think to catch it.

Maybe Brett didn't catch it this time either.

Maybe he was just as oblivious as the last time she babbled without thinking.

Camille dared a peek his way.

Only to find Brett's blue eyes locked on hers.

"How do I look, Camille?"

CHAPTER FOUR

HE'D SPENT A year thinking Camille didn't even notice he was there.

Thinking while she might see him, Camille never thought of him as anything more than one more piece of the landscape around her.

Another prop in the new world she was trying to navigate.

But she definitely saw him now, hazel eyes wide, jaw a little slack.

Like she couldn't believe what came out of her mouth any more than he did.

"I mean," she cleared her throat, "you don't look like you eat this kind of food every day." She shifted a little in the green chair he'd brought from his place earlier this morning. "You're just—" Her eyes dipped down his frame before darting away. "Fit."

"I lift hay bales all day."

"Not *all* day." Her eyes widened where they were fixed on the plate in her hand.

"No." Brett leaned back in his matching chair. "Not all day." He watched Camille closely. "I do a fair bit of riding too."

Camille shoved a bite of cobbler in her mouth, chewing slowly. When it was gone, she finally glanced his way. "You do most of the tours for the visitors to The Inn."

Brett nodded. "I do."

He'd specifically asked to be the primary guide for the groups that stayed at The Inn. And not just because he enjoyed showing people about the life he loved.

He also liked having an excuse to be at The Inn every day.

"You're a frequent topic of discussion at dinner." This time Camille didn't look his way.

"That's a shame. There's plenty more interesting things to talk about." The revelation didn't surprise him. The Inn was surprisingly popular with bachelorette parties. They usually had at least two groups of girls each month, and he almost always got hit on by at least one girl in every party.

"They like to talk about the horses too." She smiled a little behind the spoon in front of her lips. "But mostly they talk about you."

"What do they say about me?" He wasn't so much interested in what any of these other girls had to say.

What he was interested in, was what part of it Camille remembered.

She lifted one shoulder. "They just think you're nice."

"Nice?" He was hoping for something a little more...

Flattering.

"Don't you want to be called nice?" Camille slowly leaned against the back of her chair.

His chair.

"It's not the worst thing I've ever been called, but it's not the best either." Brett scooped up a pile of the blackberry cobbler he'd dished out. "Is that all they say? That I'm nice?"

Camille spooned off a corner of the brownie on her plate, chewing through it before she answered. "Some of them think you're good-looking."

"That makes me feel better."

Her brows lifted but a smile teased the corners of her lips. "You'd rather be good-looking than nice?"

"Absolutely." He leaned in to snag a bite of her cobbler. "What else?"

"That you're a thief." Camille yanked her plate out of reach, but her smile made it clear she wasn't upset.

"That doesn't seem like something they could know." He leaned close. "That's a secret only you know."

Camille held his gaze. "Are you trying to get close to my plate again?"

He almost had his spoon in her brownie. "How'd you know?"

"Because Cal does the same thing to me all the time." Her smile suddenly faltered and her mood shifted. Camille leaned away. "I should go check on Nora. See if she needs any help in the kitchen." She stood, not waiting for a response before making a beeline for the back door of the empty house.

A beeline he immediately followed.

There was something happening just now between them. Something good.

Something he didn't expect so soon.

Camille glanced over her shoulder, jumping a little when she realized he was right behind her. "What are you doing?"

"Helping you."

"Why?" She practically ran through the door and into the kitchen.

"You help everyone else." Brett went to the kitchen sink and twisted on the water before plugging the sink. "Only makes sense to return the favor."

"I don't help you."

She did. More than she realized. "You help my mother." Brett added some soap to the hot water. "My brothers." He grabbed a dishcloth from the stack in a wire basket right beside the sink. "Their wives."

"But that's still not you." Camille stood on the other side of the island, still holding the plate she'd caught him sneaking bites from.

"Might as well be." Brett turned to face her, snagging the serving spoons from the aluminum trays. "We all work as a team around here. It's the only way we can tackle the amount of work we do. No one can manage it alone." He dropped the stack of spoons into the sink. "Otherwise they'll work themselves to death."

Initially he thought Camille's incessant working was how she coped with what happened to her.

And maybe it was.

But maybe it was more than that.

"I can wash those." Camille edged in closer, eyes fixed on where he worked the bits of food loose from the metal.

"How 'bout I wash and you dry?" Brett ran the first large spoon under the tap, rinsing it clean before holding it out to Camille.

Her eyes lifted to him before dropping to the spoon between them.

He tipped his head toward the cabinet at her side. "Towels are in the first drawer down."

Camille leaned away, scooting out the drawer, eyes going to the line of folded kitchen towels inside. "How did you know they were in here?"

"I helped put the kitchen together yesterday." They'd been working on getting Brooks and Nora moved in all week. He'd spent the days working or leading tours, and the evenings helping out here. "Not sure Nora will be able to find everything, but it's all put away."

Camille pulled the top towel free. "This is a good spot for the towels." She took the spoon from him. "That's where I would have put them."

"What about the glasses?"

Camille rested the dried spoon on the counter before taking the next one. Her eyes moved to the upper cabinets, going straight to the one just to the right of the sink. "That one."

"I'm two for two then." He'd set Nora's kitchen up just like the kitchen at The Inn, using it as a guide for what should go where.

Camille had moved things around no less than five times as she got used to the space. It'd been like it was for almost six months now, so he figured she'd worked all the kinks out.

"Luckily Nora's not much of a cook, so you should be fine no matter what." Camille lifted her brows as she focused on the spoon she was drying. "Now, if it was Mae you might have had a harder time."

"I didn't touch Mae's kitchen." Brett knew better than to even attempt to tackle that feat. "I was on landscape duty."

Camille smiled a little. "Well you did a good job. Mae's flower beds look beautiful."

The compliment was as unexpected as the rest of the evening. "Thank you."

Camille nodded, falling silent as they finished washing the spoons and wiping down the counters. Brett condensed the remaining pizza into two boxes and slid them into the fridge just as his mother came into the house, Wyatt and Calvin following right behind her.

"Oh my." She rested one hand over her heart. "Someone's been busy."

"Camille and I figured we'd do a little housekeeping." Brett didn't miss the way Camille's eyes slid his way as he

47

crimped the foil back in place on the remaining peach cobbler.

"You two make a good team." His mother worked her way toward where Camille was wiping down the top of the island. "Speaking of teams." She glanced at the boys behind her. 'We were wondering if this twosome could spend the night with Pop and me."

Camille straightened. "You don't have to do that."

"It's not about having to." His mother wrapped one arm around Calvin's shoulders, pulling him in for a squeeze. "The house is so quiet." She lifted her brows at Wyatt. "And we could use some help collecting the eggs in the morning."

"Can I, Mom?" Calvin easily moved into his place within the family, seamlessly taking his spot as grandson to two people who would throw hands with anyone who said differently.

Unfortunately his momma was not as perceptive when it came to their family.

Camille rubbed her lips together, her uncertainty clear.

Brett stepped in at her side. "They won't let him eat anything he wants."

Camille glanced his way, an awkward smile flashing across her mouth. "I'm not worried."

She looked worried.

Camille shifted on her feet as everyone watched her, waiting. "If you're sure it's not an imposition."

His mother's brows came together. "An imposition to have my grandsons spend the night with me?" She scoffed, grabbing Wyatt with her free arm and pulling him into the side not currently occupied by Calvin. "Never."

Camille looked from Maryann to Calvin to Wyatt. "Okay."

It sounded more like defeat than permission.

But his mother and the boys seemed oblivious to the difference. They immediately turned, rushing off to go find his father to tell him the good news. As soon as the door closed Brett turned to Camille. "You're allowed to say no, you know that, right?"

Camille's eyes came to his, lingering a brief second before going back to the closed door. "I just want him to be happy."

"I think you succeeded." Brett moved a little closer. "But you don't look very happy."

Her smile was just as fleeting this time. "I'm fine."

"Fine and happy are two different things."

"I'm happy." Camille moved away from him, going to rinse out the sink followed by the rag in her hand, wringing it out before hanging it over the faucet.

He went with her, leaning against the counter as she stood at the sink. "I figured you'd smile more when you were happy."

"I smile." Camille didn't prove her point. "I just want to be sure Calvin's not overstepping."

His brain skidded a little at that. "Overstepping what?"

Camille dried her hands on the towel before hanging it on the handle to the stove. "Taking advantage."

He still wasn't following. "Of who?"

She turned to face him. "Your parents." Camille huffed out a breath. "All of you."

"For the love of—" Nora came through the back door, eyes going around the spotless kitchen. "What did I tell you about cleaning my house?"

Camille's lips pressed tight as Nora stood staring at the freshly-wiped counters.

"You were supposed to come enjoy yourself." Nora groaned. "Now I'm gonna have to sneak in and do your laundry."

"It's my fault." Brett moved closer to Camille's side, offering her an ally in a situation he still wasn't one-hundred percent confident he understood. "I asked her to check out where I put everything. Make sure I did it right."

"Oh." Nora's fist lowered from where she'd propped it against her hip. Her eyes went to Camille. "How'd he do?"

"Pretty good." Camille's shoulders relaxed the tiniest bit.

Nora snorted. "I mean, it's not like he was dealing with Mae's kitchen." She laughed. "Half my stuff was still in the box it came in."

Brett leaned Camille's way. "She's not lying."

"Well, thanks you two for cleaning up." Nora smiled softly. "I appreciate it."

Camille almost smiled back. "You're welcome."

"You coming out for the fire?" Nora wiggled her brows. "Brody and Boone are going to set off some fireworks."

Brett lifted his brows in question. He'd promised to take Camille home whenever she wanted. That meant this was up to her.

Camille barely nodded. "Sure."

Nora's smile widened. "Awesome." She pulled open the door and disappeared down the steps.

"Let's go watch some cowboy fireworks." Brett led the way. "Hopefully we don't have to hunt down the first aid kit."

Camille snorted out a little laugh.

She was a complicated woman. He knew that from the start.

It was part of what drew him to her.

Camille was reserved and quiet, and there was something in her eyes that made him want to get close to her.

Protect her from the things he knew she'd seen too much of.

He just had to figure out how to do it.

Their chairs were where they left them, situated close to the house and far from the fire pit Brooks was stacking with a pile of wood. Brett grabbed one chair with each hand, carrying them closer to the fire, but spaced a little bit away from the rest.

Because now that he'd managed to get Camille outside of The Inn, he was feeling more than a little selfish with her attention.

He set Camille's chair down first, making sure it was steady before settling his right beside it.

Camille stood, arms crossed, still looking uncertain as hell.

"This one's yours." He scooted the chair a little closer.

"Thanks." Camille slowly sat.

He waited until she was settled before easing down beside her, adjusting his seat on the ground, moving it closer to hers as he did.

Wyatt and Calvin were at the back of the yard, just in front of the line of trees, helping the twins manage the sparklers Mae was passing out as fast as she could get them lit. The sun was just setting as Brody and Boone set up the line of fireworks they'd picked up for the evening.

They had plenty to celebrate. Construction was finished on all the houses they currently had planned. The Inn was booked all summer and half of the next.

Everyone was healthy and happy.

For the most part.

Brett's gaze skimmed to Camille as the first firework hit the air.

Her eyes were glued to the sky and he took full advantage after a year of keeping his eyes to himself.

A year of doing his best to make her comfortable. A year of giving her time to recover.

A year of trying not to stare at a woman who drew his attention like none had before.

Camille was the most beautiful woman he'd ever laid eyes on.

Always had been.

He'd barely been thirteen the first time he saw her, hanging out with Mae and Boone after a football game.

But he was just a kid then.

A boy without the first idea how to chase someone like her.

But he'd grown up.

Learned more than he cared to admit in the years he assumed his childhood crush would always be only that.

But then fate dropped Camille in his path.

And he planned to make the most of it.

The last splash of light went dark and everyone clapped, knocking him back to the here and now.

The here and now where Camille was at his side.

"I think I'm ready to head out." His mother stood up. "What about you boys?"

"We're ready." Wyatt rushed Maryann's way with Calvin close behind.

Maryann leaned into their ears, the words she gave the boys impossible to hear.

A second later Calvin was running their way. He grabbed Camille in a tight hug. "Thank you for letting me stay with Mimi and Pop. I love you."

Camille hugged him back, eyes closing for just a second. "Be helpful."

"I will." Calvin darted away, jerking to a stop as he looked back their way. "Bye, Brett."

"Bye, Buddy. Have fun."

Camille watched as Calvin loaded into the truck, sitting in the backseat with Wyatt as Maryann and Bill waved from the front windows.

He didn't like the worried look on her face. "He'll be okay."

Camille straightened. "I know."

She didn't look like she knew that at all.

"I think we're heading out too." Brody had a baby in each arm. "Gotta get all the girls in bed so they're not grumpy in the morning."

"That includes their momma." Clara yawned. "I was ready for bed an hour ago."

Mae followed along to help load the girls into the van Clara traded her SUV for when she found out she was pregnant with twins. Camille's eyes followed as the group packed all four girls into their car seats.

Brett tipped his head her way. "You ready to go home too?"

It was odd to call The Inn Camille's home, but technically it was.

For now.

"Sure." Camille's eyes dragged from Brody and Clara. She stood from her chair, turning to collapse it. "Where does this go?"

"In the back of my truck." Brett snagged it away, tucking it under one arm as he folded his own chair. "These are the ones I brought."

"I can carry that." Camille tried to take the chair.

"I'm sure you can." He added it to the one already under his arm. "Ready?"

Camille gave him a little nod.

"See y'all later." He waved toward where Boone and Brooks sat beside the fire.

Brooks returned his wave. "Thanks for all your help."

"Anytime."

53

Camille tipped to one side as they worked their way across the uneven ground.

Brett wrapped one arm around her, hand at her waist as he offered steadying support. "Okay?"

"Yup." She continued on, but it almost seemed like she might have a little limp.

One that might be getting worse with every step she took.

When they got to the truck Brett dumped both chairs in the back end before pulling open Camille's door. The second it was open she grabbed the inside handle and hefted herself up and in.

He lifted a brow. "I'm impressed."

"It's not that tall."

He dropped his eyes down her body, stopping at the foot he'd watched her favor all night.

It was time to start doing what he said he would.

Someone needed to take care of Camille and he'd seen enough today to know it wasn't going to be her.

He stepped closer, tipping back the front of his hat as he looked her way. "It is when you've got a sore ankle."

CHAPTER FIVE

BRETT STOOD IN the open door, one hand gripping the top of it and the other resting on the edge of the opening. "You feel like admittin' you hurt yourself?"

Camille pressed her lips together, slowly shaking her head. "Nope."

This night was spiraling out of control as it was.

Somehow she'd accidentally ended up spending more than a little bit of time alone with the one man she had no business going near.

Long enough to realize if Brett knew her ankle was irritated he'd go and do something awful.

Like carry her into The Inn.

He tipped his head. "All right then."

The door closed between them.

She watched through the windshield as he made his way around the truck, her heart beating faster with every step he took.

Damn thing needed to get with the program.

Brett Pace was not for her.

She was not for him.

He was too young.

She was too...

Many things to count.

It was a truth she went to bed with each night and woke up to each morning.

But she still sucked in a breath when he opened his door and slid into the seat beside her.

Filled the cab with his scent and his presence.

That was what she struggled to ignore the most.

The air around Brett was different.

The second he walked into a room it changed.

There was something about him that soaked into the atmosphere.

And then into her.

Brett started the truck, rolling down the windows to let in the cooling air as they slowly moved along the freshly graveled lane leading to Nora and Brooks' house. He slung one hand over the top of the wheel, looking relaxed in a way she'd never been as they moved through the dark.

His blue eyes tipped her way, their color almost navy as they lingered on her face. "You have a good time?"

She had a time.

Whether it was good or not was still to be determined.

So she just smiled as much as she could manage. "Your family gets together a lot."

She avoided a night like this one at least every couple of weeks. The Paces were always collecting at one house or another for some sort of family-style fun.

"We've got a lot to celebrate." Brett's gaze spent more time on her than it did on the narrow road. "We try to appreciate all of it."

Camille forced her eyes straight ahead so she wouldn't think about the way he was looking at her.

The way his words tried to wiggle under her skin.

It was the only reason she saw the small body as it skittered across the gravel in front of the truck.

Unfortunately, all that came out of her mouth was a jumble of sounds that no one would ever call words.

But Brett must have understood at least a few of them because the truck jerked, skidding across the rock, kicking it up as he swerved in an attempt to miss whatever might have made its last bad decision.

The thump was obvious. Loud enough to make her cringe.

"What was it?" Camille leaned to one side, risking a peek in the side mirror. The brake lights illuminated patches of the ground, but there was no sign of the furry critter she'd seen.

"Looked like a raccoon." He put the truck in park and reached for the door. "I'm gonna go make sure everything's okay."

"I'm pretty sure nothing's okay." Camille leaned forward as Brett reached behind the seat. "What are you—"

He pulled out a shotgun.

The delicious cobbler she'd almost enjoyed threatened to revisit. "Oh."

"I'll be back." The door closed and the inside of the truck went dark again.

Brett slowly moved up the side of the truck, leaning from side to side as he looked around.

A soft scuffling outside her open window made her heart sink.

Camille opened her door, using the light from the cab to scan the scrappy grass for any sign of the suffering animal. "I think it's over here."

"Then get your ass back in the truck."

A movement caught her eye, drawing her out a little more, bringing her feet to the ground. "I think I saw it." Camille picked her way across the rock and grass, stepping carefully as she moved toward a spot that seemed to be shifting.

Brett was moving faster now as he came around the back of the truck headed her way. "If you don't get your pretty little ass back in that truck—"

His words cut off as the spot she thought was the mortally wounded raccoon suddenly shot her way, sending her stumbling back, irritated ankle taking her down, ass first to the dirt and dust.

As the not-so-hurt raccoon ran straight for her.

Luckily Brett ran faster.

His years as the kicker for the football team paid off when he easily connected with the furry ferociousness, punting it through the air.

"Get in the truck." Brett had her up and off the ground, hauling her the rest of the way to the still open door and shoving her in before closing it on her. "Roll the windows up."

This time she listened to him.

Probably should have in the first place.

Camille almost had both windows up when a single shot made her jump.

Then her door yanked back open. "You okay?" Brett was in her space almost instantly, hands moving over her arms, her face, her legs. "Did he get you?"

She shook her head, unable to force her tongue to do anything but stick to the roof of her mouth as Brett's slow, gentle touch moved across her bare skin, skimming down her shins.

"You're sure?" His fingers moved over her irritated ankle, the soft pressure hitting a spot that was surprisingly tender.

Brett's eyes snapped up to hers when she sucked in a breath.

Shit.

She was fine. Or would be as soon as this night was over, and the last thing she wanted to discuss was her ankle.

It would be fine in the morning too.

But one thing would not be.

"Is it dead?"

"I scared it away."

Camille tipped her head to one side as she eyed the man in front of her. "I'm not a delicate flower. You can tell me if you killed it."

His eyes lingered on hers, hanging long enough that her already struggling lungs stalled out. "I'll come back and bury him after I get you situated."

"Aren't there animals around here that will handle that for you?" She'd lived on the ranch long enough to see the circle of life in all its glory. It was the way the world worked.

Everyone doing what they needed to survive.

Brett continued to stare at her, looking like he was seeing something he'd missed.

Something new.

But she was far from new.

Camille pulled her ankle from his hands. "I should get home."

Brett stood in the open door a second longer before easing back and closing it, releasing the air trapped in her lungs.

This night couldn't get much worse. Rabid raccoons. Sore ankle.

And Brett Pace.

The last one was the biggest issue.

It would take her weeks to force her brain to forget this night.

The feel of his hands on her body. The way his eyes seemed to always find hers.

Hell, the man kicked an attacking animal to protect her. How did a woman forget something like that?

She had to find a way.

Brett opened his door, sliding the shotgun back in place, his expression something she didn't want to think on.

"Do you always have that in here?" She would control the conversation. Keep it in safe waters for the five minutes it took to get back to The Inn.

Then she'd go to sleep and wake up and start fresh.

Like none of this ever happened.

Brett tipped his head in a nod as he shifted the truck back into drive. "Not somethin' you want to be without out here."

"Do you have to use it a lot?"

"No." His eyes stayed straight ahead. "But when you need it, you need it." He fell silent.

She'd been the one avoiding conversation all night and now it was him.

Which was good.

Fine.

Fantastic.

Except the expression she didn't want to think on was still there.

Brett's jaw was set. His eyes were barely narrowed.

The laid-back Brett she was used to seeing was gone, replaced by a man with an amount of focus she'd never seen.

And when he parked right in front of The Inn that focus came her way, stalling out her lungs once again.

She was going to die of suffocation if he kept looking at her like that.

At least she was good at holding her breath.

About time that paid off.

"What's wrong?" She didn't mean to ask, it just came out all on its own.

A reflex she hadn't quite learned to curb.

"Outside of that ankle?" Brett pushed his door open. "I'm not sure anything's wrong." A slow smile worked across his lips.

She thought the look of focus was bad.

Thought it was going to be what she struggled to put out of her mind tonight.

It wasn't.

This smile. This was going to be the problem.

There was something in it she couldn't identify.

But knew was dangerous as hell.

Not dangerous in the way she was familiar with. That she could have handled.

This was dangerous in a way that might have broken her ankle if she'd seen it while she was on her feet. Might have tripped her up and sent her falling in more ways than one.

"I need to go inside." Camille shoved at her door, fighting the handle as self-preservation finally kicked in.

Brett was around the truck faster than she'd ever seen anyone move, catching her as she slid down the seat. "Just because you're not a delicate flower doesn't mean you're not breakable." He shot her a stern look. "You're putting ice on that thing."

"I will." She stepped around him, all her focus going into not hobbling as she walked to the stairs.

"I know you will." Brett skipped the steps, taking the full height of the open porch in a single leap. He pushed open the door.

"I just said I would." Camille went past him, her ability to walk somewhat normally diminishing with each step. The next one made her wince.

And since Brett was watching her like a hawk, he didn't miss it.

A second later she was scooped up, hauled into the air.

Held tight to the chest of a man she was supposed to think of as a baby. Too young to consider.

So much for that.

It was good while it lasted.

"Stubborn woman." He strode to the large sectional that dominated the sitting area of The Inn. "Gonna kill yourself trying to prove a point." His words were edgy but the way he sat her on the cushions was nothing but careful.

"I'm not trying to prove anything." She was just trying to save herself from the scenario that would most definitely play out.

She would fall for Brett Pace.

Brett Pace would find himself a woman more suited to the life he wanted.

He would be happy.

She would be sad.

And life was too short to spend the whole damn thing sad.

Brett grabbed the upholstered coffee table Nora chose to fit into the space and shoved it her way, lifting her legs and setting them on top of it before stalking away.

He rustled around the kitchen and came back a minute later with a bag of ice and a dishtowel. Both dropped to the leather ottoman as he crouched down, eyes on her ankle. "It's swollen."

"It's fine." She barely had the words out before he was unlacing her sneaker, pulling it and the no-show sock under it off.

There was no time to brace.

No time to warn him.

Brett's gaze fixed on the reason she never wore sandals. Never went for pedicures with Nora and the rest of the girls.

It was one more imperfection that made her unsuitable for someone who lacked any sort of shortcomings.

"Didn't realize you were one step away from a mermaid." He went back to the ice and towel, folding the terry cloth around the bag before wrapping it across the side of her ankle.

Hell and damnation.

Why couldn't he ever say the wrong thing?

Look something besides mouth-wateringly gorgeous?

Brett reached out to run one finger down the skin that joined her third and fourth toes. "This make you swim faster?"

She almost laughed. Almost found joy in something she'd always hated.

Because of this pain in the ass of a man.

Who was not a baby no matter how much she tried to convince herself he was.

"I've never timed myself."

"Once that ankle's better we'll race." Brett grabbed her other shoe, pulling it free along with the second sock. "You're crooked, Camille."

This time she did laugh, tucking the completely separated toes of her other foot up under her thigh. "Shut up."

He winked at her. "Make me."

She couldn't pretend he wasn't flirting with her. Being the newly-single and formerly-abused woman in town might as well have put a neon sign on her head, one that attracted any man within striking distance. She'd had no short supply of potential suitors in the past year.

Luckily she had the 'not ready to date' excuse to fall back on.

Didn't matter that it wasn't true. It sounded true and that was what counted.

Brett stood up and headed toward the front door.

Thank God.

"Thank you for the ice." She waved one hand his way. "Bye."

Brett stopped, turning her way as he reached into the half bath and flipped on the light. "I'm not leaving." He disappeared into the small space then came back a second later with a bottle of ibuprofen. "If I leave you're going to act all kinds of bad." He went to the kitchen and snagged a bottle of water from the fridge.

"Those are for the guests."

His steps slowed. "I'll dock my pay."

"There's no reason to do that." Camille scooted away from the confines of the ottoman blocking her in. "I'll just get some water from the tap."

"And that's why I'm not leaving." Brett pointed at her. "Just relax."

Camille looked from side to side.

Relaxing wasn't something she really did.

Outside of her one guilty pleasure, each day was filled with a never-ending list of shit to do. Cleaning. Laundry. Booking guests. Taking care of Calvin.

The only quiet time she had was the small window before she passed out each night. Less than an hour where she did something that helped her process where her life ended up.

Figure out how she would make sure the rest of it went very differently.

Brett cracked the lid on the bottle of water, loosening it before holding it out her way. "Do you even know how to relax?"

The truth wouldn't help her cause any. "Of course I know how to relax."

One sandy brow slowly lifted. "What do you do to relax?" He held out two gel caps.

Camille popped the pills in, swallowing them down with the icy water. "Usually I read."

It was specific enough it should appease him, but vague enough she didn't worry about judgment.

Or questions she didn't really want to answer.

Brett pulled off one of his boots. "What do you like to read?"

"Fiction." She scooted away as his other boot dropped to the floor. "What are you doing?"

"Gettin' comfortable." He leaned back and kicked his feet up on the ottoman next to hers.

"You call the couch comfortable?"

His head rolled her way. "Not as comfortable as a bed, but we're not there yet, Darlin'."

Camille couldn't even blink.

She might be struggling to separate fact from fantasy right now.

But before she could ask for clarification, Brett was pointing the remote at the television across the room. "What do you like to watch?"

Mostly him.

Sneaky peeks from the windows.

Hidden glances from the porch.

Full on stares through the binoculars Calvin asked for on his birthday.

She was a regular creeper at this point.

But telling a man you took any opportunity to catch a glimpse of him was never a good idea.

Especially this man.

The same one she wasn't supposed to even admit existed. "Funny things."

"Comedy." Brett's smile was wide and just as devastating as the rest of the night. "A woman after my own heart."

CHAPTER SIX

BRETT PULLED UP the 'on demand' screen and worked his way through the options until he found the one he wanted.

"Do you like new movies or old ones?"

Camille eyed the television for a minute before looking back his way. "I haven't really seen any new movies."

"I think we need to change that then." Brett started one of his favorite newer movies and scooted down, easily getting comfortable.

Which probably had nothing to do with the quality of the sofa under him.

"How's your ankle?" He asked knowing full well she was going to tell him it was fine, even if it wasn't.

"Fine." Camille wiggled her toes, reminding him of the surprisingly sexy seam sealing two of them together.

Hell, she could be toeless and he'd probably think it was the sexiest thing he'd ever seen.

"Good." Brett crossed his arms over his chest. It was nowhere near where they wanted to be, but right now he needed to tread carefully.

Especially since he wasn't completely sure where Camille's head was.

Before tonight he thought he knew. Thought she was still struggling with the life of abuse she suffered at her ex-husband's hand.

But earlier she'd mentioned Junior and the only people who seemed traumatized by the story were the people around her.

When it was clear their reaction embarrassed Camille, he'd done whatever it took to get her out of there. Save her from the moment that still confused him.

Made him question all he assumed.

And right now he was trying to wrap his head around what in the hell to do next.

One wrong move and he could go down like a sinking ship.

Ruining his only chance with the woman he'd wanted forever.

Based on that fact alone he should be wound tight. Add in the racoon incident and he should be struggling to sit still.

But that wasn't turning out to be the case.

He let his head fall back against the cushions. It was easy to close his eyes. Easy to relax.

Calvin was safe. Taken care of.

And so was his momma.

The sound of Camille laughing lulled him even deeper, down into a sleep he'd struggled to find lately.

Since he'd learned just how bad a man could be.

Seen the damage one could inflict on the people he was supposed to love and protect.

Brett jerked awake, an unfamiliar sound rousing him almost immediately.

The Inn was quiet outside for the sound of water rushing through the pipes as one of the guests flushed a toilet upstairs. The movie he'd started was long over and

Camille was sound asleep, her head and upper body tipped into his side as she took long, deep breaths.

He shifted a little, leaning to check the bag of water doing nothing to help the swelling in her ankle. Camille sucked in a loud lungful of air and shifted around, leaning against the pillows stacked on the other side of her slim body. It afforded him the opportunity to replace her ice, but damned if he didn't miss the feel of her against him already.

The lights in the kitchen area were still on so he padded in, pouring out the water and replacing it with a fresh batch of ice before flipping the overhead lights off and going back to where Camille was curled up on the couch. He carefully replaced the ice, making sure none of it touched her skin directly. Then he snagged a blanket from the chest that sat open in the colder months, choosing the softest of the lot and pulling it free of the stack.

Camille barely stirred when he sat back down, draping the blanket over her before retaking his spot, giving her a little space. If she came back to him, that was fine.

But he wasn't going to push.

Not yet.

****

"CAMILLE." BRETT TRIED to be as quiet as he could. Camille was out like a light, but the sounds upstairs made it clear some of the guests were early risers.

And she'd be pissed as hell if they found her here on the couch.

For a second it seemed like she was waking up.

Instead Camille rolled from one side to the other, the move bringing her closer to him as she curled against his body.

He hadn't wanted to wake her up before and now he sure as hell didn't.

But there wasn't any other option.

"Camille." Brett reached out, pushing the hair off her face.

Her eyes slowly opened, lids lifting and lowering a few times before she finally focused on his face.

Then she smiled.

The expression was fast and fleeting, disappearing almost instantly, replaced by what could only be described as panic.

Camille moved fast enough he couldn't catch her. Couldn't stop the retreat she almost managed.

But the second her feet hit the floor she went down, dropping the instant she put weight on the ankle he'd been icing most of the night.

"Shit." Brett launched across the ottoman, trying to slow her fall. Instead he ended up sliding across the low piece of furniture and going down with her, landing on the thick rug covering the hardwood. He somehow managed to be mostly on the bottom of the pile with Camille's lean body sprawled across and along his.

She rolled away almost immediately, pushing up on all fours. "Damn it."

"I didn't mean to scare you." He raised up to a sit, hooking one arm across his bent knee as she made her slow escape.

"You didn't—" Her eyes jumped to his. "It's okay." Camille continued crawling across the floor, heading toward the kitchen, mumbling under her breath.

"Where in the hell are you going?" Brett used the ottoman for leverage as he pushed up from the floor

"I need to start the coffee." Camille glanced his way over one shoulder.

Then she crawled a little faster.

"How are you going to brew coffee if you can't stand up?"

70

Camille popped up behind the island. "I can stand." She bounced to where the coffee maker sat, grabbing the carafe before hopping back to the sink.

"And you're just going to hop on one foot?" He went to the kitchen, snagging the filled carafe from her hands. "You'll end up spilling this everywhere and busting your ass on the wet floor." Brett glanced down at the floor.

That's when he noticed they had bigger issues than a wet floor to worry about.

Camille's eyes went to the same place his did, holding for a second before snapping back up. "I'm fine."

"Like hell." He dug into his pocket, fishing out his cell. He stared at Camille's ankle as it rang in his ear. His mother answered on the third ring.

"Well good morning."

"I need you to come to The Inn. I'm taking Camille into town." He hated not giving her a choice. She'd lived a life with too few choices.

But there really wasn't an option here.

"Is everything okay?"

"She hurt her ankle last night and it needs to be looked at." Brett followed behind Camille as she hopped around the island, her blonde hair bouncing along with each single-footed jump. "It's swollen as hell."

Camille shot him a glare as she worked her way to the steps.

"I'll be there in fifteen minutes." The line went dead in his ear as Camille started up the steps.

"Are you kidding me right now?"

"I'm fine." She gave up trying to make it up on one foot and went to her knees, going back to crawling. "I just need a shower. That's all."

"You're saying a shower is going to fix your broken ankle?" He'd heard some ridiculous things in his life, but that one might take the cake.

"It's not broken." Camille reached the top of the steps and continued down the hall, her voice dropping to a whisper as she made her way past the guest rooms. "You can go. I'm fine."

Brett slowly followed behind her as she made her way across the assorted throw rugs covering the wood of the hallway. "The only place I'm going is to the hospital." He waited while she reached up to unlock her door. "With you."

"I don't need to go to the hospital." Camille pushed her door wide and walked her knees across the plush carpet inside.

Brett caught the door as it started to close. "You absolutely need to go to the hospital." In any other situation he would give her what she wanted, but Camille was clearly not thinking straight. "Because that ankle is definitely broken." He'd seen more than a few broken ankles between football and ranch life, and what Camille was sporting definitely fit the bill.

"It's just irritated." She flopped over to her butt, eyes slowly moving from his feet to his head. "You're in my room, why are you in my room?"

"Because we're goin' to the hospital."

Camille huffed out a breath that carried a little bit of a whimper as she shifted the injured ankle.

It had to hurt. The pain medicine he'd given her had long worn off. "Let me get you some more ibuprofen."

Camille's attention dropped to her ankle. "This can't be happening."

"Things like this happen, Darlin'." Brett moved in closer, crouching down. "But it's all fixable. We've just got to get you there."

"But I need to work." Her eyes barely shined as she looked his way. "I have to take care of The Inn."

"The Inn will get taken care of." He kept his tone calm and even. "I'll make sure of it." He held her watery gaze. "But we've got to get you taken care of first."

Camille sniffed. "I'm still wearing what I wore yesterday."

"No one knows that but me." He gave her a wink. "And I won't tell."

"Your mother knows." Camille rested one hand to her head. "The guests know."

The chances anyone would actually remember what Camille wore yesterday were slim to none. "I bet most of them don't remember what they wore yesterday."

"Because they changed."

"What's your plan then?" He was working hard to keep his mind where it needed to stay. "I'm pretty sure you don't want me helpin' you get changed."

Camille's eyes barely dipped and her skin pinked. "No."

The word was weak and distracting as hell.

But it was the last thing he could think about right now. "You want my mom to come help you?"

"No." That time the word came out sharp and sure. Camille shifted around. "I can change by myself." She eyed the door to the bathroom. "You can wait in the hall."

She was going to make bad decisions while he was on the other side of that door, but if it sped this process up he'd have to take the risk and deal with the fallout later. "I'll be right outside. Holler if you need me."

"Okay." Camille scooted to one of the dressers in the single room where she lived, pulling open a drawer as he backed out of the space, letting the door close behind him before turning to sit down and lean back against it, keeping it from latching completely and locking him out.

It wasn't long before his mother rushed up the stairs, immediately coming toward Camille's room. "Is she okay?"

"She hurt her ankle last night." He tipped his head as the sound of the shower shut off, listening carefully for any sign the woman in the room behind him might be in over her head.

But so far Camille seemed to be a little too capable of caring for herself despite an injury.

It threatened to bring up the old anger he harbored. Make it fresh and new.

"How did she hurt it?" His mother lowered to the floor beside him.

That was the million-dollar question. He'd caught her when she stepped in a dip in the ground, but that alone shouldn't have been enough to cause the swelling he saw this morning. "Not sure."

He had his suspicions though, and they were making him edgy.

Which was the last thing Camille needed from him right now.

The door to the bathroom in her suite opened. Brett leaned against the cracked door, expanding the gap. "You doin' okay?"

"Yup. I'll be out in a minute."

His mother leaned close, eyes skimming down his front. "Those are the clothes you wore yesterday."

Leave it to her to make him a liar. "I stayed here last night. Wanted to make sure she didn't do anything to make that ankle worse."

His mother smiled softly. "Just be careful."

It was a conversation he knew was coming. His whole family was fiercely protective of Camille. "I would never do anything to hurt her."

"I'm not worried about her, son." His mother pushed up from the floor. "I'm talking about you." She smoothed down the front of her pants. "I'll go make some breakfast for you to take with you."

Brett stared ahead as his mother made her way back down the hall.

She wasn't alone in her worry.

It was something he'd tried to prepare himself for.

The possibility that Camille might never be ready to move on.

That she might never be willing to trust a man again.

It would certainly be understandable.

And if that was the case then he'd have to respect it.

But he could still be there for Cal. Show her son men weren't all like his father.

That he didn't have to be like his father.

It was the most important thing. Camille could separate herself from Junior. All it took was a judge and a divorce decree.

Cal could never do that, and that might be an infinitely more difficult thing to handle.

The door at his back suddenly shifted, catching him by surprise when the weight of it pulled away, sending him dropping backward into the room.

Camille stared down at him, her injured foot lifted off the ground as she balanced on the other. The air inside her room was a little humid and smelled intensely of the scent he always chased when she was close. She wore a pair of white shorts and a loose blue-grey top with ruffled sleeves. Her blonde hair was pulled back in a ponytail. "I'm ready."

"You look ready." She looked fucking beautiful, but that wasn't anything Camille was ready to hear from him just yet.

Brett rocked up, rolling to his feet. "My mom's here."

Camille's eyes dropped. "She shouldn't have to do this."

"It's not about having to." He eyed her. "How are you planning to get downstairs?"

The guests were starting to file out of their rooms as they made their way downstairs to where Mariah was working up their first meal of the day, so crawling or hopping were probably both bad options.

"I can maybe—" Camille started to lower her injured foot like she could hobble on it.

"Nope." Brett stepped close, grabbing her and hauling her up and into his arms before turning toward the stairs.

"You can't carry me around like this." Camille's whispered words were sharp in his ear as she smiled at the guests they passed.

One of the girls from yesterday's ride stared with wide eyes as they passed.

"People will think it's something it's not."

Hopefully it ended up being exactly what those people thought.

"They'll figure it out." Brett tipped his head as he passed a couple in the sitting area just at the top of the stairs. "Mornin'."

The woman's hand went to her chest and she gave him a lopsided smile. "Morning."

"I think you're going to be the most envied woman on the ranch." He slowly made his way down the steps, being careful not to get going too fast. Momentum wasn't your friend in times like this.

"You're probably not wrong." Camille glanced up at the top of the staircase. "Women are going to try to book the cowboy carrying service."

He couldn't help but laugh. "I'm sure a few of the hands would be happy to take them up on it." He carefully transferred her to one of the stools at the kitchen island. "But I'm a one-woman cowboy."

CHAPTER SEVEN

MARYANN STOOD ON the other side of the island with Mariah, laughing as they both worked together in the space. The older woman wrapped one arm around Mariah's shoulders, pulling her in for a sideways squeeze. "I adore you."

Mariah tipped her head Maryann's way. "I adore you back."

The moment was familiar. One Camille had experienced herself more than a few times.

But it seemed different witnessing it from the other side.

Lots of things did.

"You're in charge of this." Brett slid an insulated bag onto the counter in front of where she sat at the island watching The Inn move around her.

Without her.

Camille eyed the soft-sided tote. "What is it?"

"It's your breakfast." Maryann passed across two travel mugs. "And here's your coffee." She tipped her head toward where Brett stood at the freezer, filling an oddly-shaped bag with ice. "Once he gets your ice pack together, you're all ready to go."

"What about The Inn?" Panic bit at her insides.

This was *her* job. She was the one who was supposed to be here. Maryann didn't have the time to run the place. It was the whole reason they'd hired her.

The whole reason she had a home. Income.

Stability.

"We won't be gone long." Camille glanced over as Brett held out a set of pills. "I'm sure it's just irritated." She snagged the pain medicine and popped both into her mouth, swallowing them down with one of the coffees. "I'll be able to handle the afternoon here."

"We'll be gone as long as we're gone." Brett crouched down in front of her, carefully wrapping and velcroing the tubular ice pack in place.

Camille kept her attention on Maryann, ignoring the careful way he touched her. "We'll hurry back."

Brett picked up the bag of food and set it on her lap as he looked his mother's way. "We'll be back when we're back."

Then he hooked one arm under her knees and the other across her back, lifting her up and off the stool.

"You can't just carry me into the emergency room."

Brett walked toward the front door. "Why not?"

One of the guests opened it, holding it wide as they passed through.

Brett tipped his head in a nod. "Thank you."

"Because it's not normal." She caught the bag on her lap as it started to shift.

"Who cares?" Brett stopped at the side of his truck. "Can you get the door?"

Camille reached out to grab the handle, hanging on as Brett stepped back, swinging the door wide. "People will think—"

"People will think you hurt your damn ankle." Brett slid her onto the seat. "But I'm gonna go back to my original question." He grabbed the belt, pulling it out before strapping it across her body. "Who cares?"

"You forgot your coffee." Maryann came across the porch, her voice sing-songy as she rushed their way. She gave Camille both cups as Brett climbed into his seat. "Make sure you eat." She reached out to squeeze Camille's hand. "I love you."

Then she was gone.

Leaving Camille staring after her.

"Ready?"

The answer to that might always be no.

She was not ready for any of this.

The ankle.

The man.

The mother.

But Brett wasn't really asking.

They were barely to the end of the driveway before he started glancing her way. "What's in that bag?"

She'd forgotten about the food Maryann wanted to be sure she ate.

Which was weird. She usually never forgot to eat.

It was one of her favorite things to do.

Camille unzipped the bag and peeked inside. She pulled out the first of two foil-wrapped items.

"Breakfast burritos." Brett leaned her way as they drove down the long road leading to downtown Moss Creek. "Anything else?"

Camille passed him the first burrito before taking out the second and setting it on the console between them. Under the burritos was a container. The contents were concealed by the steam given off by whatever was inside. She worked the lid loose and the scent of potatoes and onions filled the cab.

Brett already had the foil off his burrito and was digging in.

Camille stuck the potatoes down into the larger section of the cup holder where their coffees were. Two plastic forks and a few paper towels rounded out the packed meal.

She stabbed both forks into the potato container and held a napkin Brett's way. "Your mom packs one hell of a breakfast."

"She had to feed four growing boys for a lot of years." Brett took the napkin. "Thank you."

"It's hard enough to keep Cal fed. I can't imagine feeding three more." Camille carefully peeled back the wrapping on the other burrito. "It's probably all I'd do. Finish cooking one meal and start cooking the next one."

"That's pretty much all she did for a lot of years." Brett reached for one of the forks, pulling it out along with whatever potatoes were stacked onto the tines. "It's why my dad was happy to build The Inn. She'd given up a lot for his dream. He wanted to be sure she had hers."

A year ago, it was impossible to imagine a man not only recognizing his wife's dreams but also fulfilling them. "Your dad is a good man."

It was a realization she came to relatively quickly.

There were some very great men.

Men who protected what they loved.

Put those same people first.

Provided.

Supported.

Loved.

And now she lived on a ranch with a whole slew of them.

"He is." Brett glanced her way as she took the first bite of the burrito. "What do you think?"

Camille chewed slowly, trying to figure out what all was inside the soft tortilla. It was smoky and a little spicy and filled with peppers and eggs and sausage. "It's amazing."

"She's been sneaking more spicy stuff in since Nora got here." Brett popped the last of his burrito into his mouth. "Don't tell my dad you got something spicy. He'll try to convince you to save him some next time."

"Why doesn't he eat spicy food?" Camille took another bite of what definitely ranked as one of the best breakfasts she'd ever had.

"Gives him heartburn and my mom read an article that said heartburn can lead to throat cancer." He grinned. "She cut him off that day."

Camille laughed.

She'd been on the complete opposite end of that spectrum.

The longer she'd been with Junior the more she was happy to watch him shorten his life with the alcohol that made him meaner than a snake.

Luckily, a woman stronger than she was stopped the cycle that spun her life out of control.

Brett sipped at his coffee as she finished her burrito. "How's your ankle feel?"

She leaned forward. This morning it became real clear moving it was not a good idea, so she had to gauge by sight and the dull ache settled into the joint. "Better than it looks."

"It looks pretty bad." Brett slowly coasted through downtown, past The Wooden Spoon and the window her ex-husband fell from.

She stared up at it every time she passed, right before looking at the spot where he hit the cement.

Not hard enough though.

Brett's eyes lingered on her as they stopped at the single traffic light. "You okay?"

She didn't open up much about the feelings she had toward Junior. For good reason.

Judgment.

Camille smiled. "Besides the ankle?"

Brett seemed to relax a little. "Besides that."

She forced her eyes from the spot that gave Junior only a little of what he deserved. "I'm not happy about missing work."

"I think you've more than earned a day off." Brett turned up the air as the sun started to heat the cab. "I just wish it was a day you could enjoy."

"Do *you* take any days off?" She wasn't the only one who didn't take days off. The ranch was filled with people who worked each and every day. Maybe not at the same task like she did, but Brett and his brothers most certainly worked seven days a week.

Brett chuckled. "Are you trying to catch me on a technicality?"

"I'm just saying, you act like I work too much but you work the same way." It's why she was always doing her best to earn the position they'd given her. If she worked less than them, how would it look?

Not good.

And this job meant more to her than they could ever know.

She would make sure it stayed hers no matter what.

"That doesn't mean you have to." He was making an argument he couldn't back up.

"I do what needs to be done. Just like you do."

Brett's eyes moved to stare straight out the windshield. "You do more than needs to be done."

"And you're saying you don't?" Camille grabbed the foil from her burrito and the empty potato container and went to work stacking it all back into the bag. "You slept on a couch last night and now you're driving your Inn's manager to the hospital."

"That's not what I'm doing."

Camille looked Brett's way. "Then what are you doing?"

He slowed to a stop as they reached the medium-sized hospital situated just outside the next town over. Brett's eyes came her way. "I'm taking care of you." He eased into the emergency lot. "And it's got nothin' to do with you being the manager of The Inn." His eyes pulled from hers as he found a spot near the front and fit the truck into it.

She was back to wishing she could be willfully blind.

Wishing she hadn't had any number of men try to pick her up in the grocery store.

At the gas station.

The post office.

Maybe if she hadn't it would be easy to blow this off. Pretend Brett was just being nice.

Just doing what anyone would do.

But she knew from experience this was not what anyone would do.

Even a Pace.

Camille focused on the floorboard, staring down at the damn ankle she should have gotten fixed the first time.

Ignoring it seemed like the only option back then.

Now that was coming back to bite her.

Brett came around the truck, his amble a little slower than normal. He opened her door but instead of reaching for her, his hand went behind her seat. He came back with the cowboy hat she was so used to seeing him in.

"You need that in the hospital?"

He settled the item in question onto his head before reaching in, easily lifting her out of the seat and against his chest. "The hat is a powerful thing, Darlin'. Gets shit done faster than you can imagine." He bumped the door closed before walking across the lot and through the automatic doors leading to the ER. The three women in scrubs at the desk immediately sat a little straighter.

"Mornin'." Brett tipped his head their way. "My lady here has hurt her ankle."

His lady?

There was no time to think on that too long because, like Brett promised, the hat appeared to be getting shit done.

A nurse was immediately out the door with a wheelchair, ready to whisk her away.

But Brett didn't immediately follow.

Camille turned just as the woman wheeling her stopped and gave Brett a wide smile. "You can come back."

His eyes came her way.

Camille's head nodded all on its own, leaving her to deal with the fallout.

Brett's blue gaze went to the nurse as he gave her a devastatingly dimpled smile. "Thank you, ma'am."

"Of course." The nurse swiped her badge and the door in front of them opened. "It gets boring sitting back here alone."

They walked past a line of closed curtains toward a set of enclosed rooms. The nurse wheeled the chair into the first one. Brett helped Camille out of the chair and up onto the gurney while the nurse started asking questions.

Name. Address. Phone number. Birth date.

The basics.

Followed by one she should have expected.

"Is there any chance you could be pregnant?"

Camille almost laughed.

Then she noticed the shift in the atmosphere of the room.

The change in the man sitting in the chair across from her. Brett still looked exactly like he had seconds ago.

But now there was something radiating off him.

Tension.

"No. Definitely no chance I could be pregnant."

Brett's eyes slowly lifted her way and something there sent her stomach flipping and her blood rushing.

"Ms. Shepard?"

Camille struggled to look from Brett to the nurse. "Hmm?"

"I was asking about your medical history." She quickly ran down a list of ailments like diabetes and heart disease.

"I don't have any of those."

"Is there a family history?"

It was a simple question. One that used to be easy to answer. "Not that I know of."

Losing her parents at a young age was simply something that happened. Being shut out by her sisters was what it was. There was so much other pain happening in her life she hadn't really been able to process any of it.

But the past year had given her plenty of time to reflect.

To mourn what she and Cal would never have.

"Okay." The nurse pushed her computer cart toward the door. "The doctor should be in with you soon."

She wasn't lying. Five minutes later a beautiful woman with shiny black braids wound into another, larger braid came through the door. "I'm Dr. Daniels." Her smile was warm and kind. "What brings you here to see me today?"

"I think I irritated my ankle."

Dr. Daniels' dark eyes dropped to the swollen appendage. "I would say that's an accurate assessment."

She lowered onto the stool beside the gurney. "Does it hurt when you move it?"

Normally she would say it was fine. Power through the pain to get what needed to be done, done.

But instead, the truth came out. "Yes."

"It looks like it hurts to move." Dr. Daniels gently pressed around until a jolt of pain made Camille inhale sharply. Dr. Daniels scooted back. "I think we need to get an x-ray. See what's going on in there."

"Okay." Camille blew out a breath.

"I'll put in the order now. It's actually a slow morning so they should be down to get you pretty soon." Dr. Daniels left right as the nurse came back in with a blanket.

She shook it out. "I brought this in case you get cold. It gets pretty chilly in here."

"Thank you."

"Can I get you something to drink? Maybe a cola?" The nurse spread the blanket across her bare legs, the warmed cover was soft and light and shockingly comforting.

Maybe she should have come to the ER more often in her life. "A cola would be amazing."

The nurse gave her a bright smile. "I'll be right back."

Ten minutes later Camille was tucked under a blanket, sipping a cold cola when a surprisingly attractive man came in. He was tall, dark, and handsome. The kind of man who might have caught her attention if things had gone differently.

But considering he was stuck standing next to Brett Pace the poor man looked mediocre at best.

"I'm here to take you up to radiology." He turned his attention to Brett. "I'll have her back as quick as I can."

It took at least forty minutes to get upstairs and x-rayed. By the time he rolled her back into the room Brett was pacing.

"The doctor will come in to discuss the results with you." The radiologist left and once again she was alone with Brett Pace.

An agitated looking Brett Pace.

"Did you think they lost me?" Camille shifted on the gurney. Sitting around was getting really old already.

Brett came her way, passing the chair he'd occupied earlier. "I thought maybe he was tryin' to keep you."

It was almost funny considering the man had shown her more than a few photos of his wife and daughters. "Pretty sure his very beautiful wife would have had a problem with that."

Brett came closer, his eyes focused the same way they'd been last night when she left Nora's house. "She's not the only one."

CHAPTER EIGHT

HE'D GONE A year not being able to be close to her.

Another forty minutes should have been no big deal.

But here he was. Pissed Camille was taken from him.

Even though it was only temporary.

It made him say something he probably shouldn't have, but Camille ignored it.

Just like all the other things he shouldn't have said.

"Have you heard from your mom? Is The Inn okay?" She changed the conversation immediately, dragging it back to the only thing she seemed interested in discussing with him.

"I'm sure it's fine." Brett rolled his head from one side to the other, trying to work out the tension there.

He was supposed to be supporting her.

Taking care of her.

Making sure she got what she needed.

Instead he was edgy that a man with a wedding band got to touch her.

Spend time with her.

A woman he still couldn't freely touch.

Be close to.

Claim.

"Ms. Shepard?"

The name grated on him. Reminded him a man who didn't deserve to exist had once called Camille his own.

Dr. Daniels came into the room, pushing her computer. "You definitely have some soft tissue damage." She turned the monitor around their way. "But it also looks like you've got a hairline fracture." She motioned to a barely perceptible line on the x-ray displayed across the screen. "It's right above the location of your previous break."

Brett slowly looked Camille's way. "Previous break?"

She hadn't mentioned anything about breaking that ankle before.

Camille shook her head. "I've never broken that ankle."

Dr. Daniels black brows lifted. "You may not have been treated for it, but it certainly looks like there's a previous fracture there." She pointed to a barely-perceptible shadow. "It probably happened a little over a year ago."

Camille's skin paled just a little. "Weird."

"At any rate, I spoke with orthopedics, had them check the x-ray out and right now they want you in a walking cast with a follow-up appointment scheduled for three weeks from now." She rolled the computer back to face her. "It's a pretty stable fracture so there's no need for a full cast. They'll be down to get that set up for you." She started typing. "Do you need anything for the pain?"

Camille shook her head. "I'm good."

Brett kept his mouth shut for the rest of their time in the hospital. Right now nothing he had to say was going to be good, and he'd learned long ago to shut up until you figured out what needed to be said.

And he didn't have a fucking clue what needed to be said right now.

Once Camille was fitted with an adjustable cast and given orders to stay off it for the next forty-eight hours, they were rolled back out by the same nurse who brought them in. She stayed with Camille while he went to get the truck. He pulled up to the curb and climbed out.

"Uhh." The nurse stared up at the cab.

"I got it." Brett opened the door and reached down for Camille, taking full advantage of the opportunity this truck afforded him. This time he moved a little slower, spent a little more time helping her get situated, hoping it might ease the unrest crawling over his skin.

Once she was buckled in place he turned to the nurse. "Thanks for all your help."

"You sure you don't want any crutches?"

He glanced at Camille.

She shook her head. "It would be a waste to get them for only two days."

"Okay." The nurse passed Brett the stack of papers they'd printed out. "Take good care of her."

"I plan to." It was a plan he'd been working on since the day Camille came to Red Cedar Ranch. The day he knew she was finally free of the man who never deserved a look from her, let alone all she gave him.

Brett swung up and into the truck. They were well on their way home before he trusted himself to open his mouth. "That cast helping any?"

Camille shifted her leg a little. "Actually, it is."

"Good." He didn't want to sound pissed, but right now it was almost impossible.

All he wanted to do was drive to whatever prison Junior was housed at and finish the job Mae started when she knocked him out the second-floor window of her apartment.

The bastard should have died that day.

It wouldn't have changed anything, wouldn't have fixed what he did to Camille and Cal, but at least Junior wouldn't be wasting the oxygen someone else deserved.

"Thank you for taking me." Camille's voice was quiet.

Maybe a little uncertain.

He had to get it together.

The woman was used to men acting badly when they were pissed, and the last thing he wanted was for her to associate that with him.

Brett took a deep breath, trying to calm the rage making him wish he could do karma's work and break a man's ankle. Even out the universe. "Thank you for letting me take you."

"Is that what happened?" Camille glanced his way. "Because I was under the impression I didn't have a choice."

He'd been confident that, left to her own devices, Camille would ignore the ankle.

Now he knew for a fact she would.

Had before.

"Seems to me you're not real good at takin' care of yourself." Brett slowed down as they came to a line of fast-food restaurants. "So I wouldn't expect to be gettin' any choices in that department anytime soon."

Once again Camille ignored a statement that left very little room for interpretation.

He'd worried about coming on too strong. Scaring her away.

But the woman clearly wasn't afraid of anything he had to say.

She just pretended it didn't happen.

Brett pulled up to the speaker at one of his favorite guilty pleasures. It was a local place that served any kind of milkshake you could imagine. He turned to Camille. "What do you want?"

She stared at the giant list of options. "I have no idea."

"What's your favorite dessert?"

"I like it all." Her eyes came his way. "I'm not picky."

Brett turned back to the speaker and ordered two of his favorites before pulling up to the window. Once he paid they passed them through. He handed the first one to Camille and stuck the second between his thighs.

Once they were back on the road he tipped his head Camille's way. "Try that one first."

She peered down at the blueberry crumble shake. "First?"

"You're gonna pick which one you like better." He managed a smile. "Unless you decide you want both of them."

"If I drink both of them I'll barf in your truck." She pulled the paper cap off the straw and took a sip, her cheeks hollowing as she fought the thick liquid up the tube. She stopped, lifting the cup to peek through the plastic. The ice cream was only about halfway up the straw.

"Want me to get it started?"

She immediately passed the drink his way, watching as he sucked a little of the treat free before passing it back. "The first bit's always the hardest to get out."

"Maybe you should do that one too." Camille tucked the straw that was just in his mouth between her lips. Her eyes widened, making it clear he'd succeeded in getting her what she wanted. "Holy cow." She took another sip. "That's amazing."

"They make their own custard." He sucked out some of the cherry cheesecake version then held it Camille's way. "And their own toppings."

Camille tried the second cup, lips pursing as her eyes went from one cup to the other. "This is hard." She took

93

another sip from the blueberry crumble, her lips twisting to the side. "I think I like the blueberry one better."

Brett took the cup she passed back. "How do you feel about chocolate?"

Camille sucked down a long drink of her shake. "Love it."

"Peanut butter?"

"Love it too."

Brett worked through the list of his favorites. "Lemon?"

"Also love it." Her eyes rolled his way, straw hovering right in front of her lips. "I told you. I'm not picky."

That wasn't completely true.

She was at least a little picky.

He knew for a fact she'd been hit on by every available man in town, and so far not a single one had gotten anywhere.

He'd assumed it was because she wasn't ready. Wasn't interested in dipping her toe into something that had gone so horribly for her before.

But after spending time with her he wasn't so sure that was the case.

"What about fruit and chocolate together?"

"I love chocolate covered strawberries." She drank a little more. "And cherries." Camille gave him a little smile. "And bananas." Her brows came together. "I don't love chocolate and citrus together."

"Finally." Brett slowed as they reached the edge of Moss Creek. "I knew there had to be something you didn't like."

Camille lifted one shoulder. "I don't like Junior. So that makes two things."

The way she said it was so casual. So matter of fact. It came out easily.

Like it was no big deal.

But that didn't seem possible.

The man ruined her life. Stole so much and gave less than nothing in return.

"Can't say that I blame you for not liking him." Brett resisted the urge to strangle the steering wheel. Take out his frustration on something.

Camille was quiet for a minute, sipping at the milkshake. "I try not to think about him." She scratched at a spot on the foam cup. "I don't really want to spend any more of my life on him."

She was suddenly laying out more than he expected, and it was a lot to process.

Especially considering it was very different from what he thought it would be. "Don't blame you on that one either." Brett glanced her way. "What do you want to spend your life on?"

Camille stared out the windshield. "I don't really know." She looked down at her lap. "I like working at The Inn." She paused. "And I want to make sure I give Calvin all I can."

It was the first time she appeared bothered by anything they discussed.

He'd seen her mention Junior twice now and Camille acted like what Junior did was old news.

The past.

But right now she looked upset.

Sad in a way that cut into him.

"What do you want to give him?"

She sucked in a deep breath, letting it out slowly. "Material things." She smiled a little. "I know that sounds stupid, but he did without so much." Camille's eyes moved over the landscape as they drove. "I'd like to take him on vacation." She cleared her throat. "And I want him to know I will keep him safe from now on."

It wasn't anything she really had to worry about.

No one was getting near her son. He would die before he let someone hurt Calvin.

But the way she phrased it bothered him.

From now on.

"What happened before wasn't your fault, Camille."

She turned his way. "It was, though. I'm the one who married him."

"You were young."

"But I got older and I stayed." She faced forward. "I knew Cal was suffering and I still didn't leave."

"He broke your fucking ankle, Camille. I'm sure he did more that I don't know about." His anger flared. "It sounds easy to walk away from something like that, but it's not."

"It should have been." She snorted out a bitter laugh. "What kind of woman stays with a man like that?"

He knew the answer to that. Literally.

"A broken one."

She didn't argue with the assessment, just doubled down on her incorrect opinion. "I shouldn't have let him break me."

"That's not how it works and you know it."

Camille went quiet.

Again.

Ignoring the words he offered.

Again.

The rest of the drive was a quiet one, giving him plenty of time to work through all she'd given him.

Camille's view of her past was even more twisted than he expected and it left him even more unsure of how to proceed.

He could have handled her hating men and thereby hating him.

He could have handled her having trust issues.

He could have handled waiting even longer for her to be ready for all he wanted to offer.

But he could not handle Camille blaming herself for anything that happened.

Wouldn't tolerate it.

It was past lunchtime when they pulled up in front of The Inn, which meant the place was mostly empty while the guests enjoyed a ride around the ranch with one of the hands. Mariah was gone, out doing whatever she did between meals. That meant there was only one person left inside.

And she was probably waiting by the window for them to get back.

Brett pulled right up to the front porch and parked. His mother was out of The Inn before his boots hit the ground.

She stood at the edge of the porch, watching as he walked around the front of the truck. "What did they say?"

He opened Camille's door. She stuck out her injured foot. "I broke it."

Again.

It wasn't anything he'd tell his mother, though.

Maryann Pace would go try to find something to burn down in retaliation, and considering Junior was in jail she didn't have many options.

"I thought it looked like you'd done more than just sprain it." His mother came down the stairs, wiping her hands on the apron tied around her waist. "How's your pain?" She took the empty breakfast bag, along with their empty cups, as Brett passed them her way.

"Not bad." Camille shifted around in the seat. "Better with this thing on, actually. It holds it stable." She stretched her good leg out like she thought getting out on her own was an option.

97

"She's not allowed to walk on it for forty-eight hours." Brett caught her before she could get very far.

"Oh!" His mother turned and rushed back up the steps, disappearing into The Inn before coming back pushing a wheelchair. "Mariah brought this for us to use."

"That was nice." He tried to mean it, but that damn chair stole the only reason he had to be close to Camille.

"We'll still have to figure out how to get her up the stairs, but it will certainly help." His mother parked it at the end of the porch before using one foot to lock the brakes. "There."

Brett grabbed Camille and carried her slowly up the stairs, taking longer than he needed to, stretching out the last little bit of closeness he would have with her.

His mother stepped away as he eased her into the chair, making no attempt to push Camille inside.

So he did.

"I need to run back to the house and check on some things." His mother untied the apron around her middle before taking it into the small room just beside the kitchen and hanging it up. "Can you hold the fort down for an hour or two?"

"Of course." He'd expected his mother to be at least a little difficult when she realized his intentions with Camille.

But so far she was leaning the exact opposite way, and it was throwing him a little. "Take all the time you need."

Camille spun in the wheelchair. "But—"

Brett followed his mother to the door. "We'll be just fine."

There was only one thing he really had to deal with, and even that wasn't an insurmountable obstacle. He pulled out his cell as he walked back to where Camille was sitting near the island. Brody picked up on the second ring. "How's your girl doin'?"

"Broke her ankle." He'd sent his brother to grab Duke when he realized he'd be staying the night at The Inn. "Can you hang onto Duke a little longer for me?"

"I don't have him anymore." Brody's voice carried a smile. "Told Calvin you were hopin' he'd take care of him for you. He and dad came to get him right away. Took him to the main house."

It was a brilliant idea. "Appreciate it."

Brett ended the call as he crouched down beside Camille and pulled out the other device he always had in his pocket. He pressed the alert button and waited.

He wasn't waiting long.

"Hello?" Calvin's voice carried the hint of excitement.

"Hey, Buddy. How's it going?"

"Great. I'm taking good care of Duke for you."

"I knew you would." Brett looked to where Camille was watching him. "You want to talk to your momma?"

"Is she there?"

"Right here with me." He held the walkie talkie closer to Camille.

"Hey, baby." Her eyes stayed on him as she spoke to the son she thought she'd failed. "I miss you."

"I miss you too." Calvin was a little out of breath. "We're helping Boone feed the horses."

"You're a good boy." Camille leaned closer to the speaker. "Be careful. I love you."

"I love you too."

Brett brought the walkie to his mouth. "We'll see you later on, okay?"

"See you later."

Camille's eyes followed the walkie as it went back into his pocket. Her next words were quiet. "How many times have you talked to him on that?"

He knew it might have been overstepping when he gave it to Cal, but the kid needed to know he was safe. That there was always someone right there if he needed them. "Not sure."

"Guess."

He lifted one shoulder. "Hundreds."

"Hundreds." It wasn't a question. It was a whisper.

A whisper that pulled him closer. "I want him to know I'm there whenever he needs me."

Camille's eyes held his a second longer.

Long enough for him to see the intent there.

But not long enough for him to brace for it.

CHAPTER NINE

HUNDREDS.

He'd talked to Calvin hundreds of times.

Talked her boy through God only knew how many days.

She'd kept her head up until that moment.

That revelation.

She knew Cal had the walkie. Knew Brett was on the other end.

And until this moment she'd pushed it out of her mind. Ignored the relevance of it.

But there was too much to ignore right now, and it snuck through the barriers she put up. Past the blinders she always wore.

Camille leaned forward, not really thinking through what she was doing. She'd gotten a little too good at not thinking, and now it was coming back to bite her in the ass.

Before her brain could register what was happening her hands were fisted in Brett's shirt, holding tight.

And her lips were on his.

It was a scenario she'd imagined an embarrassing number of times. Enough that her brain had it all lined up, easily executed without intent or purposeful thought.

Which was how she ended up here.

Accidentally kissing Brett Pace.

The man she was supposed to think of as a baby.

A non-option.

But the worst part of it wasn't her kissing him.

It was him kissing her back.

His hands came to her face as he leaned closer, fingers pushing up into her hair, holding her hostage as the kiss she believed belonged to her became his. Any thoughts she might have scrounged up fainted, dropping like swooning flies when his head tipped, mouth slanting as he deepened the kiss she'd accidentally started.

It had been so long since she'd been kissed. Whiskey killed any interest she'd had in Junior, smothering it out not long after Calvin was born.

A year ago she might have said she'd be fine with never being kissed again, but that thought ended quickly. Put out of its misery by a tall cowboy she wasn't supposed to want.

The same cowboy she was trying to get closer to now, leaning toward him as she looped both arms around his neck, taking anything he was willing to give her.

Unfortunately, the locks on the wheelchair under her had not been engaged.

Suddenly the chair started to move, rolling back while her body careened forward, the opposite directions feeding the momentum of each movement.

The sudden shift in her weight must have caught Brett off-guard, because he also started to tip, his crouching form falling back as she took him to the floor. Camille landed on his chest, her legs tangled with his.

Brett's hands held her in place, keeping her body from rolling off to the side as he looked up at her, his hat tipped sideways on his head. "If you wanted to roll around with me all you had to do was say so."

"Damn it." Camille tried to wiggle away, but the cast on her foot was hooked under one of Brett's boots.

"Stop." Brett held her tight. "Camille, stop."

"I can't believe I did that." She managed to get the knee of her good leg against the floor and used it to push up. "So freaking stupid."

Brett's hold on her loosened and she immediately scrambled away.

"Not sure I'd call that stupid." Brett sat up, draping one arm over his bent knee as he watched her crawl to the couch, intending to use the back of it to get on her feet.

Foot.

"It was definitely stupid. You are," she turned his way, waving one arm around, "you. I should not have done that."

"I am me." Brett stood in one easy move and slowly started coming her way. "And I think we have different opinions on what just happened."

She stared up at him. "I don't want to know your opinion."

"I'm sure you don't." He held one hand out. "That's why I'm not givin' it to you. You'll just ignore it. Same way you've ignored everything else I've said to you today."

"I haven't ignored everything you said." She'd heard every bit of it.

Unfortunately.

"Good." Brett leaned down, reaching for her hand with his and pulling her up and off the floor, bearing most of her weight as he held her a little too close. "I'm glad to hear that." His nose was almost touching hers. "But if you'd been listening then you'd know what just happened was comin' one way or another."

"It shouldn't have been."

"Why's that?"

"Lots of reasons." None of which she felt like listing out for him right now.

"Enlighten me."

"No thank you."

She was trapped in the best worst way. There was no running with her ankle the way it was.

And she should be running right now. Would be under normal circumstances. She'd evaded Brett countless times over the past year.

The man was at The Inn every day. Collecting his tours. Mowing the grass. Treating the pool. Visiting Maryann anytime she was there.

Snagging bottles of water from the fridge.

Looking for his brothers—

Hell.

"Why are you here all the time?" She shouldn't be asking. Especially since she probably wasn't going to acknowledge his answer.

Because it was definitely going to be problematic.

"You know exactly why I'm here all the time, Camille." Brett's eyes held hers. "You and Cal need someone looking out for you."

She struggled to breathe. Maybe it was how tight he held her.

Maybe it was the feel of his body pressed so close to hers.

More than likely, it was the culmination of a year's worth of fantasies all crashing down on her at once.

Brett's feet started moving, taking them toward the couch.

"Where are we going?"

"You're going to sit and relax." He all but pushed her down to the cushions.

"What are you going to do?" Camille turned, twisting to watch as Brett left her to head toward the small room just off the kitchen.

He came out tying Maryann's apron around his middle. "I'm going to do what I promised my mother I was going to do."

****

"WE BROUGHT YOU a present." Nora came into the main space of The Inn carrying a large vase of flowers tied with a floating 'Get Well' balloon.

She set it down on the center of the ottoman where Camille's injured foot was resting.

"We brought you something to occupy your time too." Mae dropped down, adding a stack of DVD portfolios to the wood tray where the flowers sat. "I pulled out everything I had that I thought you might find interesting."

Camille reached for the top set, lifting it up to read the title before turning it Mae's direction. "Snapped?"

"I figured you could identify with a lot of the women on the show." Mae was one of the only people who wasn't shocked when she talked about Junior. Maybe it was because she had her own issues with him to overcome.

Camille flipped the case over to skim the description on the back. "Too bad I didn't end up on the show."

Nora and Clara stared at her, looking a little shocked.

Not Mae. She dropped to the seat next to Camille, leaned back and got comfortable. "Nah. If you end up on the show it's because they prosecuted you. We would have made sure they didn't have any evidence to work with." She pointed to the next set of DVDs. "That's where those come in."

Camille picked that stack up. "Forensic Files?"

Mae grinned. "That's educational programming."

"It's too late now." Camille piled the DVDs in her lap. "That ship has sailed."

"We can still hope he gets offed in prison." Mae held up both hands, first and second fingers crossed. "Couldn't happen to a better person."

"I kinda hope he lives for a really long time." At first she wanted him dead.

Occasionally still did.

But right now, at this very moment, she wanted Junior to live for as long as possible.

Recoup some of the comeuppance headed his way.

Nora slowly lowered to sit on her other side. "How are you feeling?"

It was the change of subject that usually came up. She understood.

Most people didn't really know how to take conversations like this one. They expected her to still harbor the same pain she had at the beginning. The same fear. The same trauma.

But that all went away pretty quickly for the most part. Maybe because she was so tired of hating him.

The energy it took.

"Fine, actually." Camille twisted her leg, moving the walking cast from side to side. "This thing really helps. Once I can walk on it I should be back to normal."

"I'm not sure you should go right back to normal." Clara perched on the edge of the ottoman. "You should probably ease back into it."

"I have work to do. The Inn isn't going to take care of itself."

The three women around her slowly looked toward the kitchen.

Mae's eyes slid her way from where Brett stood in the kitchen, washing the dishes leftover from dinner. "Seems like you've got yourself a pretty good little helper."

Camille tried to act nonchalant. "Maryann asked him to come help."

It was sort of true.

True enough she didn't feel bad about saying it.

"If that's what you want to tell yourself." Mae scooted closer. "Doesn't make it the truth though."

Camille rubbed her eyes. She was tired.

Not sleepy.

Tired.

In a way she couldn't explain.

"Whatever you're getting at isn't an option." She felt like a broken record at this point, but eventually it had to sink back in.

"Why the hell not?" Mae spun to peer Brett's way again. "He looks pretty damn good in an apron."

"He's too young." The excuse was getting flimsier and flimsier by the minute, but she was going to wear it down to nothing until a better option presented itself.

Mae frowned, putting one hand over her heart. "Ouch."

"We're not ancient." Clara crossed her arms. "You make it sound like you'd be robbing the cradle."

"I'm older than Brooks." Nora slowly smiled. "So far it's worked out just fine."

"You're a few months older than Brooks." Camille huffed out a breath. "Not years."

"Well it doesn't seem to bother him." Mae smirked in the direction of the kitchen. "He's looked over here at least five hundred times in the past five minutes."

"It should bother him." Camille went back to rubbing her burning eyes. "I'm divorced with a kid." The truth of her own situation wedged back where she was hoping it would. "And not much else."

That was it. The reason they couldn't be together.

107

She lived in what basically amounted to a hotel room. One Brett's mother provided. She drove a used car that was the nicest thing she'd ever owned. Hell, up until the past year all her underwear was older than Cal.

She and Brett were not the same.

"You've got one hell of a body." Mae wiggled her brows. "I'm sure he's much more interested in that than what you don't have."

"I don't know." Clara pursed her lips. "She doesn't have an ex for him to deal with, and I can tell you from experience that's a pretty big perk."

"Good point." Mae poked one finger Camille's way. "No ex to deal with and you're smokin' hot and organized as hell."

"I'm sure men find organization sexy." Camille shifted a little on the couch, the weight of Brett's stare making her wish like hell she was allowed on her feet.

Because she would be gone.

Nora sighed. "We should go. I've got to go check on the house in town. Make sure the drywall finishers got it done."

"And I'm supposed to go over to Liza's." Mae stood up. "She's having a bad day."

"Is she okay?" Liza fascinated Camille.

She sort of set the stage for how Camille worked her way through the past year. Made her realize there was a way to come out of this without being bitter.

Jaded.

"Her ass is sore from having her head wedged so far up there." Mae rolled her eyes. "She's killing me."

Camille sat up a little straighter. "What's wrong?"

"She's being stubborn." Mae turned to Camille, looking her over. "Need anything before we go?"

"Can you take Brett with you?"

108

Mae grinned. "No fucking way." She started toward the end of the couch. "That problem is all yours to handle."

That was the main issue. She wasn't really sure how to handle Brett Pace.

If she even could.

Clara leaned in to give her a quick hug. "I'll see you later. Call if you need anything."

"Thanks." Camille watched them go.

Mae shot Brett a smile as she passed. "Have a good night."

His eyes slid to where Camille was peeking his way over the back of the couch. "I plan to."

Camille spun away, turning back to face the other side of the room.

The sound of the sink drain stopper popping free set her whole body on edge.

Mariah was long gone. Most of the guests were off enjoying the evening on the porch, in the pool, or roaming the grounds.

It was actually pretty surprising to her how few people were in The Inn during the day. Even in the rain they were out and about, visiting Moss Creek. Shopping in Billings. Helping care for the tour horses in the barn. Everyone seemed to love being outside and away from it all.

The sound of boots on the wood floor tempted her to turn. See what Brett was doing now.

But the answer to that became clear very quickly.

Each step that came closer sent her heart racing faster.

"Cal's comin' home." Brett leaned over the backside of the couch. "Should be here any minute." He reached out to slide one finger along the skin of her cheek, catching a bit of hair and pushing it off her face. "He's bringin' a movie he wants us to watch."

Her stomach dropped. "Us?"

"You're stuck with me until you can get up on that foot." Brett's finger didn't pull away, instead it continued on, tracing the line of her jaw. "And probably after that too."

He was getting harder to ignore.

More difficult to put out of her mind.

Especially when he touched her like he was.

The warm press of his finger stopped under her chin, tipping it up as he leaned closer. "Unless you want me to leave." His lips moved against her ear, the warmth of his breath skating across her skin. "Do you want me to leave, Camille?" She felt every word, each one warming long-neglected parts of her.

Initially she tried to convince herself it was loneliness that led her to this inappropriate fascination she had with Brett.

But she'd turned more than a few men down in recent months. Men who would have probably been more than able to offer the physical interaction she claimed to want.

Did want.

It just might not be all she was after.

"You should probably leave."

"That's not what I asked." Brett's mouth skimmed down her jaw. "I asked if you wanted me to leave."

Her lids fell as his lips reached hers, sliding across with a barely-there touch.

She wasn't supposed to be kissing him again.

Or letting him kiss her.

Whatever.

She was supposed to tell him she wanted him to go.

Lying the biggest lie she'd ever told.

Instead she leaned closer as his lips stayed on hers, warm and firm.

All that she should do rushed out in a sigh, her good intentions blowing away like the breeze as she reached for him, hands on his face, fingers against the rasp of hair peeking through his skin.

It was impossible not to want him closer. Confirm the imaginings her brain constantly provided.

But any chance of that was cut short by the sound of the front door opening and a collection of voices that filled the main hall.

Along with one set of very excited steps.

Brett moved away in a flash, putting an appropriate amount of distance between them before she could even open her eyes.

"Hey." Brett crouched down as Duke raced his way.

Except the black lab ran past Brett, jumping over the back of the couch to land on the spot right next to Camille. His doggy mouth was open wide, tongue hanging out to the side as he seemed to smile up at her.

Brett straightened, grinning as Calvin raced around the side of the couch to drop onto the cushions on Duke's other side. He went to work petting both sides of the dog's face. "I think he likes my mom."

Brett rested both hands against the back of the sofa, leaning closer. "I don't blame him." He shot Camille a wink. "I like your momma too."

CHAPTER TEN

BRETT GLANCED TO where Camille was sitting on the couch, a fresh bag of ice on her ankle as she swallowed down the anti-inflammatory pain pills he'd been giving her on the suggested schedule.

He didn't want to leave her but right now he didn't have any other option.

Brett tipped his eyes to where Cal stood in front of him, ready to help do whatever he could to take care of the woman they both cared about. "Can you stay here and take care of your momma and Duke while I go handle something real quick?"

Calvin nodded, his face serious. "Will you come back?"

Brett looked down at the little boy in front of him, more than ready to make a promise he intended to keep. "Always."

"Okay." Cal stood a little taller. "I'll make sure she doesn't walk anywhere."

"Good boy." Brett gave Cal a pat on the back. "You know how to reach me if you need anything." He tipped his head toward the couch. "Go snuggle your momma. I'll be back as fast as I can."

Calvin turned and hustled to Camille's right side. Duke had already claimed the left which meant when he came back for the night he would be out in the cold.

It was probably better that way.

For now.

Brett grabbed his keys and headed out. If he was going to be staying at The Inn, which he was, then he needed some things.

His cabin was the quietest it'd ever been when he stepped inside. Brooks had been gone for a year, but Duke was still usually there to greet him when he came in.

Not this time. This time Duke was doing much more important work.

He hurried through a shower and shave, dumping the clothes he'd been in for almost two days into the laundry basket before packing a bag with the basics. In under twenty minutes he was headed back out the door, ready to get back to where he needed to be.

His phone started to ring as he slid into his truck.

Brett connected the call, ready to answer any question she had about how Camille was doing. "Hello."

"Are you still at The Inn?"

"I came home to get a change of clothes, but I'm on my way back there now." He started the engine and backed out.

"Who's with Camille?" His mother's voice carried an odd tension.

"Besides everyone staying there? Cal and Duke. Why?"

"I'll meet you back there."

The line went dead in his ear.

It wasn't the conversation he'd been expecting, and there was something about it that made him uneasy.

Uneasy enough to kick up a decent amount of gravel in his rush to get back.

And the more he thought about it, the clearer it became.

Something was wrong.

By the time he ran up the porch steps his chest was tight and his blood was rushing. He pushed through the door, not worrying about what it might look like as he busted in.

Duke let out a single bark as Camille twisted to look his way, offering a little smile before turning back to the television.

Calvin was tucked against her, sticking close just like he promised.

Everything was fine.

He was just tired. In desperate need of a good-night's sleep.

Tires crunched on the gravel out the door he'd inadvertently left open. His dad's truck pulled right up to the porch and she got out almost immediately, her steps quick as she rushed toward The Inn.

Her eyes swept the area as she moved, narrowing as she scanned the space.

Like she was looking for something.

Maryann let out a breath when her eyes landed on him. "You're here." She looked toward the couch. "Everyone's okay?"

Brett stepped in close, lowering his voice. "What's going on?"

His mother's gaze went to Camille as she leaned his way, her words barely a whisper. "Someone came to our house."

"Who?"

She shook her head. "I don't know. It was a woman I've never seen before."

He glanced at the mother and son cuddled close as they watched one of the many superhero movies he'd made sure to stock The Inn with. "What did she want?"

His mother stared at him for a few long seconds. "She was looking for Camille."

"Why?" People didn't drive down a lane a mile long for no reason.

"I don't know." His mother rubbed her hands up and down the skin of her upper arms. "I didn't get a good feeling from her, so I told her I had no idea who she was talking about."

"And she left?"

His mother nodded.

He turned to look back at the woman who might hold more secrets than he realized. "Do you think she owes anyone money?"

"Junior spent every dime he had." Maryann's lips tipped to a frown. "And then some."

"Maybe that's all it was." Brett hesitated before asking the question that really mattered. "Did she know you?" His mother had been in Moss Creek long enough that she knew just about everyone there and for sure everyone knew her. Between the ranch and The Inn everyone in town knew the Pace family.

She shook her head. "I don't think so."

That meant the woman wasn't from there.

His mother moved closer. "Are you staying here tonight?"

"I was planning on it."

"I think it's a good idea to have someone with her." Maryann eyed his bag. "At least until we figure out who that was."

"I'll work on it." He set his bag down. "You get any footage?" They'd installed interactive cameras when The Inn went in, just in case visitors got turned around and ended up at the wrong door. It made it easy to let them know where to go even if no one was at home.

She nodded. "I'll send it to you."

"I'll find out what I can." In some places this might be a normal occurrence, but not here. Strangers didn't just show up on your doorstep. Not without a reason. And it usually wasn't anything good.

Which explained his mother's concern.

A concern he now shared.

Maryann gave him a pat on one shoulder. "I'm glad you and Duke are here." She backed toward the door, quietly going out without disturbing Calvin and Camille.

Brett watched out the window as his mother got into his dad's truck and they pulled away. Maryann Pace wasn't prone to overreacting and his father was even less inclined, so Bill Pace's presence lodged concern deeper in his gut.

And the fact that Camille and Calvin stayed in a building that always had unlocked doors suddenly seemed like a bad fucking idea. Unfortunately, based on the nature of the business, there were no other options.

He turned away from the front, ignoring the desire to flip the deadbolt as he went to drop his bag off at the base of the stairs. Duke's tail wagged, flapping against the couch as he watched Brett come closer.

Brett sat down on the other side of the sectional. Camille, Calvin, and Duke were stretched across most of the other portion, eyes glazed as they watched the movie.

He tried to relax and watch with them but ended up checking his phone every minute as he waited for his mother's text.

After fifteen minutes it finally came through. The series of video clips showed a dark-haired woman driving an older-model sedan slowly pulling up in front of the main house before getting out. She moved off camera for a few minutes before reappearing and going to the porch. He turned the volume down so it was impossible to hear what she was saying to his mother during the two-minute conversation. She smiled the whole time, but something seemed off about the expression.

And the woman was definitely no one he'd ever seen before.

It all gave him the same feeling his mother had.

Something wasn't right.

And there wasn't shit he could do about it right now.

So he had to focus on something he could do.

He set his phone down and leaned forward, lifting away the melted ice from Camille's ankle. The swelling looked to be going down quite a bit already. "How's it feeling?"

"Pretty good, actually." Camille wiggled her toes. "It's a little sore when I move it, but that's it."

"Good." He stood up. "Anyone want a snack?"

Calvin sat up straight. "I do."

"What kind of snacks do you like?" Brett headed for the kitchen.

"I like all kinds of snacks." Cal stood at the island while Brett dug into the fridge. "I like chips, cookies, cake..." Cal's eyes snapped to where his mom still sat on the couch. "Fruit."

Brett laughed. "That's a good list." He pulled out a gallon of milk. "What about cereal?"

"At night?"

"That's one of my favorite bedtime snacks." Brett opened the door to the large pantry and went in to look through the assortment of cereals they kept on hand for guests to choose from. Containers of cornflakes, Cheerios, and a few sugary options lined the shelf. "You like cereal?"

Calvin peeked into the room. "Sometimes."

Brett snagged the Cheerios from the shelf. "What kind of cereal do you like?"

"Any kind, I guess." Calvin backed away as Brett came back out to the kitchen.

"You like bananas?" He pulled out two bowls and set them on the counter.

"Yeah." Calvin watched closely as Brett pulled a banana from the fruit bowl and went to work slicing it over the two bowls.

"I eat this almost every night before bed." He poured a serving of cereal out into each banana-filled bowl before topping them off with milk. He dropped in spoons and passed one Calvin's way. "See what you think."

Calvin pulled the bowl along as he took a seat at the island. He took a bite, chewing slowly.

"If you want to play sports then you've got to be good at fueling your body and cookies and cake and chips taste good, but they aren't real great at helping you get stronger." He took his own bowl and sat down beside Calvin. "You've gotta eat protein and fruits and vegetables. Stuff that gives your body what it needs."

"What does it need?" Calvin took another bite.

"Vitamins and minerals and enough carbs for all the energy you're going to need." Brett scooped in some of his own snack. "I gotta do it too since I work all day on the ranch."

He'd always struggled to keep weight on. What he put in his body was something he had to always think about, otherwise he lost mass and strength.

And strength was important in his line of work.

Calvin nodded along, eyes wide as he continued to plow through the bowl in front of him.

Calvin was a lot like Brett had been. Skinny and scrappy.

The kid ate any and everything and stayed a string bean.

But it was easy to end up taking advantage of the system and filling up on bullshit since weight gain wasn't a fear.

Unfortunately, weight gain wasn't the only problem to come out of a poor diet, and when you played sports or did manual labor all day, malnourishment caught up with you real quick and everything suffered.

"What you put in your body matters, Buddy. We only get one of these things and we need to take care of it." His father was a good example of why it was so important to start young. After years of eating anything he wanted because mother nature gifted him with a metabolism that never stopped, Bill had acid reflux, high blood pressure, and pre-diabetes.

Which meant his mother cracked down.

Hard.

It was a lesson Brett decided to learn along with his dad.

And maybe could pass on to Calvin. Give him even more of a head start.

"Will it make me run faster?" Cal tipped his bowl to scoop out the last of the cereal.

"It will help, but you've still got to put the work in." He'd spent the past year trying to show Calvin how men are supposed to act. The way they're supposed to treat the people around them.

He wanted Calvin to know he had a choice in what kind of man he grew up to be. It might not be important right now, but one day Camille's son would realize Junior was as much a part of him as Camille was, and if he didn't have a good foundation that knowledge could fuck his whole world up.

Calvin moved his spoon around the milk remaining in his bowl. "I heard Wyatt and Brody talking about a football camp. Wyatt's gonna go."

Brett glanced up to where Camille sat on the couch. They hadn't had time to finish their discussion on the camp, and until Camille signed off on it he couldn't make any promises to Calvin. "I'll talk to your momma. See if it's something she thinks would be a good idea for you."

"Really?" Calvin's whole face lit up.

Like he'd never had anyone go to bat for him before.

Maybe he hadn't.

"I'll talk to her, but the decision is up to your mom." Brett tipped back the remaining milk in his bowl before setting it on the counter in front of him. "She calls the shots." Camille had spent too much of her life at someone else's mercy. He'd be damned if he took any power from her now.

Brett stacked Calvin's empty bowl into his before taking them to the sink. The dishwasher was still running, so he quickly scrubbed both bowls and spoons clean before drying them and putting each back in its assigned place.

By the time he was done Camille had sent Calvin up to bed and she was working the Velcro straps back in place across the cushioned cast stabilizing her second ankle break. She finished and carefully lifted from the couch before dropping down into the wheelchair he'd made sure was close by.

"One more day of this." She used her good foot to push herself backwards across the floor.

"It'll be worth it when that ankle heals." He caught the chair by the handles, leaning down. "Again."

Camille's hazel eyes tipped his way.

"What happened to it, Camille?"

"You don't want to know."

She wasn't necessarily wrong, but that didn't mean he wasn't willing to pretend. "Try me." Brett rolled her toward the front door.

Camille didn't say anything as he opened the door and pushed her out onto the porch. He sat down in one of the chairs while Duke did his nighttime business, sniffing around for a good place to pee.

"He shoved me down the porch stairs." Camille's eyes came his way, holding. "I tried to catch myself and stepped funny on my foot."

"Why didn't you go to the doctor?"

She looked out over the darkened landscape. "If you get hurt too much people start asking questions."

"And you didn't want them asking?"

Her gaze fell to her lap. "I wasn't strong enough to deal with what was happening." She scratched at the side of one of her fingers. "So I just pretended not to notice."

It sounded familiar.

He'd seen her do it to him more than a few times in the past twenty-four hours.

It looked like Camille could ignore just about anything if she set her mind to it.

"But then Calvin got bigger." She rolled her lips inward. "Older."

Something in her tone sent a chill down his spine.

But before Camille could tell him any more Duke rushed back up onto the porch, immediately going to rest his head right on Camille's lap, tail wagging as she smiled down at him.

"I think you've got a new best friend." Brett made a quick visual sweep of the area around The Inn before standing to push Camille back inside. He parked the chair at the base of the steps before locking the brakes. Camille was out of the chair before he could stop her, crawling up the stairs.

"You better hope none of the guests come down to get something to drink from the kitchen." He picked up his bag. "You'll scare the shit out of them climbing up the stairs like that."

The dim light from the kitchen cast a shadow that gave her form an eerie edge as she made her way up, making it look straight out of a horror film.

Camille snorted out a laugh. "I'll be able to walk up them tomorrow."

"If you think that then you didn't hear the same instructions I did." He followed her up the stairs and down the hall to her room.

"They said two days. Tomorrow is day two."

"Pretty sure that's not how math works." He waited while she unlocked her door, then he pushed it wide, holding it as Camille crawled in. "You're off it for 48 hours, Stubborn."

"I shouldn't have turned down those damn crutches." Camille stopped, slowly backing out of the room to look at the item sitting just outside. "What's that?"

"That's a rollaway bed."

The Inn was full. There were no rooms left for him to occupy.

And sleeping on the couch wasn't an option in a place like this.

Camille stared at the bed. "Where is it going?"

Brett leaned against the door casing, waiting while she worked her way through the situation. "I guess it'll fit in the laundry room." He tipped his head into her room. "But I'd rather roll it in here."

CHAPTER ELEVEN

LIFE WAS FULL of tough choices.

But this.

This was just evil.

How did one simply decide to send the man who just spent one of the sweetest moments she'd ever witnessed with her son to sleep in a laundry room?

"I don't—" Camille swallowed down the panic that might actually be closer to excitement and tried again. "I thought—"

This was the downside to ignoring important things. You ended up unprepared to deal with the shit that came your way.

She didn't think Brett would be sleeping at his place tonight.

It was pretty clear what his plan was.

But like so much else in her life, she'd blocked it out of her mind, refusing to allow herself to consider a possibility she wasn't sure how to deal with.

Especially since her initial plan was failing so miserably.

One of the doors in the hall opened and a young woman from the bachelorette party darted out, her feet stalling when she saw Brett standing in the hall wearing only a pair of jogging shorts and a tank top that showed just how much his normal t-shirts hid.

But Brett's eyes never left her. He tipped his head toward her room. "Can we talk about this inside?"

Being alone with Brett in a room with a bed seemed like a terrible idea. An idea that sent her head spinning into all sorts of premapped territories.

Camille pressed one hand to her head. "Can I just have a minute?"

"You can." Brett leaned closer. "But you should consider how this looks."

She'd been so busy trying to figure out how to ignore this new development that she hadn't really thought their current position through.

Brett stood at the door to her room.

And she was on her knees in front of him.

Like she was going to...

Going to...

Brett's bag hit the floor with a heavy thud and a second later she was up off the floor being dragged into the room. He deposited her on the bed before backing away.

"I thought you said I could have a minute?" Camille struggled to look away from where her eyes accidentally got stuck earlier, fixed to the way the front of his pants draped across an area she might have thought about a little too often. When she finally managed to find his face Brett's blue eyes were dark and staring her way.

"You lost that option when you licked your lips."

She didn't do that.

Couldn't have.

But then it accidentally happened again.

"Hell." Brett wiped one hand down his face. "I'm sleeping in the laundry room." He turned to go.

"No." She reached one hand his way in a reaction that definitely surprised him as much as it did her.

She didn't mean to say it. To reach for him.

Didn't mean for what she kept inside to make its way out.

But now that it was, the word and all it meant hung in the air.

Teasing her with the reality she faced.

A reality that was difficult to handle.

"I mean." Camille cleared her throat. "I don't think that bed will fit in the laundry room."

She wanted to ignore him.

This whole day and the night that came before it.

But it suddenly seemed impossible.

"Does that mean you want me to stay in here?" He was so cautious. Careful to always make sure whatever happened was her decision.

It was something she might have noticed long ago if she hadn't blocked it out immediately, filing it away with all the other little things Brett did.

And now she had an overflow problem.

"I don't know what I want." She'd worked so hard to stuff it all down.

Pretend none of it was happening.

Ignorance was bliss.

Which meant right now she was caught in whatever the opposite of that was.

"Then I'm going to the laundry room." He went to the door.

The laundry room wasn't far.

It was much closer than he usually was.

But the thought of him, wedged in there, sleeping on a cot...

A cot that was not near where she was.

"You can stay." She swallowed. "Here." One hand went to smooth down the fabric of her shorts. "With me."

Brett turned back to face her, his eyes moving over her face. "I think we should maybe get a few things out in the open."

No. They should not do that.

He slowly came closer, each step ramping up her heart. "I'm not trying to sneak into your bed, Camille."

A surprising amount of disappointment hit her right in the gut. "You're not?"

Brett shook his head as he continued to come her way. "No."

"Why not?" It might have been the boldest question she'd ever asked in her whole life.

It was also an accident. One more thing her overfilled brain spit out because of whatever the mental version of muscle memory was.

If there was a fantasy to be had, she'd imagined it.

And Brett Pace always had a starring role.

It seemed harmless at the time.

But now...

Now it seemed like her brain was using it all against her.

While the question might have been shocking to her it did not seem to surprise Brett in the least.

He reached where she sat and leaned forward, one hand pressing into the mattress at each side of her as his eyes met hers. "If I do this right I won't have to sneak into your bed." He came closer, the whisper of his words warm as they moved over her lips. "Because you'll be dragging me there."

She swallowed out of reflex. A full-on gulp at what was about the least likely thing to ever happen.

Dragging Brett Pace to bed would involve admitting that she very much wished to have Brett Pace in her bed.

It would also require a level of forwardness she'd never possessed. Not even on her best day.

But before she could explain any of that Brett straightened, going to the door that connected her room to Calvin's. "He locks his doors at night, doesn't he?"

"Yes." She assumed he wanted to be sure Calvin wouldn't walk in and find them there. Together.

But Brett walked right past the connecting door and back to the one leading to the hall. He opened it, using his bag to prop it in place before slipping out. He was back seconds later, rolling in the folding cot. "It's locked."

Of course it was locked. "We're in a house full of strangers. He knows he has to keep his room locked at all times."

Brett pulled his bag from its position as temporary doorstop, letting the door slide closed.

Then he locked it.

The click of the deadbolt into place seemed to echo around her.

In her.

She was locked in a room with Brett Pace.

Watching as he stretched out the collapsed bed he planned to sleep on.

"Those aren't very comfortable." It was mostly an observation.

Mostly.

"I've slept in worse places." He dropped his bag onto the expanded mattress.

He probably didn't mean it the way she took it.

But like every other second she spent with him, this one was ending up infiltrated with inappropriate thoughts.

It was how her infatuation with him started.

Completely carnal.

And it was supposed to stay there. She might have been fine if it had.

Unfortunately he had to go and start doing things that took that interest and made it grow.

Spread.

Like wildfire.

And now it was getting impossible to control.

Contain.

Camille tapped her fingers against the blanket covering her mattress, uncertain what in the hell to do now.

"I'm going to go get some water." Brett backed toward the door. "You want anything?"

She wanted so many things. Things she should feel much more guilty about. "I'm good."

"I'll be back." He left the room, the sound of a deadbolt sliding into place, sending her leaning to look toward the door.

He'd locked it behind him.

Which was a little strange.

A little overly cautious.

But dwelling on that would only cut into the precious minutes she had until he came back.

Camille hopped to the dresser, digging through her pajama drawer, looking for something that would fit over the cumbersome brace. Unfortunately, none of her pants were wide enough at the bottom.

So she was left with one option.

It was an item she'd bought but never wore, lured in by the pretty floral print of the fabric and the lace trimming the edges.

And the thought of wearing it in front of Brett made her heart race.

Made her wonder how he might look at her. Where his eyes might go.

Where they might linger.

Camille shoved the drawer closed before she could talk herself out of it.

It was just a nightgown. That's all.

He probably wouldn't even notice.

She went to the bathroom to brush her teeth, scrub the makeup from her face, and change into her harmless nightgown and the matching panties that came with it.

But it turned out the thing was shorter than she realized, the hem of it barely clearing her upper thighs.

That couldn't really matter though. It's not like she was planning to sleep on top of the covers.

Camille hopped her way back to the bed, dropping down on top of the blanket she should be wiggling her way under.

But her skin suddenly felt hot. Warm in a way that made her wish she had a fan.

She might have to invest in one.

Or two.

As she was deciding where the hypothetical fans would be placed for maximum cooling the lock on her door flicked open.

A soft knock came a second later. "Can I come in?"

There was no reason not to let him in. "Yes."

Brett came in carrying his glass, immediately relocking the door before turning to face her.

He stopped dead in his tracks.

She should have been thinking about this moment instead of focusing on the fans she didn't have.

Should have let herself really work through the ramifications of this nightgown.

Of being on top of the covers instead of under them.

Then she might have done things differently.

Or not.

Brett was silent for a very long time, his eyes dark as they stayed on hers, never wandering to the flowered cut of the dangerously low neckline. The lacey drape skimming the skin of her thighs.

But it was clear he'd seen it.

And what was once warmth ignited, turning the heat creeping over her skin to a full-fledged inferno.

Brett slowly set the water down, placing it onto the floor beside the cot he was supposed to sleep in.

But the thing was so uncomfortable. She'd slept on it for weeks when they first came to The Inn. When Calvin wasn't used to having his own room or the different sounds of their new home.

"Um." Camille smoothed one hand down the gown that suddenly felt smothering. "I usually watch television when I go to bed."

"That's fine." Brett still hadn't moved from the spot he'd stopped in. "So do I."

Camille shifted around, pushing up toward the pillows before leaning back against them in a way that accidentally lifted her chest higher. "If you wanted to come over here to watch so you can see better you can."

"Are you inviting me into your bed, Camille?" His voice was low and deep in a way that snaked down her already hot body, reaching places that hadn't been touched by anyone else in years.

Places she once thought were DOA.

Until she happened across something that shocked them back to life.

"Yes." The word was breathless.

She was breathless.

Starving for air and a list of things she'd been ignoring.

But nearly everything on that list had one thing in common.

Brett Pace.

"What are you inviting me to your bed for?" His eyes finally shifted, moving slowly down the line of her body. "Specifically."

That was a question that could take hours to answer. Especially now that she knew the options available to her.

This past year she'd gotten an education in something she thought was a pretty basic art, thanks to the kindness of Moss Creek's resident librarian.

"I don't know." It was a truthful lie.

She technically knew all the things she would want Brett Pace in her bed for, the issue was her brain's willingness to convert any of that into actual coherent thoughts right now.

"That's not good enough." His eyes came back to hers. "You're gonna have to make it real clear."

It was impossible not to be irritated. Frustrated. "Why?"

His lips lifted in a slow curve. "Lots of reasons."

"Like what?" Getting answers from him seemed much easier than having to offer her own.

"I don't plan to only be in your bed once, Camille." Brett took a single step in her direction. "So I'm happy to wait as long as it takes to get there."

Wait?

He wanted to wait?

The thought ramped her frustration up to a level she'd never felt before. "What are you waiting for?"

The intensity she'd seen in his eyes as she drove from Nora's house was back and sharper than ever before. "I'm waiting for you to be ready for all I want from you."

"What do you want from me?" Part of her knew she shouldn't ask. That she was probably just going to ignore whatever he said anyway.

But another, larger part of her, wanted to hear it.

Needed to hear it.

Just in case she might decide to listen.

The slight curve of his lips lifted to a heart-stopping smile. "All of it."

"You're going to have to be more specific." She dug her fingers into the blankets as he continued to slowly come closer.

"Now you're ready to talk specifics?" Brett reached the foot of her bed and her head started to spin.

"Yes." The answer wasn't well-thought-out, but nothing in her life was.

"Really?" His brows barely lifted.

"Mm-hmm." Whatever kept him moving closer.

"Okay." His fingers trailed up the mattress. "Then, specifically, I want to be the only man in your bed." His eyes lifted to hers. "Your turn."

Her eyes watched as the tips of his fingers dragged closer to her foot. "What was the question?"

"I want to know what you're inviting me to your bed for." He was so close to touching her. "Specifically."

She hadn't blinked in so long her eyes burned. "I want you to touch me."

The words might have accidentally come from her mouth instead of staying in her brain where they were supposed to be.

But it almost didn't matter when the heat of his skin reached hers, the pads of his fingers almost rough as they skimmed across the top of her foot. "I want to be the only man who touches you." The slide of his hand moved to her ankle. "Specifically."

"Okay." There was no reason to explain that might have already been the case.

She'd had countless offers from men.

And turned every one of them down.

For one, very specific, reason.

None of those men were Brett Pace.

"I want to be the only man who kisses you." Brett's hand continued along her body, tracing the line of her shin, the dip and swell of her knee. "I want to be the only man you kiss."

Also easy to agree to considering he was the only man she'd kissed in years. "Okay."

He reached her thigh and she stopped breathing, every bit of her focus going to the spot where he touched her.

"Camille."

"Hmm?"

"Look at me."

It took everything she had to look away from where his fingers pressed to her body. To force her eyes up to meet his.

"If I touch you then you can't pretend I didn't."

He was probably more right than he realized.

She would have definitely tried, but there was a one-hundred percent chance it would be impossible to forget.

It was still a deal she shouldn't make. Shouldn't even consider.

"Okay." The word barely made it out of her mouth before Brett's lips smothered it out.

Sealed it off as his wide body came to hers, heavy and hard, pressing her into the mattress and pillows.

She'd never wanted like this.

Never considered it an option.

And now that it was...

She felt very greedy.

Like there was so much time to be made up for.

So much missing to be found.

Reclaimed.

Brett's hair was soft as her fingers went into it, holding tight as she spread her thighs, making room for his body to press against the aching throb between them.

She sucked his lower lip, using her uninjured leg to pull his body closer. Tighter to hers.

Brett groaned as the hard length of him rubbed against her, the ragged sound pushing her need higher.

Speeding the spinning of her head and the racing of her heart.

This was something she'd only read about. Imagined.

At length.

She should have been more prepared for what it would do to her.

What it would turn her into.

Because right now she felt like a different woman in the best way possible.

"Brett." Camille grabbed at his shirt, trying to lift it up.

See what was under it.

Touch what was under it.

Lick what was under it.

His breath was sharp and short as he caught her hand with his, lacing their fingers before pressing the back of her hand into the mattress beside her head. His eyes were unbelievably dark as they looked down into hers.

"I'm goin' to need you to take a deep breath." He followed his own directions. "Specifically."

CHAPTER TWELVE

"I DON'T WANT to take a deep breath." Camille's other hand went for his shirt. "I want to touch you." She managed to get her hand under the hem, her fingers immediately splaying across his stomach. "You said you wanted to be the only man I touched."

"I said I wanted to be the only man you kissed."

Her hand traveled higher. "So does that mean you want me to touch other men?" Her fingers slid over his nipple, forcing him to suck in a breath at the unexpected touch.

"You probably should only touch men you want me to kill." He grabbed her wrist as she made another pass across his now-hard nipple. "Especially if you touch them like that."

He'd expected a lot of things from Camille.

This was none of them.

He thought she would need him to go slow.

Expected to take a few steps back here and there.

He did not expect to come into her room and find her laid across the bed in a nightie so short there was no missing the matching panties beneath it.

"If I promise not to touch anyone else will you let me touch you?"

That seemed like a trick question. "No." He dragged her hand from under his shirt. "I thought you wanted me to touch you?"

The leg wrapped around his hips flexed. "Yes."

"Me touching you is very different from you touching me."

"Then I want to touch you too." The tip of her tongue slid along her bottom lip like it had when she'd been on the floor in front of him earlier. "Specifically."

"You're in an awful big hurry." He'd rushed into plenty of beds.

And learned that the faster you get in, the worse things seemed to go.

"I'm not." Camille sounded like she believed what she was saying, even as she pressed up against him, the line of her nightgown threatening to release its precarious hold on her perfect tits any second.

She certainly appeared like a woman on a mission.

But maybe that mission wasn't what he was thinking it was.

Maybe this wasn't just about getting something from him physically. Maybe her sudden desperation was for something else.

Something significantly more important.

Brett brought one of the hands he held to his lips, running them along the velvety softness of her inner wrist. "If you want me in this bed then we've got to put down a few ground rules."

"You're already in the bed."

"I got in before I realized how fucking dangerous you are." He nipped at the inside of her elbow as he worked his way toward her shoulder. "Now I'm thinking you need corralled."

"I'm not dangerous." There was a hint of hope in her voice. Like maybe some small part of her desired to be that woman.

The one who brought men to their knees.

The fact that she didn't know she already was might be the only reason he was still holding his own.

Once she figured it out he was fucked in the best possible way.

"You are most certainly dangerous." Brett kissed along her shoulder, intending to make his way to her neck, but the slight arch of her back broke what little hold the lace of her nightie had and the pink of a nipple peeking out lured him down. He worked closer, covering every bit of creamy skin that was exposed as she fought the hold he still had on her hands. When his mouth finally closed around her puckered tip Camille let out a low sound that shot straight to his aching dick.

She pushed higher, breasts fully releasing from the gown pinched between their bodies, freeing both to his mouth.

And he took full advantage, worshiping each one until she was writhing under him.

But in order to do anything else he had to release her hands. "I'm going to let go, but you've got to keep your hands to yourself."

"Why?" She twisted a little in his grip, making it clear as hell that she had no intention of listening.

"Because those are the rules." Brett finally made his way to her neck, running his nose along her skin as he took a slow breath. "And if you can't play by the rules then I'll have to go back to my little bed."

"Why do you get to make the rules?"

"I don't get to make all the rules. Just mine." Brett took another deep breath, this one against the silky weight of her hair. "You get to make rules too." He

137

relaxed his grip on her hands, almost expecting her to immediately reach for him.

She didn't.

Instead her hands rested against the pillow beside her head, palms up, fingers relaxed as she watched him. "Now what?"

"I guess that's up to you." He eased down her body, hoping it made his intentions a little clearer. "You come up with any rules for me?"

She slowly shook her head as he continued working his way lower, catching one of her breasts with his mouth as he passed.

Camille needed to know he was capable of giving without taking.

And he sure as hell wanted to give right now.

Offer up anything that might make her willing to let him here with her again tomorrow night.

And the night after that.

His fingers caught the elastic of her panties, dragging them down her legs. He managed to get them free from one foot, but the cast on her other ankle trapped them.

So he let them stay, instead focusing on the fabric still between him and where he wanted to be.

He slowly pushed the bottom of her nightgown up, inching it higher to reveal the slightly tanned skin of her upper thighs. His heartbeat throbbed in his dick as the first glimpse of her pussy came into view, teasing him with yet another surprise.

"Jesus." Brett shoved the fabric up to her waist, unable to maintain the slow drag once he caught sight of what awaited him.

He shoved her legs wide, shock and desire making him forget his plan to be patient.

His eyes lifted to where she watched him.

This woman.

This sneaky seductress.

The nightie.

The matching panties.

Now this.

He was clearly not the first one to decide this moment would happen.

Brett reached out to run one finger down the seam of her perfectly waxed mound, tracing the triangle of closely-cropped hair that was the only bit remaining. "What's this, Camille?"

"If you don't know then I might have a rule."

Was that a joke?

"You know what I mean." He put more pressure behind his touch, sliding down to find the bit that made it clear he knew exactly what he was dealing with. "Who did you do this for?"

Maybe he was wrong. Maybe all of this was innocent. Something she always did.

Camille's eyes rolled closed as he teased across her clit. But even half naked and unseeing she was still able to take him down with a single word.

"You."

A year of waiting.

Wondering if it was all for nothing.

Worrying Camille would never see him the way he saw her.

Never give him a chance after all she'd been through.

Hoping she might be ready one day.

Only to find out one day might have passed him by, left him sitting with his dick in his hand, counting down wasted time.

No more.

His mouth was on her a second later, slicing time into two separate sections.

Before.

And all the rest.

Camille's back bowed off the bed as he lapped at her clit, intent in a way he'd never been before.

Because this wasn't the end of anything. It was the beginning of everything.

And he wanted to start off right. The path he intended to make clear enough Camille couldn't ignore it.

Her hands fisted in his hair as she rocked against him, thighs locked around his head, pinning him in place.

Not that he planned to go anywhere. He'd been with this woman for a year. Right beside her.

She just didn't know it.

She came too fast, leaving him wishing he'd been just a little less eager. A little less focused on proving himself.

Her whole body sagged, legs dropping, hands falling to the mattress.

He slid back up her body, lips dragging over her stomach, across the silvery lines etched into her skin by a sacrifice he couldn't begin to imagine.

But hoped to one day witness.

He was on top of the fucking world. Finally feeling like all he'd waited for was within reach.

But then he lifted his head, expecting to see a slack and satisfied woman collapsed against the pillows.

Instead Camille stared at the ceiling, eyes open wide and unblinking.

"Camille?"

One hand went to her forehead. "Shit."

Not the reaction he was hoping for.

"What's wrong?" She came. There wasn't a doubt in his mind.

"Damn it." She sat up, wiggling away before scooting toward the end of the bed.

Brett crawled after her. "Stop."

She was on her feet before he could catch her, hobbling along on the foot she wasn't supposed to be walking on.

"Where are you going?"

She stopped, spinning in place as she looked around the room. "I don't know."

Brett held both hands out her way. "Okay. Just take a deep breath." He slowly worked off the edge of the bed, inhaling loud and long, hoping she would follow along.

She did not.

So breathing wasn't going to help anything. That meant he had to try to get her to talk to him, which was even less likely to work than the breathing. "What's wrong, Sweetheart?"

Her eyes snapped to his. "What did you call me?"

"I called you Sweetheart." He slowly crept her way.

"Oh."

He stopped as what was happening registered.

He'd expected her to need him to be slow earlier. Physically.

But the physical wasn't turning out to be her problem. Not really.

She was trying to shut down. Figure out how to block out what just happened.

Put it somewhere she could ignore it until it went away.

He couldn't talk her out of it. Couldn't convince her to do otherwise.

All he could do was power through. Keep piling it on until there was nowhere to store it all.

"Come on." He held one hand out while the other snagged the remote, switching on the TV. "Let's watch television."

Her eyes went to the hand stretched her direction, holding there a second before lifting to his face.

She was silent long enough he started to worry she might be better at this than he realized.

That Camille might succeed in stuffing this away.

"Okay."

He barely wiggled his fingers. "Okay."

She slowly lifted her hand to his, the slide of her palm slow and steady as it fitted into place.

He gently pulled, easing her closer, waiting as she took lopsided steps his direction, each one forcing him to fight the urge to grab her and lift her onto the mattress. Get her off that damn foot.

Once they were close enough he reached for the covers, pulling them back, making a space for her to sit. As she swung her legs up he noticed something he'd forgotten.

The panties that matched her nightie still dangled from the boot strapped to her foot.

Camille's eyes landed on the flowery bit of fabric right as his did.

He snagged the free leg opening of the garment, straightening out the tangle and holding it open. "Here."

She hesitated just a second before sliding her foot through the hole.

He skimmed them up her legs, past her knees and along her thighs.

It was the first time he'd ever helped a woman into her clothes.

Camille snagged the waistband of the panties from him, barely lifting her butt off the bed to slide them into place. "Thank you."

Brett lifted the glass of water he'd used as an excuse to give her privacy from the floor before switching off the light. He held the drink her way. "Thirsty?"

She looked from it to him then back again. "That's yours."

"It's ours." He moved it closer. "Take it."

Camille wrapped the fingers of one hand around the sweating glass, watching as he made his way around the foot of the bed. She took a sip as he slid under the covers beside her, watching him over the rim of the glass.

Then she kept drinking, downing half the large cup before passing it back his way. "Thank you."

"You're welcome." He swallowed a little before setting it onto a coaster on the table next to his side of the bed.

The glow of the television was as familiar as the rest of the room.

It looked identical to every other room in The Inn.

Not a single thing appeared to be different.

No photos. No personal items.

It was like Camille was simply a guest in the place she lived.

He passed her the remote. "What do you like to watch?"

She didn't make any move to change the channel. "You're going to laugh."

"Maybe. But you could tell me anyway." He wanted to lighten the mood. Let her see nothing she could do would upset him.

She eyed him in the dim glow of the screen. "I watch The Joy of Painting on PBS."

"Let's watch some happy little trees then." He'd witness way worse than Bob Ross to sleep beside her.

"The bushes are happy too."

That was two little jokes she'd made. "What about the birds?" Brett snagged the remote from her, pulling up the smart aspect of the television and punching in his Netflix pass code before moving through the screens to find the show she enjoyed. "There. Now you can watch it whenever you want."

And he planned to watch it along with her.

Brett stretched out, hooking one arm behind his head. The bed was comfortable and, while there might not be any outward evidence this room belonged to Camille, the whole place smelled like her. The combination relaxed him instantly, making his limbs and lids heavy. After getting nowhere near enough sleep last night he was beyond exhausted. Five minutes into Bob's rendition of a bridge in the middle of the woods, his eyes were closed more than they were open.

Nothing against Bob, he just didn't hold a candle to a strict bedtime and a sweet-smelling woman.

****

BRETT TRIED TO shift on the bed, move from the heat of the spot he was in, but something was pinning him in place.

No. Not something.

A long-legged blonde in a foot cast.

Camille was stretched across him, curled into his side, one arm thrown across his chest and one leg hanging over both of his. A line of drool soaked into the shoulder of his shirt, making it stick to his skin.

Netflix's home screen played across the television, rotating through the shows they were currently trying to reel watchers into.

He squinted at the clock on the dresser, blinking a few times as he tried to focus on the numbers.

It was almost six. An hour past when he should have been up and moving.

He eased out from under Camille, carefully working a pillow into his place.

Using her bathroom would certainly wake her up so he quietly unlocked the door connecting Camille's room to Calvin's, creeping in. Duke's tail thumped against the bed as Brett walked in.

"Come on." He kept his voice low as he silently patted his leg, hoping to bribe the dog out.

Luckily Duke was probably ready for a potty break and immediately jumped off the bed, tail still wagging as he followed Brett back into Camille's room.

After closing the door to Cal's room he quietly opened Camille's door, locking it behind him before heading down the long hall toward the stairs. Most of the guests slept until at least six-thirty, so he had a half hour to check in with his mother and brothers before getting himself together and figuring out what he needed to do to keep The Inn running. He was halfway down the stairs when something odd caught his attention.

Fresh air.

The downstairs smelled like the outside.

He snapped his fingers, stopping Duke short.

Brett held his breath, listening for anything out of place.

He slowly moved toward the base of the stairs, leaning down to look toward the entry hall.

Sure enough the front door stood wide open.

He'd been the last one in after they took Duke out and he was positive he'd closed the door.

Even considered bolting it.

Maybe it was the wind. Maybe he just thought he got the door closed.

He'd been distracted as hell.

Brett crossed the space, looking out over the quiet porch and front drive while Duke did his business, checking for any sign something might not be right.

But everything seemed fine.

When Duke was finished he closed the door, paying extra attention to how it latched, looking for any sign of how it might have accidentally opened.

145

"Brett?" Calvin's voice from the stairs sent him spinning around.

"Yeah, Buddy?"

Calvin was still in his pajamas, eyes sleepy as he padded across the wood floor. "Are you going to have a healthy breakfast?"

He smiled. "Sure am. You want some?"

"Yes, please." Calvin slid onto one of the stools at the island as Brett went to the pantry. He yawned, long and loud.

"You still tired?"

"Yeah." Calvin reached down to scratch Duke's ear. "I had a dream that someone was knocking on my door and it woke me up."

Brett stopped. "You did?"

"Yeah." Calvin yawned again, this time stretching his arms over his head, making the yawn more of a grunt. "I dreamed they knocked and whispered my name from the other side."

CHAPTER THIRTEEN

CAMILLE JERKED AWAKE, head snapping up, vision obscured by the mass of hair covering her face. She swatted at the strands, smacking them to one side as she twisted to look around the room.

It was empty.

Not empty. It was just missing the cowboy she thought might be there.

There were signs of Brett though. His bag still sat on the cot he didn't sleep on. The cup he brought up was still on the nightstand.

And the smell of his skin still whispered through the air.

Camille turned her head to one side, sniffing.

She lifted the front of her nightgown to breathe against the fabric.

It wasn't the air that smelled like him.

It was her.

Probably because she'd practically sexed him last night. Would have if he'd been willing.

God only knows what her freak out after that would have been like.

She dropped back to the mattress, pulling the pillows over her head so she could groan into them quietly.

She was a full-grown woman, not a horny teenager driven by hormones.

Except last night apparently.

Last night she was not herself.

She was oddly confident.

A little demanding.

Strangely willing to take what was offered her.

And it was...

Wow.

Wow enough to send her into a panic.

Maybe that was normal after your first non-self-induced orgasm.

"Good morning."

Camille slowly dragged the pillow covering her face to one side to peek out at the man upending her life. "Morning."

"You ready for breakfast?" Brett came toward the bed, fully dressed in his standard jeans, t-shirt, and cowboy hat.

And carrying a tray.

This couldn't be real. She had to still be asleep.

Men like this didn't exist outside the confines of her clandestine closet library.

She whipped the pillow away. "What's happening?"

"I brought you breakfast so you could eat before you get up and moving." He stood beside the bed. "You ready?"

No.

Definitely not.

"You didn't have to do this." Camille worked her body up the mattress. The second she was upright he set the tray across her lap, the folding legs at each end balancing it in place.

"I know that." He leaned down and pressed a kiss to her forehead. "I wanted to."

She stared at the tray of food. "What is this?"

"It's my best attempt at French toast." He shot her a wink. "Mariah helped a little."

French toast was her favorite. Specifically, French toast with bananas and cinnamon.

Which this was.

"Calvin told me it was your favorite." He eased down onto the mattress, reaching out to pour coffee from the carafe into the cup prefilled with cream and sugar.

"It is." She stared down at the meal. "I can't believe he remembered that."

"You're his momma. Of course he remembered it." Brett ran one hand down her leg, rubbing it through the layers of sheet and blanket. "He even knew you liked the bananas on top and not inside."

"They get all mushy when you cook them."

Brett smiled. "That's what he said."

She sniffed at the emotion making her nose run. "He's a good boy."

"He's one hell of a good boy." Brett's hand paused. "And I promised him I'd talk to you about football camp."

She took in a slow breath, working to ease the tightness in her throat. "Okay."

Brett reached out to snag the bundle of flatware. "It's a week long. Goes every day from eight to five at the high school field."

"I meant okay he can do it." She'd failed her son in so many ways. If this was something he wanted, then she'd do whatever it took to make it happen for him. "I just have to figure out how to get him there."

Brett unrolled the fork from the napkin and held it out. "He can ride with me if that's okay with you."

She took the fork without really meaning to. "With you?"

"I'm one of the coaches, Sweetheart." He stretched across the foot of the bed. "That's how I got Cal in this late."

She couldn't look away from the man relaxing at her feet. He suddenly took up so much space.

In her room.

In her head.

And other places.

Places she hadn't intended to let him go.

Body and mind, those felt safe.

But Brett was already spilling out of the wells she made for him, spreading to areas less capable of surviving the flood.

"Thank you." She forced her eyes to the food, fought her focus to the act of eating.

But even that wasn't safe.

Wasn't untouched.

"How'd I do?" The easy smile on his face said Brett knew darn well how he did.

"Does your mother know you can cook like this?" She picked up a thick slice of the peppered bacon served every morning with breakfast.

"I can't take full credit for that." His hand stretched across the blankets, coming back to slide across her thigh. "Mariah had to tell me what to put in the batter."

"I might see if she can add this to the menu." Camille relaxed just a little as the sweet taste of eggy bread and banana warmed her belly.

"I bet she'll do anything you ask her to do." Brett's thumb stroked against the blanket. "She loves you."

"I love her." Mariah was one of her favorite people. They spent most of the day together, working in the kitchen at The Inn. Talking about things no one else would understand. "She's an amazing person."

"She says the same thing about you."

Camille took a sip of coffee, watching Brett over the rim of the cup, swallowing down as much of the hot liquid as she could manage before setting it back on the tray. "I'm glad."

"She also said you have some fantastic ideas that we should implement here." His eyes were very focused as they fixed on her face.

Camille continued cutting through the slices of battered bread, planning to ignore the conversation. She wasn't in any position to tell anyone how they should run their business. She was just here to make sure it ran the way they wanted it to.

An employee. Just like Mariah.

Brett reached up to steal a strip from the stack of bacon on her plate. "Would you tell me some of them?"

She lifted one shoulder. "I was just talking, that's all."

"So talk to me." His voice was quiet and calm. "You're the one here day in and day out, Camille. If you think there are things we could be doing better then we need to hear them."

Need?

She moved around one of the bananas on her plate. "I was just thinking the guests might like it if we offered a picnic lunch they could order."

Camille slowly lifted her eyes to where Brett was watching her with a wide smile on his face. "That's a brilliant idea."

"It is?"

"Absolutely it is." He sat up and reached for another strip of bacon. "What else?"

"Well." She stabbed the tines of her fork into the last bit of bread and stacked on the final slice of banana. "It's sort of along the same lines, but what if we offered charcuterie trays they could have delivered to their rooms?" She chewed through the bite. "It would be things

COWBOY SEEKING SOMEONE TO LOVE

we keep on hand anyway and they would have to order it in the morning for the evening." She swallowed. "I think there are lots of people who would love to have a quiet night in their room instead of having to come down to dinner."

"I agree." He leaned closer. "What else?"

"We have a lot of bachelorette parties that come here." She set her fork across the empty plate. "What if we had some sort of working relationship with a limo or party bus service that would come pick them up and take them out for the night?"

"Have you written these down?" Brett worked his way closer, coming to lay right at her side.

Camille shook her head. "No."

"Can you?"

"I don't want your mom to think I'm trying to—"

"My mother will be thrilled to have your input." He eased in a little more. "She can't think of everything, and this is a new venture for us. We need all the help we can get to make this place the best it can be."

"I don't want to overstep." She tried again to explain. "I'm just—"

"My mother trusts you. You run this place better than anyone else could have. She needs your input." Brett was right beside her now, the warmth of his body sinking into the side of hers. "It takes all of us to run this place, so don't be shy about puttin' your two cents in."

Her two cents might not be worth what they paid for them, especially considering she was still laid up and unable to do the work she'd been hired to do.

"You ready to get up and get movin'?" Brett's nose ran along the side of her neck. "Or you want to stay here a little longer?"

Her lids fell as his lips replaced his nose, going to the spot just below her ear. "I'm supposed to be downstairs."

"You're supposed to be stayin' off that foot." His hand slid up the covers, sinking into the valley between her thighs before continuing up.

Higher.

Higher.

Each inch he gained sent her heart racing faster and her brain struggling to stay online. To stay focused on what she should.

Because she was supposed to be...

Supposed to be...

Brett's hand tucked under the covers as his teeth caught the lobe of her ear. His tongue flicked it, reminding her of last night.

The act she was supposed to forget happened.

When his fingers slid into her panties her legs pushed apart, opening for more of his touch.

She was incapable of pretending she didn't want it. Didn't crave anything he was willing to offer.

Her head tipped back, dropping to the headboard as he immediately found the tiny bit of flesh the previous man in her life didn't seem to know existed.

Back when she was willing to let him close to it.

Which was clearly a huge waste of time when there were men like Brett in the world.

He stroked against her in perfectly paced passes that dug her heels into the mattress and pulled her hips from the bed as she tried to steal more.

Just in case it was the last she ever got.

Her body tensed, clenching tight a second before releasing all the air from her lungs and all the tension from her limbs.

But they didn't go alone.

They stole a little of the fear she held close.

The caution she used like a shield.

The hesitation she brought to every conversation. Every interaction.

And it left her exhausted.

Drained.

A little empty.

She meant to inhale but yawned instead as her body melted down the headboard.

"Maybe you should stay up here." Brett pulled the covers up her chest. "Take a nap."

"I'm supposed to—"

"Stay off your foot for one more day." He curled in closer. "Tomorrow you can do all the things you want to do."

"I have so much to do." She yawned again.

"We do have a lot to do." His voice was low in her ear. "But we have plenty of time to get it all done."

****

CAMILLE SNAPPED AWAKE for the second time.

She sat up straight, sucking in a breath.

The clock across from her said it was nearly lunchtime.

"Shit." She'd slept four more hours after Brett brought her breakfast.

Breakfast and...

For the second time she fell back against the pillows, pulling them over her face as she tried to smother out all her decisions over the past twelve hours.

She was a terrible employee.

Physically incapable of doing her job.

And fraternizing with her boss's son.

Definitely not a good look.

Especially since there hadn't been any technical fraternizing.

Brett hadn't gotten anything out of it besides...

Nope. Nothing.

If she was a wondering kind of woman, she'd definitely be trying to figure this situation out.

But that would involve thinking about things she didn't want to think about.

Like why she was letting it go on like she was.

So instead, she whipped back the covers and swung both feet over the edge of the mattress, carefully keeping as much weight as she could on her good leg as she moved to the dresser to pick out panties and a bra.

Her options were actually pretty decent after having a year to slowly replace the ones she'd been wearing since before Calvin was born. Her hand hovered over the stacks as she considered what she might wear with them.

She snagged a navy-blue set, chewing her lip as she went to the closet, pulling open the doors and sliding the navy t-shirt dress she'd just bought from its hanger. It wasn't anything fancy, but it was comfortable and cool in the summer heat.

And it would look okay with the boot she was stuck with for the foreseeable future.

Camille went into the bathroom, unstrapping her boot while the water warmed up. It was surprising how much more her foot hurt without the extra support, so she was careful not to put any weight on it while she showered, washing her hair and body before shutting off the water and drying off as much as possible before sitting on the edge of the tub to swing both legs out. The process wasn't too terrible considering she didn't have to shave.

Waxing was one hundred percent worth the effort and mess, which after doing it for a year, was minimal.

She strapped on the boot first, ready to get her ankle back into it as fast as she could.

Unfortunately then she was left trying to get her panties over the damn thing. After some maneuvering she was ready to stand up, working them into place before adding on her bra and the buttery soft dress. She quickly dried her hair and added a little makeup, then went out to find a shoe that might keep her hobble to a minimum. It took a few tries to find one that had a sole thick enough to even out the added height of the boot, but a pair of slightly wedged espadrilles she had worked pretty perfectly.

Half of a pair of espadrilles.

She was just finishing tying the fabric around her ankle when there was a knock at the door. A second later it cracked open, but not enough for her to see who was on the other side.

"Camille honey, are you awake?"

"I am." She forced a smile as Maryann came in, the nerves twisting her stomach making it nearly impossible to keep the expression in place.

"Don't you look beautiful." Both Maryann's hands came to rest over her heart, one stacked on top of the other. "How are you feeling?"

Camille started to give the same answer she'd offered every person who'd asked since she moved to The Inn, usually with pity in their eyes.

But fine didn't sit right.

"I'm good." She started to stand up.

"Oh! Wait." Maryann disappeared out the door, coming back a second later with a pair of crutches. "Look what I found." She hurried Camille's way with the well-worn set of supports. "And thank goodness I did. That pretty dress would be hell to hop around in." She held the crutches out. "See if they fit. We guessed on the height."

Camille carefully stood, tucking the cushioned pads under her arms before grabbing the hand supports. "I'm not sure where they need to be."

"You shouldn't have to stretch into them, but they should also give you a little room to swing that foot."

Maryann stepped back. "Take a few steps and see how they do."

They were awkward and clunky, but she managed to move herself from the bed to the dresser.

Maryann smiled wide. "Perfect." She leaned in at Camille's side to give her a sideways hug. "Brett said that was the right height. I should have figured if anyone would know how tall you were it would be him." She went to the door, pulling it open wide. "You ready for lunch?"

"Yup." She took that little bit of problematic information Maryann gave her and stuffed it away.

Unfortunately, it didn't really stay there.

And it knocked something else loose.

I want it all.

That's what he said to her last night.

Right before he...

Another bit fell out, dropping from its hiding spot out into the open.

Into the unavoidable.

"After lunch I was thinking we could talk about the picnic idea you have." Maryann pulled the door closed and locked it with the key she could have only gotten from one person.

The same person who was leaving his mess all over the place, mucking up the tidy way she chose to live.

It's no wonder she broke her ankle.

Probably tripped on the way Brett looked at her when he saw her holding Faith.

Suddenly it was right there, front and center. Another memory she tried to smother out staring back at her.

The look in his eyes.

The set of his jaw.

I want it all.

What he'd said and done wasn't a mess.

It wasn't haphazardly strewn everywhere, thrown messily around.

It was all lined up, one next to the other.

Like dominoes.

Ready to fall.

And she was standing at the end of the line.

CHAPTER FOURTEEN

HIS BROTHERS' TRUCKS were lined up in front of the barn at the main house, just like his mother said they would be when she came to fill in for him at The Inn.

Brett parked next to Brooks and headed straight for the open doors. It was almost lunchtime so everyone was collected together, meeting up from whatever they spent the morning working on.

"Look who decided to come get his hands dirty today." Boone grinned his way. "Not that I can blame you for skipping out on us. I'd take bein' with my woman over this too."

"How's Camille doing?" Brody scrubbed one hand down Edgar's cheek as he passed the horse's stall.

"She's okay." Brett moved deeper into the barn, doing a visual sweep, making sure they were alone in the space.

Not that he didn't trust the rest of the men who worked on the ranch, this was just something that needed to be kept as quiet as possible. If Camille found out from someone other than him...

Brody's eyes narrowed. "Somethin' wrong?"

"Someone came to the main house lookin' for Camille last night." He leaned against the panel of wood between two of the stalls. "A woman."

"A woman Mom didn't know?" Brooks picked up on the primary issue right away.

Brett dipped his head in a nod. "That's right."

Boone dropped the bale of hay he was carrying. "She say why she was lookin' for her?"

"No." He'd watched the video over and over, listening to the conversation his mother had with the woman. "Just asked for her by name."

Brody wiped one hand down his face. "Not many reasons a person would come all the way out here."

"Not many *good* reasons a person would come all the way out here." Brett clarified his brother's statement. "And if she was here for a good reason I'm sure she would have explained it."

That was his primary concern. The woman was nice as hell to his mother.

Friendly.

Polite.

Sweet.

To the point it was overkill.

"What all did she say?" Brooks hooked one arm over the door of the empty stall beside him.

"Started off complimenting the place. Tellin' Mom how nice it was out here. How pretty the house was." Brett dug into his pocket, fishing out one of the snacks they kept on hand for the horses. "Then she asked if she could talk to Camille Smith."

"That doesn't sound like she was asking for her." Brody stepped back as Brett offered Edgar the treat. "That sounds like she was sayin' she knew Camille was here."

"It might get worse." Brett smoothed one hand down Edgar's neck as the horse chewed through his snack. "Cal told me about a dream he had last night. Said someone knocked on his door and whispered his name."

Brody went very still. "You think someone was really there?"

"Front door was open when I got up this morning." He fought to keep himself calm.

Calm was the best thing a man could be in the face of anything, but this day was already testing him.

And it was barely lunchtime.

"How would someone have known which door was Cal's?" Brody was trying to talk himself out of the possibility, just like Brett had done.

"Hell if I know." Brett pulled off his hat to run one hand through his hair. "Who would be looking for him at all?"

"Maybe it really was a dream." Boone's expression was serious. "Kids have strange dreams all the time."

"I hope you're right." He met Boone's gaze. "But we need to be ready in case it wasn't."

Boone's frown was deep and sharp. "If this has anything to do with that son of a bitch I'll—"

"If this has anything to do with Junior then we'll handle it." Brody was calm and cool. "Same as we'll handle it if it's not got to do with him." He turned to Brett. "Has Camille called her attorney? See if he's heard anything?"

This was where shit got sticky. "I haven't told her yet."

She was just starting to let him closer. Reminding her of the not so distant past risked losing any headway he'd made.

Brody's brows lifted. "You've got to tell her."

"I can handle this." Camille had been on her own so long, even when she was still married to Junior. It was time for her to have someone take on the hard shit. Keep it off her plate.

Out of her mind.

"It's not about handling it." Brody's expression was serious. "It's about taking shit on as a team. You can't come in and act like you're in charge of how her life goes." Brody tipped his head. "Even the bad parts."

The advice would be easy to blow off. Ignore.

But Brody had dealt with a similar situation with his own wife.

"I don't know if she can handle it." It was his number one fear. That this would send Camille ten steps back.

And she'd come so far.

"That woman is stronger than you'll ever be." Brody smirked. "And I bet you she knows it." He pointed one finger Brett's way. "Tell her and see what happens."

Brett glanced at Boone. "You gonna tell Mae?"

Mae and Camille were tied by a common enemy.

More than a year ago Camille's ex-husband tried to take his frustration at Camille leaving him out on Mae.

But he found out the hard way Mae was meaner than he was. Junior ended up knocked out a second story window after taking a cast-iron pan to the face.

But not before he managed to take a shot at Boone.

Boone tipped his head in a nod. "She'd kill me if I didn't." He straightened. "And I spent too long on her shit list as it is."

Brett huffed out a breath. "Damn it."

He didn't want to tell Camille. Not even a little bit.

"We're gonna have to start locking up The Inn at night." Brody shook his head. "I'm not riskin' Cal's safety so people can come and go as they please."

He'd been thinking on that all morning. "We should install the same system we put on Mom and Dad's place but add in the digital locking system." It would make it possible for someone to remotely unlock the door so he could easily check ID and let visitors in from his room.

Camille's room.

Which was another thing he needed to talk to her about.

And maybe one discussion would fuel the other.

"I think that's a good idea." Brody pulled out his phone. "I'll call Curtis and send him that way now."

It was a perk of having so many hands on deck. The men who worked on Red Cedar Ranch could do just about anything between them. Curtis had worked in alarm systems for a few years and was able to handle everything the ranch needed in that department.

Which it looked like might end up being quite a bit.

"Send him to my place next." Boone pulled out his own phone. "I'm headin' into town for a minute." He hurried out the open door.

"Go talk to Camille. Maybe we're gettin' all upset over nothing." Brody slapped him on the back as he headed for the hay Boone abandoned. "Welcome to marriage."

"Not yet." Brett turned to follow Boone out. "Gotta talk her into it first."

"Some are easier than others." Brody shot him a wink. "Hopefully you'll end up like Brooks and not Boone."

"I had to ask her twenty times before she said yes." Brooks grinned. "I don't think any of them make it easy."

Brett threw one hand up in a wave as he headed out the door. "I'll let you know what I find out."

Boone's truck was already out of sight when he reached the drive, the dust from his rushed departure still hanging in the air.

It was understandable. Mae was about as easy to find as it got. If someone wanted to get to her for any sort of reason all they had to do was show up at The Wooden Spoon.

Which meant whoever this was wasn't also looking for Mae.

So hopefully that meant this had nothing to do with Junior.

Brett eased his truck down the gravel drive as he headed back to The Inn, making a stop at his cabin to grab all the clothes he could. He'd been worried about what would happen once Camille was back on her feet and there was no longer any reason for him to stay at The Inn.

It'd been the worst-case-scenario in his head.

Now he knew it wasn't.

By the time he got back to The Inn Curtis was already there, looking around the front door while his mom and Camille watched.

Brett made his way across the gravel toward where the women were watching as Curtis took a few measurements.

His mother was the first to glance his way, doing a double-take when she saw him. "That was fast."

"I'm a fast mover."

She gave him a little smile. "We'll see."

"So this is for what now?" Camille's brows came together as she watched Curtis.

"We're putting a camera on here like we have on the main house." Curtis was one of the older hands on the ranch. He'd been there since Brett and his brothers were too small to be much help.

"Why?" Camille was balanced on a familiar-looking set of crutches as she watched Curtis mark a spot on the cedar right beside the door.

Brett moved Camille's way, wanting her attention as much as he needed it. "Have you had lunch?"

She gave him a quick glance, her cheeks pinking up just a little. "Not yet."

"Let's go get something then." He rested one hand on the center of her back. "We'll get out of Curtis's way so he can do what he needs to do."

From experience he knew their camera wouldn't be up and running for a few days. The unit had to be ordered and even with rush shipping it took at least two days to be delivered, but there was electric work that had to be done in preparation and Curtis could knock that out in an afternoon. That way all he had to do was hook everything up once it came in.

"Okay." Camille gave Curtis one last long glance before finally turning to head back into The Inn. She moved easily on the crutches which wasn't surprising. Cal got his athleticism somewhere and it definitely wasn't from Junior.

Curtis moved back as she passed, tipping his head in a nod. "Ma'am."

She gave him a little smile. "Do you want something to drink?"

"I'll get it." Maryann moved in right behind them. "You two go get something to eat."

"What about Calvin?" Camille scanned the space. "Where is he?"

"He's with Bill and Wyatt." Maryann went to the fridge and pulled out the pitcher of tea that always sat on the top shelf. "They are helping with today's riding tour."

He'd lined it up so Calvin would be both closely watched and far from anyplace accessible to the general population. The only way to get where they were now was by ATV or horseback so the little boy was as safe as he could be.

Just in case.

"Oh." Camille smoothed down the side of the dress draped softly around her body. "I hope he's not in the way."

"I sent him out." Brett set his bag in the small room just off the kitchen before pulling the door closed. "I think he'll be a good addition to the team in charge of the tours." Everyone on the ranch had a job and it was time for Calvin to find his.

Because he was one of them.

"It helps the kids be less scared when they see another kid riding." It was why they'd started taking Wyatt out anytime they had children going on a tour. "He's a strong enough rider now that he can handle helping."

It'd taken almost six months for Calvin to really feel comfortable on a horse. Luckily the horse he chose for Cal was about as user-friendly as it got, so at the beginning he could just get on and go.

"Really?" Camille seemed surprised.

"He might be a cowboy yet." Brett tipped his head toward the door. "Let's go get you some lunch."

Camille's eyes went to where his mother was working in the kitchen, wiping down the counters as she chatted with one of the women staying overnight. "I should stay here."

"You should enjoy a day off when you get it." Brett moved in a little closer. "Cause tomorrow you'll be back on your feet and it'll be forever before I can sweet talk you into sneaking out for another lunch." He leaned into her ear. "But I'll be happy if I can just bring you breakfast in bed."

Her breath barely hitched, the small sound just enough to make it clear Camille's thoughts weren't on banana French toast.

"Get out of here." His mother waved one hand at him, shooing them away. "I need you back before dinner. We've got things to get in order."

That got Camille moving. "We'll hurry."

"I didn't say hurry." His mother propped her hands on her hips. "I said get a move on so you have plenty of time to enjoy your lunch." She winked at Camille. "Have fun."

Camille looked from Maryann to him, then back to Maryann. "Okay."

She didn't sound committed to the fun his mother suggested, but that was all right. Camille definitely had a work ethic that put his to shame, so it was no surprise that fun and relaxation didn't come naturally to her.

She was surprisingly fast on the crutches he used for six weeks freshman year when he broke his own leg during a particularly rough football game. He had to walk fast to keep up with her, even on the gravel. "You could win a race on those things."

"It'd be the only race I could win." Camille glanced his way. "I haven't gone running in years." She focused back on the ground in front of her. "Not since high school."

"You ran in high school?"

He'd been far enough behind Camille in school that by the time he made it to high school she was already graduated.

And pregnant.

And married.

"Cross country." She stopped at the end of his truck, letting him go ahead of her. "Sometimes I miss it." Camille barely smiled. "I used to love it."

"It's not too late to pick it back up again." He glanced down at the crutches tucked under her arms. "Probably not for a couple months though."

"You mean in all the free time I have?" She carefully moved down the space between his truck and the minivan parked beside it. "I barely have time to read."

"You'll have more free time eventually." He opened Camille's door, waiting as she worked her way into the gap. "You ready?"

167

She turned to face him. "I'm starting to feel like your truck is so tall for a reason."

"Smart woman." He gripped her at the waist and lifted her up into the seat. "You're the first one to figure it out."

Camille's hands braced against his shoulders as he settled her back away from the edge. "Does that mean once you settle down you'll put running boards on the side?"

He shook his head. "I'm not giving up any excuse I can get to have my hands on you."

There was no room to read anything into his words.

The point of them was clear.

He still fully expected Camille to ignore it. Refuse to admit what was between them. It was how she handled things she wasn't ready to deal with.

But this time she didn't immediately turn away from him.

Didn't instantly change the conversation.

This time her eyes stayed on his, holding for long enough he could see the war happening behind them.

"I'm—" She took a quick breath. "I don't think—"

He caught her face in his hands, closing the little bit of space still between them to catch her lips with his.

She melted against him almost immediately, her body relaxing as she tipped closer.

Close enough she started to slide.

The weight of her body hit his surprisingly fast as she shot down the side of the leather seat.

Her legs latched on, hooking around his waist as she tried to catch herself. He managed to get one hand under her ass and one arm across her back, keeping both of them from hitting the gravel or the van behind him.

Camille pressed her lips tight together, hiding a smile that continued to fight its way free.

He glanced at the truck behind her before leaning back to meet her gaze. "Maybe I'll lower it a little."

CHAPTER FIFTEEN

IT WAS IMPOSSIBLE not to laugh.

It was a little funny.

And it was better to focus on the funny part than it was to think about the rest of it.

Specifically the settling down part.

She was dangling mid-air, dress definitely not covering her ass, unable to do anything to save her own skin.

And cracking up over it.

The ridiculousness.

The insanity.

The bizarre way her life had gone off the rails in less than forty-eight hours.

She used to have a routine.

Work.

Work.

Work.

Work some more.

Read.

Sleep.

Repeat.

Now everything was a mess. Scrambled up and dumped back out looking nothing like how it started.

"Hold on tight." Brett's arm tightened across her back as he lifted her back up and into the seat, scooting her farther into the cab than he had before. He still stuck close, arms bracketing her in. "You gonna stay in there this time?"

"It's slippery." She ran one hand over the fabric of her dress. "Especially in this."

Brett's eyes dipped down her front, slowly making their way along the line of her body. "I like it."

Heat crept along her skin at his blatant perusal. "Thank you."

"Any particular reason you picked a dress today?" He came in closer, one of his hands coming to the side of her thigh, fingers inching up under the hem of the soft fabric.

"No." She was used to avoiding the truth.

Was pretty good at it at this point.

At least she used to be.

A few days ago she would have believed the lie that came from her mouth.

Would have gone to her grave swearing it was the truth.

But not today.

"You sure?" Brett's hand crept higher. Sliding along her skin.

"About what?" She already lost track of the conversation. All her attention was focused on where he touched her. The closeness he offered.

"I think you wore this dress because of me." His lips skimmed over her jaw. "I think you wore this so I could do exactly what I'm doing right now."

She'd be an idiot to impede a man like Brett Pace. If he was willing to do the things he had then why would she do anything to make that more difficult for him?

It was just common sense.

She was simply being smart.

The tips of his fingers traced along the crease where her thigh met her body, creeping inward toward her—

"Ahem."

Camille jumped, eyes flying open at the sound of a man clearing his throat.

But Brett didn't move. His wide body kept her blocked in, barricaded in place, as he glanced toward the back of the truck. He barely shifted back, one hand coming to smooth her dress down before catching her legs and swinging them into the truck. He gave her a wink and a smirk before closing her into the cab and heading to where one of the visitors to The Inn was waiting to get into the van parked beside them.

She resisted the urge to peek at the man who interrupted a moment she maybe should have stopped.

But it was way too late for any of that.

She didn't stop Brett last night.

Or this morning.

And, being completely honest, chances were good she wouldn't stop him the next time either.

Brett opened his door and slid her crutches behind the seat. "What sounds good for lunch?"

"We could go to Mae's."

"Normally I would say that sounds like a great idea." He easily climbed up into the truck. "But today that might not be our best choice."

"Mae's is always the best choice." Mae made the best food in twenty miles. It was comfort food elevated.

Brett backed out and headed toward the unlined road leading to town. "Not today."

The way he said it was unsettling.

Camille fingered the bottom of her dress. "Why?"

Brett's jaw suddenly seemed very tight. "Something happened."

Camille tried to swallow around the tightening in her throat. The last time something happened to Mae it was because of her.

Because she finally stopped ignoring.

Finally stopped avoiding.

Finally faced the truth.

It didn't go well for her.

Or Mae.

Brett took a deep breath she wished she felt. "A woman came to the main house last night looking for you."

"For me?" She relaxed a little. "Who was it?"

Brett shook his head. "Don't know." He glanced at her. "My mom didn't recognize her."

"Oh. Wow." If Maryann didn't know this woman then she definitely wasn't from Moss Creek. "What did she look like?"

There were a handful of options of who it could be. Someone from her attorney's office.

Someone trying to track down anyone who could be on the hook for Junior's debts.

"I've got a video." He passed her his phone.

She stared down at it as he rattled off the passcode, allowing her full access. She smiled at the photo of Duke centered across the screen. "He's such a good boy."

"He slept with Cal last night." Brett seemed almost relieved by it. "Open up the messages. The video's from my mom."

She tapped the text icon and did her best not to look at anything outside of what he instructed. "Okay." The text string from Maryann had a set of three videos in it. She started the first one in line, watching as an older-model sedan pulled up and parked. A woman with long dark hair got out and slowly crept around the other cars parked there before disappearing off screen.

In the next video she reappeared, looking around as she made her way to the porch to ring the bell right beside the camera.

Camille paused the video. It was surprisingly clear and the woman was standing literally right in front of the camera so the shot of her was fantastic.

Unfortunately she wasn't anyone Camille recognized.

"I don't know her." Camille restarted the video, watching as Maryann came out.

The final video was the conversation Maryann had with this unknown woman. The woman was clearly trying to sweet talk her way into some information, but Maryann shut her down at every turn.

"She doesn't live here."

"But you know who she is?"

"Of course I know who she is. Everyone knows everyone around here." Maryann looked the woman up and down with narrowed eyes. "And I don't know who you are."

"I'm just an old friend."

"If you were an old friend you would be from here." Maryann crossed her arms. "And you're not from here."

That was when the woman started backing up.

Probably realized she was in over her head which meant she had to be at least a little smart.

"That is so weird." Camille shook her head as the woman hurried off the porch, jumped in her car, and drove away.

"You don't have any idea who it could be?" Brett was very serious about what was not really that big of a deal.

"Probably someone hired by a credit card company." She closed out the text app and passed his phone back. "They used to come to our house all the time."

Junior owed everyone and their brother money. He'd mortgaged the house his parents bought them within an inch of its life, borrowing against it to make tiny payments on his existing debts.

And then spent the rest of it on booze and whatever woman was his current side piece.

Not really *side*. Side insinuated she was the main piece.

Or a piece at all.

But she hadn't been physical with Junior in almost a decade. Not since she found out he'd been trying to pick women up at a bar in Billings.

It was one of the few times she put her foot down.

It was also the only time she'd ever threatened to cut off a man's penis.

Apparently she'd seemed serious enough that he'd never tried to touch her again.

Not sexually anyway.

"Are you responsible for his debts?"

"Only if my name was on it too." That meant once the divorce was done she was responsible for the house and a handful of credit cards. "And I paid all that off not long ago."

She'd gotten lucky when Brooks wanted to buy the house. There was no way she could have afforded the payments and done the repairs the house needed. Not if she wanted to save money for things like football camp.

"So why would a debt collector be looking for you?"

"They try to get money from anyone they can. That's their job." Camille lifted one shoulder. "They used to go to Junior's parents all the time too."

Brett was silent for a minute but, based on the squint of his eye, he wasn't done with the conversation.

But neither was she. "Is that why you're putting a camera on The Inn?"

Brett tipped his head in a nod. "That's part of the reason." He shifted in his seat, switching hands on the wheel. "When I went downstairs this morning the front door was open."

"That happens all the time." The latch on the door was a little wonky, especially in humid weather. "The door doesn't always close right."

"I'm the one who shut it last night." He looked her way as they sat at the light downtown. "I'm sure it was shut right."

"I'm usually the one who closes it and I always make sure it's shut." She lifted one shoulder. "But sometimes it still comes open."

Brett's eyes narrowed. "When was the last time it came open?"

She thought back. "One day last week."

"Was anything missing?"

She almost laughed. "You think someone drove all the way out there to try to take something from The Inn?"

The building wasn't easy to get to. Not only was it almost three miles down an isolated road that led only to Red Cedar Ranch, but it was also another mile down the gravel drive. There was only one way in and one way out.

And almost everyone there was armed.

Planning a robbery at Red Cedar Ranch would be idiotic.

It was the primary reason she'd gone there when she left Junior.

Which was the primary reason Junior targeted Mae. She was easier to get to.

"I think that woman drove all the way out there for a reason." Brett's eyes went back to the road as they passed through town, heading out in the same direction as the small hospital he'd taken her to the day before. "And I'm not convinced she's lookin' for money."

"What would she be looking for then?" The whole thing was weird, she could admit that.

But it wasn't as serious as he was making it out to be.

"Cal said he had a dream that someone was outside his room last night, knocking on his door."

"He's had that dream before." As nice as their new home was, there was still some adjusting to be done. She and Cal had slept together his whole life, so even though he was ready to move into his own space, there were some growing pains along the way.

"When was the last time he had that dream?"

She blew out a breath. "I don't know. Maybe..." Camille thought back, trying to remember a point of reference for the last time her son rushed into her room. "It was back when Nora and Brooks were hanging drywall in the house downtown."

"That was last week, Sweetheart." Brett's voice was slow and even as he asked a question she didn't want to consider. "Was it the same night the front door was open?"

"No." Camille pushed the word out fast, so she didn't have to think about whether or not it was the correct answer.

Whether or not her son was sleeping in her bed the morning she found the front door open.

"Are you sure?" It didn't seem like Brett was really asking.

It seemed like he already knew the answer.

So she turned to the window, looking out at the landscape as it blurred past the window.

It was what she'd been doing for years.

Watching the world pass while she sat.

Stagnating.

Avoiding.

Suffering because she struggled to face certain truths.

But she hadn't been the only one who suffered.

"It was the same night."

She'd let her son down so many times over his short life.

Given him a terrible father.

Allowed him to witness abuse.

Experience it.

All because she wasn't strong enough to stand up for herself.

For him.

But it still hadn't been enough to stop her from burying her head in the sand.

Hiding from all the things that scared her.

And one of them was the man watching her with a sharp gaze.

"We should go see Grady." Camille couldn't even fight in a breath, but she still managed to force out the words. "Show him the video."

"Grady won't be able to fix it right away." Brett paused. "I think we need talk about ways to keep you and Calvin safe until we figure out what's goin' on."

She nodded, fear making it hard to do much else. The bite of it was intolerable. The chill of panic racing across her skin as she fought the dump of adrenaline in her veins.

But then Brett reached for her, grabbing her hand in his and holding tight.

And anchor in a sea she'd refused to weather.

"I'm stayin' at The Inn." His thumb dragged across her skin. "With you."

"Okay." The word was shaky and strangled.

"And Calvin can't be alone. Not until we figure out what's going on." He sounded confident. Ready and capable of dealing with whatever this might be.

"Why would someone try to find him?" She tipped her head back, widening her airway in the hopes she might get more air in. "Just to try to find me?"

178

"We'll figure this out." Brett turned into the same milkshake place they'd stopped at the day before. He pulled up to the speaker and ordered a mudslide shake and a peanut butter pie shake before pulling around to the window. He set both into the cup holders built into the console between them before pulling away.

They were back on the road before something occurred to her. "Could it be someone his parents sent?"

"They know where you are." Brett shook his head. "And I can promise you they wouldn't be stupid enough to send someone out to Red Cedar lookin' for you."

"They wanted custody of Calvin. They tried to get the court to give it to them during the divorce." It was one more thing she had to ignore. Pretend wasn't happening so she could sleep at night.

Eat during the day.

Function.

"I didn't know that."

Camille stared straight ahead. "No one did."

She didn't tell anyone what went on. That usually included herself.

"They didn't get it though."

She shook her head. "No."

They hadn't even come close. She'd poured every penny she had to spare into the best attorney she could find, and he'd shut their bid for custody down before it even had legs.

"That explains where Junior gets it from." Brett turned into the lot of the police station and parked in the spot right next to Grady's blue pickup.

He was out of the truck a second later, coming to her side carrying the crutches Maryann brought over this morning. Camille grabbed Brett's shoulders as he lifted her out, gently setting her on her feet before passing over the crutches. Then he snagged the two shakes and closed the door, doing a quick scan of the lot before turning toward the entrance to the station. He tucked the cup in his right hand into the crook of his elbow, his free hand immediately coming to rest on her back as they made their way into the station.

Grady was standing behind the desk, along with Wes Eldridge. Both men were a year behind her in school and both had gone into the military before coming back to protect and serve Moss Creek.

Which now included her.

"You got a minute?" Brett led her right around the counter and straight toward one of the interrogation rooms along the back wall.

She'd spent a few hours in one answering questions the day Mae knocked Junior out the window of her apartment above The Wooden Spoon. Unfortunately her answers probably hadn't been as helpful as they could have been.

She hadn't lied.

She'd just held back the truth.

Because she pretended it didn't exist.

"What happened to you?" Grady gave her a wide smile. "You break it giving this guy the ass-kicking he deserves?"

It was a funny comment. One that was definitely meant to lighten the mood.

But she'd been doing that long enough. Finding any way she could to avoid the weight that came with life's difficulties. To downplay what happened to her.

And hurt her son because of it.

Camille stood as tall as she could manage on the crutches and looked Grady right in the eye, before spilling out a little of the truth she was drowning in.

"I broke it in the same place Junior broke it."

CHAPTER SIXTEEN

"HOW YOU DOIN'?" He reached across the console to grab Camille's hand. Partly for her, but mostly for him.

"I don't know." She stared straight ahead, barely blinking. Her eyes slowly came his way. "How are you?"

"Better and worse." Grady had the video and was able to send a few stills out to the rest of the force, along with the basic description of the car she was driving.

So that was good.

But Camille dumped out a lot of information he wasn't expecting to hear.

She didn't stop talking the whole time they were there and the woman laid out more than a little of Junior's bad behavior.

And it was probably only the tip of the iceberg.

"It sounds like Grady is on top of this. If that woman comes into town he'll find her and then maybe we'll figure out what in the hell she's up to." He was trying to calm Camille. Soothe the nerves making her jumpy. "And maybe she's exactly what you thought. Maybe she's just trying to trick you into paying money Junior owes."

"Or maybe it's something else." Camille wiped her free hand down the front of her thighs. "Maybe she's from the courts. Maybe his parents are trying to sue me for visitation."

"Whatever it is, we'll deal with it." He pulled her hand to his lips, holding it there as they drove to the ranch.

"How long will it be before the camera is set up at The Inn?" She continued stroking down her thigh, smoothing the fabric over and over.

He was going to have to figure out a way to help her relax.

"Brody ordered it and it should be here in two days." Luckily they had a few volunteers to help keep things safe until then. "But I think we've got something else set up in the meantime." Brett stroked his thumb across her skin. "You've got nothing to worry about, Sweetheart."

"What if someone did come into The Inn?" She was talking faster than normal, her voice a little pitchy as she spoke around short shallow breaths. "What if they come back?"

"If they come back then they'll be dealt with." He caught her eyes as they turned onto the gravel drive. "You and Calvin won't ever be alone."

She stared at him for a few long seconds before finally nodding. "Okay."

It was soft and barely a whisper, but hopefully she understood what he meant.

She'd ignored so much. Not just bad.

Good too.

And right now he was hoping she'd see the good as well as the bad.

Because even in the face of this, the good sure as hell outweighed the bad.

His mother's car was still parked at The Inn when they pulled up, along with Mariah's Jeep.

The place smelled fantastic when they walked in and a line of visitors was already collected down the stools of

182

the island, drinking blended drinks while they watched Mariah assemble what appeared to be beef enchiladas. Camille went straight to the kitchen, moving carefully on the crutches she'd soon be done with.

His mother's face split into a wide smile when she saw them. "How was your lunch?"

"Good." Camille answered before he could, her eyes moving to the people seated around her. "How's everything here?"

"Not as smooth as it is when you're in charge." His mother wrapped one arm around Camille's shoulders. "But we're managing." Her eyes stayed on Camille. "You're so organized that it's been pretty easy."

Camille smiled a little. "I try to stay on top of things."

"You do an amazing job." His mother shook her head. "I always think I can't be more impressed with you and then I am." She looked down. "How's your ankle feeling?"

"It's actually fine." Camille moved her whole leg from side to side. "I'm really surprised at how much this boot is helping."

"It's the stability." His mother's gaze held Camille's. "Stability makes all the difference."

"This margarita is amazing." One of the young women at the island sucked down the last of her drink. "Can I have another one?"

"Coming right up." His mother turned to the blender set up behind her and started dumping in the ingredients lined down the counter. "I think I missed my calling." She pressed the button to whirl it all together before coming back to pour the concoction out into the woman's glass.

"You should have tiki bar nights." The young woman's eyes went wide. "That would be amazing."

Maryann pointed at the woman. "I think you're onto something there." She set the container back on the blender base. "Sounds like I'm going to have to find another set of hands to work here on a permanent basis." Her eyes came his way, one brow lifting.

It was an offer he wouldn't turn down. "Sounds like."

Camille loved running The Inn. A person didn't put in as much effort as she did unless there was a certain level of enjoyment.

But she was already doing too much. Hiring Mariah helped some, but there was still too much work for one person to manage.

"There's a bunch of towels up in the dryer, would you two have time to pull them out and fold them for me?" His mother gave him a little smile. "Please?"

"Definitely." Camille was already on her way to the stairs, moving surprisingly speedy on the crutches.

"You're welcome." His mother shot him a wink.

He wasn't one to look a gift horse in the mouth, so he did as he was told following Camille to the base of the steps, catching her just as she was trying to figure out how to negotiate the stairs with the crutches.

"One hand on the rail." He snagged the crutch under the arm closest to her uninjured leg. "Brace yourself on the crutch while you jump up the step on your good foot using the rail for balance."

Camille hesitated, eyes going from the rail to the step.

"I'll catch you if you fall."

"I don't want to fall."

"No one does." He moved in close behind her. "But it happens."

Camille took a slow breath, her hand finally going to the rail. She slowly pushed up, lifting her good foot to the tread of the first step.

"See? It's not too hard." He moved up the step as she climbed to the next one.

"How do you know how to do this?" Camille's focus moved between the steps and the rail as she worked her way up toward the second floor.

"I broke my leg freshman year. Had to wear a cast for eight weeks." Brett pressed his hand to her back as she wobbled a little. "You got it."

The desire to grab her was strong. Carry her the rest of the way.

Save her the strain and the struggle.

But maybe that wasn't the best he had to offer her.

Maybe Camille didn't need him to bear the weight.

Maybe she just needed to know there was a net.

Then she could step off the edge. Jump without fear of what was coming.

What might happen.

She stopped, turning to look at him over one shoulder. "So these are your crutches?"

"I'm hopin' not to need them again." He grinned. "So that makes them yours now."

Camille faced forward and took another step. "Hopefully I don't need them again either."

"We should hang onto them since it seems like neither of us is good about knowing their limits." She sure as hell wasn't, and he admired the hell out of her for it.

The woman took everything on head-first. Wrangled any task into submission, going above and beyond on anything she did.

They made it to the top of the steps without a single misstep. Camille smiled wide as she blew out a breath. "I'm glad I don't have to do that for long."

"Yeah. It got real old, real fast." He pushed open the door to the laundry room, letting her go into the small, detergent-scented space first.

Camille opened the dryer and dumped the contents out into one of the rolling baskets they used to move the large quantities of linens around the upstairs. "I need to get caught up on so much."

"We'll get caught up." He snagged the basket and rolled it out the door. "Let's do this out here so you can prop that foot up while we work."

The seating area at the top of the stairs was vacant, so he pulled the basket right up beside one of the chairs. Once Camille sat down he scooted the small table close enough she could lift her foot into place. Then he snagged the second rolling basket and put it on her other side so they could line the folded towels into it.

Camille lifted a brow at him. "You thought the whole process through, didn't you?"

"I've gotta prove I can hold my own so you don't try to convince my mother to let someone else help you run The Inn." Camille's ability to ignore things she wasn't ready to deal with made it easy to give her the full truth.

If she didn't want to hear it, she wouldn't.

And he'd tell her again later.

She pulled out a hand towel, folding it slowly before lining it into the empty basket. Then she did the same with another one.

As she set it on top of the first her eyes came his way, holding a second before going to the stack of towels. "Don't you like working on the ranch?"

"Of course I like working on the ranch." Brett grabbed a bath towel. "If I didn't like it I wouldn't be here."

Camille's attention came his way. Like she was surprised by what he said. "You could have left?"

"Sure." He finished the bath towel and set it into place before going for the next one, leaving the smaller towels for Camille. "My parents didn't assume we'd stay here and work the ranch."

"But your mother got mad when Boone left."

"My mother got mad because of *how* Boone left." He shook his head. "Not that he left."

"So you always wanted to stay here and work on the ranch?"

"Always." He finished the last large towel. "But it wasn't so much about wanting to work the ranch. I wanted to be here with everyone else." Brett grabbed the last washcloth from the basket. "I wanted to raise my kids like I'd been raised."

She smiled a little. "It's a nice place for kids to grow up."

"It's the best place for kids to grow up." He was skirting something important. Something he needed her not to ignore. "I'm happy this is where Cal will get to finish growing up."

Camille held his gaze for a few long seconds before her shoulders lifted on a little breath. "Me too."

Pushing the conversation any farther would risk losing her, but he was willing to take that risk. "I'm makin' plans, Camille." He set the final bit of laundry in place. "And my plans include you and Cal."

"I know that." She pressed her lips together, rolling them inward before rubbing them together. "You're taking him to football camp."

"It's more than that." He leaned down, resting his hands on the arms of the chair as he lined his eyes with hers. "My plans go a lot longer than the summer."

Her throat worked as she swallowed.

But she didn't look away so he kept going. "And you don't have to be ready for it right now. We don't even have to talk about it after this, but I need you to know I plan on makin' you mine."

Camille didn't blink, but the slight move of her chest made it clear she was still breathing.

Otherwise he might have questioned how still she was sitting.

"Mom!" Cal raced up the stairs, his feet hitting the treads as he ran their way, a second set of lighter steps mixing with his.

Brett straightened away from Camille just as the little boy reached the landing, Duke right at his feet.

Cal smiled wide when he saw them. "I helped Pop lead the tour."

"That's great, Buddy." Brett held his hand out for a high-five that Calvin immediately slapped. "I'm proud of you."

The praise no longer shocked Cal like it used to.

He grinned. "Thanks." The little boy went straight to his mother's side. "And Pop says next time I can lead all by myself." His mood settled just a bit. "How's your foot?"

"Really good." Camille grabbed the crutches at her side and used them for leverage as she stood up. "It doesn't hurt at all now."

"Did you get washed up yet?" Brett grabbed the basket of folded towels and rolled it toward the closet.

"I'll go do that now." Calvin turned and raced down the hall toward his room, using the key always chained around his neck to unlock the door before he and Duke disappeared inside.

"He shouldn't have to lock his room all the time."

"He's used to it. He's always had to keep his room locked." Camille's eyes snapped to his.

Like she expected him to react.

Instead he nodded, keeping any sign of the anger snapping at his skin from showing. "That makes sense."

Camille chewed her lower lip for a second before letting it slide free. "Junior took anything worth money and sold it."

"Sounds about right." Brett glanced down at Calvin's door. "But Cal deserves to live in a home that's his." He looked back toward Camille. "And so do you."

She almost smiled. "Technically the house ended up being mine."

Her ease at discussing what happened with Junior was at odds with what he knew about how she dealt with things she wasn't interested in acknowledging. It didn't really make sense.

But that was okay. At least she was talking to him.

"It did, didn't it?" He stacked the towels in place before reaching in to switch the items from the washer into the dryer.

Camille stood in the doorway of the laundry room, balanced on her crutches, watching as he worked. "I'm just glad I was able to pay off the mortgages when I sold it to Brooks."

"Me too." He tried to act unfazed by the peek he was getting into her past. "Would you have kept it and lived in it if you could have?"

She shook her head. "No. It's too far from here." She lifted one shoulder. "And there's really no reason to stay somewhere else when I can stay here."

"But it doesn't feel like your home." He set the dryer and switched it to start. "You can't go to the kitchen in your underwear."

She laughed. "I could, I'm just not sure how much the guests would appreciate it."

"I'm sure some of them would pay extra for that service." Brett flipped off the light in the laundry room before pulling the door closed. "Our visitor demographic might change a little."

"You mean instead of a bunch of women fawning all over you it will be a bunch of men who stake out the kitchen hoping to catch me in my panties?"

"That's exactly what I mean." They headed down the hall toward the stairs, staying at Camille's side as she navigated the area rugs slowing her stride. "But I guess whatever gets them here, right?"

She tipped her head back in a laugh. "I'm not sure that's a sound business plan."

"What's not a sound business plan?" His mother appeared at the top of the stairs, carrying a large basket over one arm.

"Letting Brett walk around in his underwear to bring in more visitors." Camille didn't miss a beat as she easily twisted their conversation, a hint of a smile playing on her lips.

His mother's expression stayed serious. "How many more visitors do you think it would bring in?"

"At least ten more a week." Once again Camille didn't hesitate.

Maryann's brows went up. "That's a lot."

"I'm not walking around in my underwear."

Both women's serious expressions started to crack and a second later they were laughing.

"I feel like I'm going to have to separate you two." He looked from his mother to Camille as they continued to laugh.

It was fucking amazing.

Finally Camille was starting to relax. Starting to see her place in this family was already established and occupied.

They were all just waiting for her to realize it.

"Don't be a baby." His mother shoved the basket his way. "I want you to try this out."

He reached in to pull back the fabric folded over the open top. "What is it?"

"It's the picnic Camille suggested." His mother leaned into Camille's side. "Brilliant by the way."

Camille's whole face changed in an instant, softening into something that made his heart hurt. Something that was almost identical to the expression he'd seen on her son's face the first time he told Cal how proud he was of him. "Thank you."

"Nothing to thank me for." His mother pulled back the fabric, revealing a number of containers lined down the inside of the large basket. "You're the one who thought of it." She pointed to the largest of them. "There's enough in here for all three of you."

"Perfect." Brett flipped the fabric into place. "We'll be your test dummies anytime."

His mother gave him a wink before backing toward the stairs. "You should. This place is your responsibility now."

CHAPTER SEVENTEEN

"WHICH ONE OF these do you think is yours?" Brett lined up the sandwiches wrapped in clear film.

Calvin pointed to the skinniest one. "Mine's always the smallest." His finger went to the one on the right. "My mom's is usually the fattest because she likes everything on her sandwich." he leaned close like he was telling Brett a secret. "Even jalapenos."

"I like jalapenos too." Brett snagged the fattest of the subs before holding it Camille's way. "But this one's got double meat on it too."

Camille accidentally wrinkled her nose. "No." She grabbed the only sandwich left. "Everyone knows double cheese is the only way to go."

Calvin grinned from his spot at the foot of her bed where they were enjoying the first picnic meal offered at The Inn at Red Cedar Ranch. "I like double cheese too."

"I bet yours has double cheese on it then." Brett went to work pulling the film from around his sandwich. "Your Mimi remembers what everyone likes."

Calvin tore into the wrap on his own sub, ripping it away before separating the bun and looking down at the layers of turkey, cheese, and lettuce. Sure enough there was an extra set of cheese slices lined down the bread. "How does she do that?"

"She's magic." Brett set his unwrapped sandwich onto the paper plate in front of him before pulling out a container of potato salad and setting it on the center of the mattress. "You want some potato salad, Buddy?"

"Just a little." Calvin waited patiently while Brett scooped out a small serving onto his plate. Next he added some of the baked beans and a handful of chips.

"There you go." Brett moved to Camille's plate next. "You still like everything?"

"I still like everything." She smiled a little. "Except liver."

Brett added some beans to her plate. "You won't have to worry about that with me." He wrinkled his nose as he moved on to the potato salad. "I can't handle liver." His nostrils flared. "At all."

She picked up her sandwich, trying to hide a smile behind the sub loaded with any veggie Maryann could find in the fridge, along with turkey and extra cheese.

Brett lifted a brow at her. "I feel like you're laughing at my pain."

"I would never do that." She bit off a chunk, trying to chew around the smile she couldn't seem to stop.

"Savage." Brett shook his head.

"I've just never seen you look like that." She choked a little between the food and the laugh trying to come out. "I thought you were going to gag just thinking about it."

"Maybe I was." Brett coughed a little.

"Are you gonna throw up?" Calvin inched closer to her side of the bed, eyes on Brett.

"Not as long as we stop talking about liver." Brett grabbed one of the bottles of water and cracked the top, tipping it back as he swallowed it down.

His eyes were watering a little as he screwed the lid back into place.

"I feel like that about beer." She turned her attention to her plate, moving around a few beans. "The smell of it makes me sick."

So far Brett was the only person who didn't seem shocked when she talked about her past and it made her want to offer more of it up.

For a handful of reasons.

"I'll keep that in mind." Brett sucked in a breath through his nose.

She smiled again. "Thank you."

Brett's blue eyes met hers. "Of course."

Cal seemed oblivious to the conversation going on behind their words as he sat at the end of the bed, happily plowing through his dinner.

"You want to go out and get a little practice in after dinner?" Brett settled against the headboard, plate balanced on one hand.

"Yeah." Cal talked around a full mouth. "Can Wyatt come too?"

"I figured he would." Brett glanced at her before looking back at Calvin. "I've gotta get you boys ready for camp."

Calvin's eyes lit up. "I can go?"

Brett turned his head her way but didn't make any move to answer Calvin's question.

Because he was letting her be the one to give her son the news.

Camille nodded her head. "But you've got to promise to be a good listener and do everything Brett asks you to do."

"I promise." Cal was practically bouncing with excitement as he wolfed down the rest of his food.

Once they were finished eating, he and Brett packed everything back into the basket, keeping the trash and containers separate. Brett grabbed the repacked basket from the bed as Cal and Duke ran to the door. He shot her a wink as he followed them out. "I'll let you enjoy some peace and quiet." The door clicked shut a second later.

And the sudden silence felt odd.

Peace and quiet was normally a hot commodity. Something she'd only gotten to experience recently.

And up until now she'd taken full advantage, spending every minute she could in the first hobby she'd ever really had.

The same hobby that helped her process the life she lived before coming to The Inn. Helped her see a light at the end of the tunnel.

Camille sat on the bed for a minute after they left, taking a few deep breaths.

She definitely needed some processing now because this day had been a lot.

A lot.

She worked her legs off the side of the bed and carefully stood up, keeping all her weight on the foot still strapped into an espadrille. She only needed one crutch to get to the closet where her most valuable assets were lined along plastic shelving she'd ordered online.

Normally she couldn't wait to dive into a new world.

A new life.

But right now it was a struggle to focus on anything but the one she was in.

Camille snagged one of her most favorite books and pulled it from the shelf, tucking it close as she made her way out into the hall. The upstairs was quiet. It was Sunday after dinner and most of their guests were scheduled to leave tomorrow morning, with a near complete turnover of their entire capacity happening all at once.

That meant this was the calm before the storm. Usually they had a near constant flow of check-out and check-ins, but occasionally the whole inn would turn over at once.

Like tomorrow.

Normally this would be the perfect time for her to find a quiet spot and spend a few hours reading about a love she'd never been lucky enough to experience.

Instead she found her way downstairs and into the kitchen where Mariah was still working. The guests from earlier had cleared out of the space. A few were out at the pool. Some were lined near the horseshoe pit Brett installed earlier in the spring. The rest were off in unseen spaces, enjoying the home that felt more like her own than Brett realized.

Mariah glanced up when Camille walked into the space, giving her a wide smile. "Hey. How was your picnic?"

"Good." Camille slid onto one of the stools, propping her crutch against the counter. "You should try it sometime."

"A bed picnic with a hot cowboy?" Mariah tipped her head in a nod. "I agree."

"I'm assuming you won't want Cal to chaperone yours." Camille rested both arms against the cool granite.

"Definitely not." Mariah chopped her way through a stack of celery stalks. "If I ever manage to find myself in bed with a cowboy I plan to take full advantage."

"There's plenty here to pick from."

Mariah wrinkled her nose. "I don't generally like to mix work and cowboy sex, so the search continues." Mariah added the chopped celery to the large stainless bowl at her elbow.

"Red Cedar isn't the only ranch in town." Camille wiggled her brows at the woman she'd spent countless hours talking to over the past few months. "You could go hunting at one of the other ones."

"I don't have time for hunting." Mariah tipped a bowl of roasted chicken breasts out onto her cutting board. "Between working and taking care of my mom I'm booked solid." She glanced at the book sitting on the counter in front of Camille. "One of your fictional boys is about all I have time for in my life."

Camille glanced down at the well-worn cover. The book was the first one she'd read since school.

And in the time since she'd picked it up at the library surplus sale for fifty cents she'd read it countless times, going back over the parts that she'd once thought were pure fantasy. "Here." She scooted it Mariah's way. "Take it."

"I'm not sure I can handle the pressure of taking one of your books." Mariah grinned as she peeled back the skin from one of the breasts, stacking it off to one side before shredding the chicken.

"You've watched my son for me."

"But this is one of your books." Mariah dumped the chicken into the bowl. "They are what got you through all the Junior bullshit."

She was partly true. "I know, but I think it's time to pass them on." She smiled. "At least a few of them."

"Really." Mariah dragged the word out, giving her a disbelieving stare. "Wowza."

"Wowza?" Camille leaned forward. "What's wowza mean?"

"Wowza means I definitely want to spend a little time in bed with a cowboy one day. Especially if they can live up to what's between the covers of those books."

Camille traced a line in the granite with one of her fingers. "I thought it was all made up." She lifted her eyes to peek at Mariah. "I mean, it's fiction, right?"

"I would be hellaciously jealous if it happened to anyone but you." She smiled. "But since it's you I'm freaking thrilled." Mariah wiped her hands on the towel tucked into the apron tied around her waist as she turned to the fridge. She pulled out a small pitcher of clear liquid. "I made us something to celebrate."

She set two stemmed glasses onto the counter between them.

"What's this?" Camille wiggled in her seat, sitting up straighter.

She and Mariah had a lot in common.

Unfortunately.

Initially she just loved having someone else who wasn't a Pace around. Someone else who was exactly what she was.

Just an employee.

But it didn't take long to realize Mariah was so much more than that.

"I steeped simple syrup with lime and jalapeno." Mariah pulled out a plastic container of coarse salt and pulled off the lid. "I didn't want everyone but us to have something fun to drink." She snagged a baggie of lime slices from the refrigerator, running one around the edge of each glass before dipping it into the salt.

Camille smiled. "Thank you."

"Thank *you*." Mariah poured some of the syrup into each glass before topping it off with a pour from a can of lime sparkling water and a squeeze of lime. "You're the first person who didn't look at me like I was crazy when I talked about my mom."

"How's she doing?"

Mariah shrugged. "As well as any dying alcoholic can do." She scooted one glass Camille's way before lifting the other one.

"What should we toast to?" Camille picked her own glass up, holding it right in front of Mariah's.

"We're toasting to you finally boning Brett."

"I haven't actually done that." Camille gave Mariah an exaggerated cringe.

"What?" Mariah set her drink on the counter. "That's an outrage." She scoffed. "I'm so disappointed in you."

Camille lined her drink up next to Mariah's and wiped both hands down her face. "It's complicated."

"Exactly how long has it been since you've had sex, because I'm happy to make you a few diagrams if you need them." Mariah shook her head. "It's really not that complicated."

"I know how to have sex." She picked up her mocktail and took a sip. "Technically."

She knew the nuts and bolts of how things happened.

But her experience with it was very limited.

"Listen." Mariah pursed her lips. "If I tell you something will you freak out?"

"Probably."

"I'm gonna tell you anyway, because I know you can handle it and I think it will really help you." Her head tipped to one side. "Or it might make everything way worse, but I'm willing to take that chance."

Camille took another drink. "It seems like I'm the one taking the chance."

"Potato *potato*." Mariah looked from one side to the other, like she was about to disclose some hugely-guarded secret. "Brett Pace has been in love with you since he was thirteen."

Camille stared at Mariah.

Then she started to laugh.

"I'm serious." Mariah looked almost offended. "He really has been."

Camille couldn't stop laughing.

Because what in the hell else do you do in a situation you have no clue how to handle? "I believe you."

Mariah frowned, the space between her eyebrows shrinking. "Then why in the hell are you laughing?"

"Because this is insane." She smashed both hands into the sides of her face. "Things like this don't happen."

"They happen sometimes." Mariah snagged the book from the counter. "Otherwise no one would know to write about it."

Camille dropped her head back to look at the ceiling. "What in the hell am I supposed to do?"

"First," Mariah took a swallow of her drink, "you bone him." She rocked her head from side to side, the dark red bun on the top of her head bobbing along with the motion. "Probably a few times to make up for lost time." She smiled. "And then you let him keep bringing you breakfast in bed and teaching your son how to play football and helping you do laundry."

"He's so young." The argument was about as flimsy as they came, but it was the last one she was left clinging to.

A tiny bit of barrier she might be able to hide behind.

"Why are you trying to come up with reasons not to be with him?" Mariah downed the last of her drink before rinsing the glass and setting it into the top rack of the dishwasher.

Camille picked at a bit of salt that had fallen to the counter. "I don't know."

"You should probably figure it out." Mariah grabbed a container of mayo from the fridge along with a bag of purple grapes. "Because that man has his shit together and knows what he wants." She scooped some mayo out and added it to the bowl of chicken and celery. "If you aren't sure about him then you need to tell him."

"I'm sure about him." The defensive-sounding response came out fast and easy.

Easier than the next bit. "It just feels strange for things to be good."

Mariah's hands dropped to the counter and she stared at Camille. "Shit." Her eyes dipped to one side. "Now that I think about it, things going right does feel wrong."

Camille nodded. "Right? It's not just me?"

Everything was wrong for so long that it was normal. Wrong was right.

And as messed up as it sounded, that meant that right was wrong.

"I never really thought about it." Mariah's lip lifted on one side, nose scrunching up. "Is this how people self-sabotage?"

Camille picked up her drink. "Yup."

She walked away from her marriage to Junior with less than nothing, which sounded bad to most people, but nothing also included love.

She didn't love Junior. Maybe ever.

Definitely didn't like him.

Her life with him was loveless, sexless, and abusive.

In short, it was bad.

Unfortunately, somewhere along the way bad became normal, and she'd done whatever it took to stay in her normal.

That meant pretending nothing was wrong.

She didn't lie to people so they wouldn't find out what was happening.

She lied to them so she wouldn't.

Mariah pursed her lips, pushing them out in a thoughtful pout. "We might be fucked-up."

Camille nodded along with the sentiment. "I think I'm tired of it though."

Tired of ignoring the bad. The scary. The problematic.

It led her to making bad decisions.

And if she wasn't careful she'd do it again, only realizing how much she fucked up in hindsight.

Like she had with Junior.

"Good." Mariah grinned as she added the grapes to the salad, giving it a quick toss. "Then I can live vicariously through you." Her eyes lifted toward the door leading out to the pool as Brett and Cal came in with Brody and Wyatt right behind them. "Speak of the devil."

"Mom." Cal rushed to her side, his cheeks pink and his hair sweaty. "Can I stay with Wyatt tonight?"

She glanced Brody's way. "Were you invited?"

His head bobbed in a nod. "Uncle Brody said Duke and I should come stay the night at their house."

Uncle Brody.

She'd probably heard it a hundred times. Technically.

But it was one of many things she'd ignored, unable to really process the possibility that she and her son might find their way into a place they'd never been.

She'd tried to keep a line of separation, but once again her refusal to see things as they were could hurt a little boy who deserved so much better than she'd given him.

Camille pushed on a smile, fighting through the urge to preserve the wrong that felt right. "Sure." She glanced at Brett. "If you're sure it's okay with Uncle Brody."

CHAPTER EIGHTEEN

SOMETHING WAS DIFFERENT.

Something had changed.

And whether it would be a good thing or bad remained to be seen.

"Why don't you boys take the rest of these cookies with you." Mariah grabbed a plastic container and passed it across the counter to Calvin. "I made these so we would have extra just in case no one liked the tres leches cake I made for dessert tonight."

"I take it they liked the cake?" Brody snagged the cookies from the counter.

Mariah grinned. "They ate all of it but a couple pieces." She looked Brett's way. "Those are packed up in the fridge."

The Inn's resident chef added the last few dishes on the counter to the washer before switching it on. "I'm gonna head out for the night." She disappeared into the small room just off the kitchen, coming back out with her purse and keys. "I'll see y'all in the morning." She wiggled her brows in what appeared to be Camille's direction before turning to make her way to the front door.

The sound of her yelp carried in from the entryway.

Brody rushed toward the sound.

"I forgot to tell her Clint and Elijah were on the porch." Brett reached the front door just in time to find Mariah propped against the frame, hand over her heart.

"You two scared the shit out of me." She huffed out a breath. "I'm not used to anyone being out here when I leave."

"We'll be here the next two nights, ma'am." Clint stood up from the chair he'd been parked in. "Can I offer you an escort to your vehicle?"

Mariah gave him a wicked smile. "Not right now, cowboy." She shot him a wink. "Maybe some other time."

"I look forward to the opportunity." Clint stayed on his feet as Mariah crossed the gravel drive, whistling out a tune as she made her way to where her Jeep was parked near the back of the lot.

"I'd stay away from that one. She might chew you up and spit you out." Brody shook his head as the music from Mariah's speakers blasted across the quiet of the evening.

The sharp beat of The Men Who Rule the World by Garbage followed her out into the dusty light from the setting sun.

"I'd let her do it." Clint crossed his arms as he watched Mariah's retreating vehicle. "Might even go back for seconds."

"I'm not gonna fault you." Brody turned to the two hands taking the first rotation on the porch. "You need anything before I head out?"

"Not a thing." Clint eased back down in his seat. "We've got a cooler full of beer and a deck of cards. We'll be just fine."

Brody tipped his head in a nod before heading back into The Inn.

Brett closed the door behind them, leaving Clint and Elijah to their game.

"The next shift starts in three hours." Brody kept his voice low enough Cal and Wyatt couldn't hear. "We had more than enough volunteers so everyone should still get a decent night's sleep."

"No one wants her to ever feel like she did before again." They'd told the men what was going on and pretty much every single one offered to come spend a few hours on the porch, making sure no one got to Camille or her son.

"Ben Chamberlain called. He and everyone at Cross Creek offered to come too." Brody snorted out a little laugh. "Including Liza."

"That doesn't surprise me at all." The owner of Cross Creek Ranch was a force to be reckoned with. "But I think we've got it under control."

"That's what I told him." Brody held his hands out as they walked into the kitchen. "You boys ready?"

"Yup." Wyatt carried the container of cookies as the three of them filed out the front door, Duke sticking close to his new best friend.

"I think you've been ditched." Camille eased off the stool, wincing a little as she stood.

"Is your foot hurting?"

"No." She worked the crutches under her arms. "It's actually the only part of me that's not hurting." her movements were a little slower as she made her way to the stairs.

"Using crutches works all sorts of different muscles." He followed her as she made her way upstairs.

Camille needed to stretch out. Work the kinks loose.

"What if we get in the pool?"

"The pool's closed." She peeked his way over one shoulder, a smile playing at her lips.

"I don't know if you heard." He moved ahead of her, unlocking her door before opening it wide so she could walk right in. "But we're in charge here."

It was clear Camille needed another set of hands around here, and they might as well be his.

Camille went to her dresser. "I may or may not have taken advantage of that a few times already." She opened the top drawer and pulled out a handful of something bright orange.

"Camille Shepard is a rule breaker?" Brett grabbed his bag from the floor. "I never would have thought it."

She lifted one shoulder. "You learn something new every day." She pulled out another drawer, grabbing something floral before going past him and into the bathroom.

Once the door was closed he peeled off his clothes, trading them for the swim trunks he packed just in case the opportunity to get into the pool came up.

It was one of his favorite things to do in the world. There was nothing as relaxing as the feeling of weightlessness and the warm lap of the water.

And now he got to share it with her.

Hopefully it was the first of many things they got to share.

A few minutes later the bathroom door cracked open. Camille peeked out, her hazel eyes skimming his bare chest before dipping lower.

Her gaze was slow and purposeful.

Blatant.

"Are you ready?"

Her eyes came to meet his as she fully opened the door, revealing the flowery pattern of her coverup. "I am."

He slowly moved toward her, feeling a little less sure of himself than he did a few minutes ago. "Good."

206

Camille's head barely tipped to one side, the edges of her mouth lifting the tiniest bit. "It is good."

Brett opened her door, waiting as she worked her way out into the hall before closing and locking it behind them. The walk downstairs was quiet as they moved past the occupied rooms. It was late enough that most people were tucked way, exhausted from the early mornings and fresh-air-filled days.

The downstairs was silent and shadowed, most of the lights switched off by the timers in place.

He pushed open the door leading to the pool area, snagging a couple towels from the shelf before stepping out into the warm night air.

Camille took a deep breath, her eyes lifting to the sky.

"It's a pretty night." Brett set their towels onto one of the many chairs around the pool before toeing off his flip flops.

Camille's attention stayed on the sky a second longer. "I never noticed how many stars you can see out here."

He looked up. "This is nothing compared to how many you can see if you ride out to the west end of the ranch." Brett stepped closer, his eyes falling to the woman who'd held his attention for as long as he could remember. "I can take you out there sometime so you can see it."

She turned her head, looking right at him. "Okay."

No avoiding.

No ignoring.

"You ready to get in?"

Camille pulled her crutches free, tipping them against the chair holding their towels. "I am."

She took a tentative step, moving carefully along the concrete toward the edge of the pool. She was about halfway there when her hand came to his arm, reaching out for support.

He wrapped one arm around her waist, taking some of the weight off her injured ankle as they finished the few steps remaining.

Once they were there Camille looked from side to side. "I should probably sit down to take this thing off."

She lowered down, stretching the foot strapped into the brace out as she settled onto the cement.

While she worked the Velcro loose he eased into the warm water. "I can't believe we waited so long to put in a pool."

Camille slid the brace free then turned to dip her feet into the water. Brett caught her leg, lifting it up so he could get a good look at her ankle. Most of the swelling was gone and only the barest hint of a bruise stained her skin. "It looks pretty good." He carefully lowered it back into the water.

"Thanks." Camille smiled a little at him.

"Are you coming in or was all this a ploy to get to see me in just my trunks?"

Her head tipped back and she openly laughed.

It was something he'd never heard before.

It was light and soft and a little husky.

And it shot straight to his dick.

Camille wiggled a little on the cement, pulling the fabric of the flowy gown out from under her ass before lifting it up, dragging it over her head and down her arms before dropping it onto the cement, revealing the tiniest bikini he'd ever seen.

She slowly edged forward, lowering into the water right in front of him, her hands coming to slide down his chest as her body moved the water around him.

The tips of her fingers trailed along the hair covering his pecs.

"I didn't expect you to have this." Her touch moved up, sliding over his shoulders.

"Are you disappointed?"

She shook her head. "No." Her eyes stayed on his. "Not at all." Her hands eased around his neck as she came closer, the line of her body sliding against his.

"What are you doing, Camille?"

She still hadn't looked away. "I'm embracing the good." She inched closer, her legs tangling with his in the shallow water.

He caught her around the waist, holding on as he pulled them into deeper water. "What's the good?"

When the water reached the middle of his chest she stopped trying to walk with him, instead lacing her legs around his waist, letting him carry her through. "This place is the good." She chewed her lips for a second. "You're the good."

"Maybe you're the good." Letting Camille think of her life as two separate sides didn't sit right.

Her head tipped, watching him as the water reached his shoulders.

"You have to be the good." He relaxed his legs, letting the buoyancy of the water keep them upright. "Look at all you went through." He reached out to push her hair back from where it clung to her shoulder. "And you are still kind and gentle and sweet." He smoothed down her arm. "Most people would have come out of that angry and bitter."

"I think it helped when Mae rearranged his face." She said it deadpan. Completely serious.

"I could see how that might be helpful." He shook his head. "I'd still do terrible things to get a few minutes alone with him."

"There's no reason to waste the energy." She held to him as they slowly moved around the pool.

"Can I ask you something?" He waited, making sure it was okay.

Camille nodded. "You can ask me anything."

"Why aren't you angrier?"

She traced a droplet of water as it moved across his skin. "Because it's over." She stared off into the water around them. "If I wasn't mad about it when it happened then I wasn't going to be mad about it when it was over."

"You weren't mad about it when it was happening?"

"No." Her eyes lifted to the sky. "I didn't feel anything when it was happening. I couldn't."

"That doesn't mean you can't still be mad about it now."

She smiled a little. "I don't want to be mad now." Her arms tightened around his neck. "I want to feel the good, not the bad." Camille pulled closer. "I just want to be happy now."

"I want you to be happy." He ran the fingers of one hand along her cheek. "That's all I've ever wanted."

Even after giving up his teenage fantasy of being with Camille Smith, he'd grown to a man who just wanted her safe and happy, whatever that looked like for her.

Because for a long time it was clear he wasn't the answer to that.

But then she came to the ranch.

He saw her day in and day out.

Saw her as a mother.

As a friend.

As a woman.

She was everything he wanted.

Still.

And what was once the dream of a kid became the plan of a man.

"I've wanted you for as long as I can remember." He traced along her jaw. "Knew I could treat you better than anyone else could."

Her eyes moved over his face but didn't stray.

Because she was listening. Hearing what he said.

"I'm gonna build us a house right here, behind The Inn."

A year's worth of dreaming, thinking of all that could be, was waiting to come out.

Waiting to be offered. "We'll work it together." He slid his hand into her hair, his wet fingers sliding along her scalp. "We'll raise Calvin. We'll be a family."

It was all he'd ever wanted.

Even as a kid. Young and naive enough to think that's what everyone wanted.

Camille's fingers ran along his face, sliding down his skin as the tip of her nose ran along the side of his, lips achingly close.

But he'd made his move. Offered up all he planned to give—

And take.

The next move had to be hers.

Brett held her close.

Breathed in her air.

Waiting.

Because for the first time he needed something from her.

The tip of one finger slid across his lips, dragging slowly from one side to the other. "You have perfect lips."

Camille's focus followed her touch, moving over his face, tracing the line of his jaw.

The slope of his nose.

She looked at him closer than anyone ever had. Like she was seeing him for the first time.

"I never noticed how handsome you are." Her lips quirked a little. "I know that's weird to say considering I've seen you every day for the past year." Her eyes drifted to his. "But I tried not to realize you were there."

"I know."

Her brows lifted. "You know?"

Brett slowly eased them toward the shallow end of the pool, toward the stairs built into the side. "I showed up here every day, Camille. Found any reason I could to be in front of you."

"You wanted me to see you."

"I wanted you to know I was there." His foot hit the bottom stair. "I wanted you to see that I'd show up for you and Cal." Camille's legs dropped from his waist as their bodies rose above the water. "Every day."

She leaned against him as they stood on the cement edging the pool, her eyes locked on his. "I've known that from the beginning."

CHAPTER NINETEEN

THE ADMISSION SEEMED innocent enough.

But the look on Brett's face was anything but.

"Why are you looking at me like that?" Camille tried to fight in a shaky breath but her lungs refused to cooperate.

"The beginning of when?" Brett's eyes were dark as they stared down into hers.

"Always." It was the simplest answer she had to offer him.

She'd known his family forever. Seen the way his father treated his mother. The way his brothers treated their wives.

The way he treated everyone around him.

She'd known that Brett was there forever.

The only forever that mattered anyway.

"I couldn't admit it, though." How in the world did you explain the fact that you didn't want to see the good things happening around you? "I didn't know how to deal with it." Camille managed to hold his gaze. "I didn't know how to deal with you."

That was only the partial truth.

The full truth was that she didn't know how to deal with *any* of this. The job. The family. The man.

The entirety of her new life was filled with only good.

And good was terrifying.

Bad was known. Something she was used to. It's why finding out about the strange woman showing up at Maryann's door actually made her feel a little better.

It felt normal.

Which was really fucked up.

Then again, so was she.

Was. Past tense.

"There's nothing to deal with, Sweetheart." Brett's voice was soft and quiet. "All you have to do is show up." His hand curved against the side of her face. "I can do the rest."

That hardly seemed fair.

It actually wasn't fair at all. Much like the time they'd recently spent together.

And that needed to change.

"I'm not okay with that."

Never in her life had she expressed dislike of a situation. Especially not to someone she cared about.

And she most definitely cared about Brett.

"I don't want to just show up." Camille stood a little taller, being careful to keep the weight off her injured ankle. "That's all I've done for the past ten years."

Every day she woke up and did what it took to get through.

She didn't live. She didn't enjoy. She simply existed.

It was surprisingly exhausting.

"I want to learn how to be happy." She thought on that a second. "I want to learn how to be happy being happy."

That didn't sound any better.

"I want to be happy. I want to actually live my life, and I haven't done that in a long time." Camille reached out, letting the tips of her fingers slide up the center of Brett's chest.

"I can make you happy." Brett sounded confident in his ability.

Rightfully so.

But expecting someone else to make you happy was the same as expecting someone else to do all the work for you.

And if there was one thing she wasn't afraid of, it was work.

"I don't expect you to make me happy." Camille traced a path across his shoulders and down his arms. His skin was warm and wet from their time in the water. Stretched tight across muscles built on hard work and consistency.

It was one of the many things that made it impossible for her to ignore him.

Brett worked as hard as she did.

At everything.

His responsibilities on the ranch. Taking care of his family.

Watching over hers.

The way he took care of Calvin was her undoing. The reason she could never seem to push him out of her mind.

"I didn't want to like you." She dragged her fingers back up, over the corded strength of his forearms and across the tight knot of his bicep. "I tried to think of you as a baby." Her eyes slowly lifted to meet his.

She expected him to be at least a little annoyed at being considered a baby, but the quirk of Brett's lips made it clear he was anything but annoyed. "How'd that work out for you?"

She smiled back. "Not well."

"I can't say that I'm sorry for that."

"Me either."

Brett suddenly backed away, stealing the hard planes of his body from under her touch. "Let's go get you out of that wet suit."

He didn't say *and into dry clothes*, which was promising.

Camille reached down, intending to pick up her cast and dress, but Brett beat her to it. "Nope."

"What do you mean *nope*?"

Brett straightened, passing over her boot and gown before immediately hooking his arms around and under her and lifting her off her feet. "Tomorrow you're allowed to walk around again and I'm not missing out on my last chance at this."

His eyes slid her way as they walked toward the door. "At least for a little while."

"I don't plan on breaking my ankle again, so hopefully it's your last chance for a long while." Camille hooked her arms around his neck as he used the fingers of the hand across her back to pull open the door.

"I'm not talking about carrying you because of an injury, Sweetheart." Brett moved quietly through the main area of The Inn. He leaned into her ear as they started up the stairs. "The carryin' I'm thinking about has more to do with a threshold than an injury."

It used to be so easy to pretend.

So simple to ignore.

Not now. Somehow Brett managed to break that part of her.

But that didn't mean she was ready to admit it. Especially when it came to something like that.

Marriage. Kids.

A man who would treat her the way Brett did.

The thought of it was still overwhelming.

"I'm not ignoring what you said." Camille chose her words carefully, hoping she could explain something that made no sense, even to her. "I just don't know how to wrap my head around it."

Brett gave her a slow smile as they reached the top of the stairs. "You've got plenty of time to work on that." His words were quiet enough no one else would hear as they walked down the line of doors toward her room at The Inn. "I'm not in a hurry."

She smiled back. "Okay."

Brett paused in front of her door and stared at the lock as he shifted her around.

"You need some help?"

"I didn't think this all the way through." He leaned to peer down at his side. "The key is in my pocket."

"Seems like you're going to have to put me down."

"I don't want to." His frown was deep.

For some reason the situation made her happy, the lightness of joy replacing the weight that usually rested in her chest. "What if I promise to let you carry me to bed again tomorrow?" Camille chewed her lower lip, struggling to take it a step further. "And maybe again the day after that."

Being happy in the moment was one thing.

But making plans to be happy again tomorrow and even the day after that?

That was a whole different ball game.

But it was one she wanted to learn how to play. To learn what it was like to look forward to the future.

And to finally believe that Brett would be a part of hers.

"Those are some awfully big promises." He slowly lowered her to the ground. "But I'm not one to look a gift horse in the mouth." Brett dug one hand into the pocket of his wet swimming trunks. He pulled out a key to her room and shoved it into the lock before swinging the door open.

Camille slowly made her way in, carefully working her way into the bathroom just inside the door. She peeked at herself in the mirror. "Holy cow."

Brett came into the bathroom and stood behind her, resting his hands on the counter at either side of her hips as the front of his body slowly pressed into the back of hers. "Something wrong?"

She ran her fingers across the skin under her eyes, trying to wipe away the smudge of makeup darkening the area. "I look like a raccoon." She lifted her eyes to meet his in the mirror. "And I've seen what you do to raccoons."

"Sweetheart, I will shoot anything that looks at you cross-eyed." His expression was surprisingly serious. "And I won't feel even a little bad about it."

Even if she didn't already know Brett Pace meant everything he said, she would still believe the words that just came out of his mouth.

Because it was clear he meant every one of them.

But he wasn't the only one who should be saying things he meant.

"You'll have to teach me how to shoot. Just in case I ever have to return the favor." She thought the offer would make him happy. It clarified her position where he was concerned.

But Brett did not look happy.

He looked something very different, and significantly more dangerous.

His hands slowly pulled from the counter and came to rest on her hips, the tips of his fingers pressing into her flesh as he leaned closer. "I think that might be the sweetest thing anyone has ever said to me." His lips were so close they brushed her ear as he spoke. "And I'm happy to teach you anything you want to know."

It almost seemed like he might be offering to teach her things much more indecent then shooting a gun.

But she already knew all those things. In the past year she'd gained an education that would hopefully serve her well.

Because right now she was more than interested in returning certain favors.

Not because she believed he expected it, but because she wanted to give it.

And her reasons weren't completely selfless.

Camille relaxed back, letting her head drop against Brett's shoulder as she barely arched her spine, bringing her ass right against the line of his cock.

It'd been so long since she'd been wanted.

Desired.

And thinking that this man felt that way about her made her feel something she'd never felt in her whole life.

Powerful.

Brave.

Strong.

"Camille." His voice carried a hint of warning.

She was going to ignore it.

Imagine that.

It was about time that worked in her favor.

Camille twisted, spinning to face him in the small bathroom.

He'd offered to teach her things. Maybe Brett needed to find out she was capable of more than he realized.

Maybe even more than she realized.

Her front brushed his, nipples pulling tight under the chill of her wet suit, causing a tiny shiver that lifted goosebumps across her skin.

Brett's eyes immediately dipped, pupils dilating as they fixed on where the pebbled tips pressed against the damp fabric.

Camille slowly reached to her back, finding the dangling tie of her top and giving it a little tug. The triangle cups immediately went slack, moving away from her skin but still holding their position.

Brett stood very still, barely breathing as her fingers went to the tie behind her neck.

Another tug and the top dropped down, falling as the knot slid free.

She thought he might reach for her, but Brett held his ground, only touching her with a gaze heavy enough to feel.

It made her want to continue on, claim more of his attention.

His desire.

But right now she had something to prove.

A point to make.

To Brett.

To herself.

"Your turn."

His eyes snapped up to hers, stormy with the same focus she used to run from.

Not anymore.

For a second she thought he might argue with her. Refuse like he had the night before.

But his hands slowly went to the laces at the front of his trunks, deftly working them loose with a skilled touch she'd been lucky enough to experience.

When his thumbs hooked in the waistband her breathing stopped, anticipation making her heart race.

In one easy move he pushed the clinging wet of the fabric past his hips and down his thighs, letting the trunks hit the rug under their feet before kicking them away to a spot she didn't see.

Mostly because all her attention was otherwise occupied.

The long line of his cock bobbed free, smooth and thick.

And significantly larger than she expected.

The bravery she'd been feeling faltered.

That thing seemed like a choking hazard.

Definitely something only an experienced driver could handle.

And most of her experience was of the textual variety. Found on the pages of the hundreds of books she used to find the sanity she almost lost.

The hope she never had.

"Your turn again, Sweetheart." Brett's rough words dragged her eyes up and away from the most intimidating thing in the room. She met his gaze.

It was so familiar now. The look lingering there.

What she used to think was intensity.

Focus.

And maybe some of it was.

But it was also something else she was too blind to see before.

Maybe too scared to recognize.

Need.

A need so deep it touched everything, tainting it all with a stain she would never be able to wash away.

A stain that would penetrate her whole life.

Her whole world.

Color it all.

Forever.

Camille slowly shook her head. "No."

She wanted more of his need. She wanted all of it.

Wanted to claim it as her own.

The need and the man.

They were hers now.

Hers always.

Camille spread her hands across his chest, dragging her fingers over his nipples, the sharp intake of his breath spurring her on.

She'd known Brett long enough to realize this was a game she had to play perfectly. Anything she did had to be done with purpose and intent. If she gave him the chance he would shut her down.

Steal this opportunity to prove all she'd become.

All she could still be.

Camille reached between them, ignoring the urge to hesitate, the urge to talk herself out of the bravery pushing her forward. As her hand wrapped around him, Brett's eyes shut as he sucked in a hiss of air.

There was no time to overthink. No time to consider she might be lacking. No time to worry about the good or the bad.

She dropped to her knees and slipped her lips around him, reveling in the velvety smooth feel of him under her tongue as she sank over the steely line of his shaft.

The sound of his ragged groan heated her blood.

Made her want to earn another.

Made her want more. All he was willing to give.

She held him with one hand, sliding deeper, swallowing down as much as she could before pulling back.

Then taking it all again.

The sweet man who'd brought her breakfast in bed, iced her foot with the gentlest of touches, and carefully carried her wherever she needed to go, let out a string of profanities that would make a sailor blush.

It made her heady with power.

And greedy for more.

She curved the fingers of her free hand under the weight of his sack, tracing the delicate skin with a careful touch as the sharp swearing continued above her.

But she didn't just want to hear what she was doing to him.

She wanted to see it.

Witness an undoing she would remember forever.

Camille lifted her eyes.

Brett's jaw was clenched. His brows were drawn low. Every muscle in his body was tight, arms straining where his hands gripped the counter behind her.

She could stare at him like this forever. Soak in the power and restraint he possessed.

Suddenly his eyes opened, dropping to where she was, nostrils flaring as he held her gaze.

His balls pulled tight under her touch and a second later Brett had her, fingers tight in her hair as he pulled her off him.

He lifted her up, hauling her off her knees and against his chest, pulling her legs around his waist.

"I wasn't done."

"You've been cut off." His eyes flicked to her face. "Indefinitely."

"That's not fair." She'd only tasted the smallest hint of what she could do.

What she could own.

No way was he taking it.

"I don't care." Brett grabbed at his bag where it sat on the small cot still tucked into the corner of her room, fishing around a second before dragging her onto the bed they'd shared last night, crawling over her as he scooted her up toward the pillows.

Camille scoffed. "I care." She reached between their bodies, finding the object of her desire, only giving it a single stroke before he pulled away from her touch.

"I knew you were stubborn." He grabbed her hand. "Just didn't expect it to come out so soon." Brett snatched her other hand before she could even get close to touching him and added it to the first. He managed to pin both her hands with one of his, keeping them tight together as his gaze moved down her body.

His free hand went to the ties at the sides of the bathing suit bottoms she still wore, yanking them loose before pulling the whole thing free and throwing it over the side of the bed. "That's better."

He didn't hide his blatant perusal. Didn't pretend he was doing anything but looking at every inch of her. "God you're perfect." His hand splayed across her stomach before dragging down to palm her hip as his lips came to hover over hers. "Remember what I said last night, Camille?"

"Yes." She probably remembered everything he said ever. It seemed like she'd ignored it all, but that wasn't what really happened.

What really happened was she filed all his words away, stacking them into neat little rows, just waiting for the day they would all come back to take her down.

"What did I say?" Brett's fingers slid over her skin, tracing a line up her side and along the barely-there crease under her breast.

"That you wanted to be the only one to touch me."

His eyes came to hers. "What else did I say?"

He said a lot, but one thing stood out. One thing pushed the limits of the way she lived.

"That if you touched me I couldn't pretend you didn't."

His head bobbed in a slow nod. "That rule still applies."

She held his gaze. "I know."

"There's one more thing." One of his light brown brows lifted.

"You remember what it was?"

Camille couldn't stop the slow smile as it crept across her lips. "That you didn't plan on being in my bed just once."

CHAPTER TWENTY

MAYBE HE SHOULDN'T have been as open with her as he had been.

Especially seeing the way it could come back to bite him.

It never occurred to him that he might end up in over his head with her.

Camille seemed so sweet. So soft and quiet.

Cautious.

Hesitant.

But the woman staring up at him with hooded eyes was definitely not hesitant.

Maybe not even sweet.

One of her legs hooked around his, sliding up in a way that made it hard to think of anything besides how close he was to having her the way he'd always wanted.

But there was a problem.

He didn't just plan on having her.

He planned on keeping her.

"This is about more than just bein' in your bed." He struggled to keep his free hand from moving across her skin, skimming over the dips and swells of her body. "This is about bein' in your life."

She gave him a slow nod, her glassy eyes holding steady on his. "I know that."

He wasn't so sure she did.

"I'm not just here for a quick fuck, Camille." He hoped the coarse language would sink deep enough she would hear it.

And based on her sharp gasp he was inclined to think she did.

But the way her body rocked under his made it seem like she was anything but offended by it.

The leg wrapped around him slid higher, binding across his lower back. "I know." She licked her lips. "I'm not here for a quick fuck either."

He shouldn't like the sound of that word coming out of her mouth.

Definitely shouldn't want to hear her say it again.

"What are you here for?" He palmed down the outside of the thigh pinning him close.

Camille's hazel eyes moved over his face. "I'm here for you."

It was a simple answer. Only four little words.

But they were everything he needed to hear.

Everything he'd waited so long for.

And it made him forget something important.

He didn't realize it. Not when he pulled her close, covered her mouth with his, hands roaming the skin he would never get enough of, the body he would worship every chance she gave him. All he could think of was the way she felt. The way she smelled.

The way she tasted.

It wasn't until her hand closed around him that he remembered the woman under him was dangerously capable of ruining all his plans.

Brett tried to catch her hands again, but this time Camille knew he was coming and she managed to catch his first, holding tight to his wrists as she smirked up at him.

This was supposed to be his show to run.

He thought he'd be able to come in and prove all he could do.

All he could offer.

"What's wrong, Cowboy?"

"You're only causin' problems for yourself right now." He leaned close, running his nose along Camille's neck. "Don't you want me to touch you?"

"You know I do." She sucked in a breath as his lips closed around a nipple, pulling it deep into his mouth. "But I want to touch you too."

Brett pulled free of her breast, holding the suction as it slipped from his lips. "You can touch me next time."

She lifted one brow, looking more than a little skeptical. "Promise?"

He didn't want to make the deal, but right now it was his best option.

His only option.

"Promise."

Camille held him a second longer before letting go, looking a little disappointed.

"What's wrong?" Guilt tugged at his gut, putting a damper on what should be the highlight of his fucking life right now.

Her lips pressed together, twisting to the side. "I just thought..."

Damn.

He'd been so focused that he'd done exactly what he swore never to do.

He took away all her options.

Decided she would get what he wanted her to have instead of what she chose.

Brett eased off her, rolling to his back, putting his hands behind his head and locking his fingers together.

He was trying to look relaxed.

Calm.

In control.

Even though right now he was none of those things.

He tipped his head her way. "Do your worst."

Hopefully she didn't take him up on that.

Camille's eyes skimmed the line of his body. "Really?"

"Really." He took a slow breath, trying to force down the anticipation already pulling his balls tight.

Camille slowly sat up. "What am I allowed to do?"

"Anything you want." He was an absolute idiot for doing this. The amount of suffering he was about to endure was unexplainable.

But somehow he had to get through it.

Prove he was man enough to handle whatever she could dish out.

Her lips curved in a smile that twisted the anticipation and dread fighting through him, tying them together in knots. "Why?"

"I wasn't being fair." He tried not to notice as she came closer, inching his way. "If you want to bore yourself touching me then I should let you do it."

Camille came up to her knees. "And you think touching you would be boring for me?"

"I can't imagine it could be more fun than letting me touch you." His fingers itched to prove his point. "Which I'm still happy to do if you changed your mind."

Camille's hands came down at his sides as she swung one leg over his body, knee pressing into the mattress as she straddled his hips. "Why does it have to be one or the other?" She leaned closer, the soft swell of her breasts brushing his chest. "Why can't we do both?"

The heat of her pussy pressed to his straining dick. It took everything he had to keep from thrusting up against her, seeking out some sort of relief from the ache setting in. "I'm not sure I can handle both, Sweetheart."

Her head tipped to one side as her brows came together.

He saw the second that realization dawned.

The instant Camille understood exactly how much power she held.

Her body slowly lifted from his as she pushed up to her knees, palms dragging down his chest as she went. He held his breath as they moved lower, her touch soft but purposeful as it moved over his skin.

But then it was gone, leaving him aching for the contact he'd been dreading.

His dick flexed, looking for the attention it was expecting.

But Camille was focused elsewhere, her eyes fixed on a spot near the edge of the mattress.

For a second he was confused, but only until she grabbed the item he'd forgotten was there. Snagged in a moment of brilliance as he carried her from the bathroom.

Camille held it between them, the foil pouch pinched in her fingers as she stared at it.

Then her eyes refocused to find his. "I don't know what to do with this."

He plucked it away, tearing it open and pulling out the rubber inside before rolling it into place. She watched him with an interested gaze.

Her lips slowly tipped down. "Too bad I didn't learn about them sooner."

Brett reached for her, hands at her face as he pulled her close. "Then you wouldn't have the best thing in your life."

Camille's frown softened. "But then maybe I could have done that with you instead."

It was the first time she'd even hinted at thinking of their future. It would figure she went straight past love and marriage to the thing he was trying not to focus on.

Trying not to push for.

"There's plenty of time for us to do anything we want." Brett laced the fingers of one hand into her still-damp hair as he reached between them. He barely brushed against her before Camille grabbed his hand and yanked it away.

"Somethin' wrong, Sweetheart?"

Camille rocked a little, sliding against his sheathed dick in a move that dragged out a groan he couldn't control. "Maybe you're not the only one who can't handle too much right now."

He flexed up, digging his heels into the mattress as he pressed toward her, earning a little gasp. "I wish I could say I was sorry for that." He nosed along her neck. "But I waited a long time for you to want me the way I wanted you."

Camille's palm pressed to the center of his chest as she pushed up. "It wasn't as long of a wait as you thought it was." Her hips rolled then angled.

Suddenly he was lodged against her.

Camille's eyes closed as both hands splayed across his chest, using it as leverage as she inched down, making a little headway before easing away, slowly engulfing his body with hers. Her bottom lip tucked between her teeth as she worked herself onto him, the tips of her fingers digging into his skin more with each bit she claimed.

Once she was fully seated all the air rushed from her lungs and her head dropped forward. "Holy shit." She ground down a little. "I don't remember it feeling like this."

All he could do was stare up at her, watch as Camille set a slow but steady rhythm. It took all he had to maintain his focus.

Contain his thoughts.

Because if they got involved then he was fucked.

He gripped her hips, hands sliding higher to curve under the barely-there swell of her breasts. He pulled her down until she was close enough to catch one in his mouth.

Camille sucked in a breath. "That. I like that."

He pulled at her, working the nipple with his tongue and lips as she started to go faster.

When he moved to the other one his hand eased between her thighs to find the tiny bit of flesh he planned to exploit the hell out of for the rest of his life.

Her legs tightened at his hips as he circled her clit, working the pad of his thumb against it with each glide of her body onto his.

Camille's hand fisted in his hair, holding him close as she started to shake, her whole body tight as she rocked onto him, the sound of her low, raspy moan shooting straight to his dick.

Heat pooled in his balls, making him clench his teeth, fighting for a few more seconds.

"Brett." His name was on her lips as her pussy fisted, thighs jerking as she came, dragging him down with her.

Pulling him under until she was all there was.

All there ever would be.

****

"CAMILLE." BRETT KEPT his voice low, hoping not to startle her awake as he ran one hand through the length of her hair.

The weight of her head shifted a little where it rested on his shoulder. "Hmm?"

"I need to get up, Sweetheart." He rested his lips on her forehead, breathing deep as he savored the final seconds of the most perfect night he'd ever had.

Camille's legs stretched under the covers. "What time is it?"

"It's almost five." He'd been slacking the past few days, taking full advantage of the opportunity, but there was too much to be done for it to continue any longer.

"Okay." Camille sucked in a breath as she slowly eased up, twisting to drop her feet toward the floor.

"Where are you going?"

She bent over and he heard the rip of the Velcro closures on her cast as she worked it onto her foot. "I finally get to work again." She stood up and turned to look at him, the t-shirt she slept in swinging around her thighs, her face lit up with a sleepy but dazzling smile.

"You genuinely like working here, don't you?"

"I love it." Camille lifted one shoulder. "It makes me feel like I'm something besides what I used to be." She stood a little taller. "It's the first time in a long time I've been proud of myself."

"You should be proud." Brett moved the covers to one side as he got out of bed. "You run this place better than anyone else could."

Camille's lips pressed tight together as she twisted the fabric of his t-shirt in her hand. "It was a little easier at the beginning."

"I can imagine." Brett kept moving, hoping it might make her more likely to finish the admission he hoped was coming. "This place got real busy real fast."

"It did." Camille watched as he pulled a fresh set of clothes from his bag. "Some days I can barely get it all done."

"I believe that." He turned to face her. "It's well past time for an extra set of hands here."

They should have noticed sooner, but Camille was so good at hiding the truth from everyone.

Including herself.

But the fact that she was comfortable enough to admit that she needed help settled him in a way little else could.

Brett reached out to push her hair from her face. "Let's take a shower and then you can tell me what I need to do today."

Her lips barely lifted at the edges. "Okay."

Thirty minutes later they were showered and dressed and headed downstairs. He would have liked to make it forty-five minutes that included a little more together time, but it was clear Camille was itching to get back to work.

Excited about it even.

And he could wait. Especially now that he knew she understood where this was headed.

What it would become.

"How's your ankle?" Brett followed her down the stairs, watching for any sign of a limp as Camille took the treads one at a time.

"It's actually doing pretty well." Camille glanced his way over one shoulder, giving him another of the beautiful smiles he hadn't seen enough of. "It doesn't hurt at all."

"That's good news." He stayed right with her as she reached the base of the stairs and went toward the entryway. "Cause we got a lot to do today."

Camille pulled open the front door and peeked out onto the porch.

"Morning." Two deep voices greeted her.

Camille's smile widened. "You boys want some coffee and breakfast?"

Two seconds later both the ranch hands who finished out the last shift were up and out of their chairs and headed inside.

Camille leaned out the open door to scan the area in front of The Inn before slowly closing it and turning his way. "Seems like it was a quiet night."

"Seems like." Based on the fact that no one came in and woke him up he was inclined to believe it was true, but he'd wait until he heard it directly from the men who spent the night making sure Camille was safe.

Camille was already at the coffee pot when he made it into the kitchen. She chatted idly with the cowboys seated at the counter as she filled the large maker with grounds and water. "What do you boys want for breakfast?"

"Beggars can't be choosers." Ezra, one of the newer ranch hands, shot her a smile across the counter. "I'll eat anything you serve me, Miss Camille."

Brett scowled Ezra's direction as the hand smiled at Camille. He might have to kick Ezra's ass before the morning was over.

Brett moved in close at Camille's side. "Miss Camille isn't the only one serving breakfast anymore." He dropped a kiss on her head before turning to the fridge to snag a carton of eggs. "How many eggs can you eat?"

"I'll eat as many as you serve me," Ezra's grin moved Brett's way, "Darlin'."

Brett forced his shoulders down as he slid the eggs onto the counter. He needed to calm down. Ezra was a good man and a good hand and he'd dragged his ass out of bed early as hell to prove it. "I appreciate you staying out there last night."

"It was purely selfish." Carter took a cup of coffee as Camille passed it his way. "We knew the last ones would get coffee and breakfast."

"Course we did think our breakfast would come from Mariah." Ezra took a sip of his own coffee. He leaned against the counter as his eyes trained on Camille. "Does Miss Mariah have herself a male companion?"

Camille lifted a brow as she passed the next cup of coffee Brett's way. "I don't think Mariah is currently looking for company."

Ezra clicked his tongue as he shook his head. "That's disappointing."

Brett understood where he was coming from. "Sometimes you just have to bide your time." He glanced Camille's way. "Patience pays off."

"Maybe not in this circumstance." Camille started up another round of coffee. "Mariah wouldn't date anyone where she worked anyway." Her eyes snapped to Brett before bouncing away. "It doesn't always work out well."

Brett didn't miss the hint of uncertainty in her gaze.

It was something he hadn't really considered.

In her mind Camille was putting everything on the line to be close to him.

So maybe he needed to prove there was no line.

Because, whether she knew it or not, Camille was a Pace the second she set foot on Red Cedar Ranch.

CHAPTER TWENTY-ONE

"THEY LOOK REALLY good." Clara stared across the field as she bounced Ella on her lap.

"I'll take your word for it." Camille watched as the lines of sweaty boys moved around the stations set up on the grass. "I'm not real sure what I'm looking at."

She'd never been into sports. The closest she got was her cross-country days, but that was more of a solitary endeavor that basically consisted of getting yourself from point A to point B as fast as possible.

Football was a whole different beast.

"You'll figure it out." Clara smiled her direction. "I'm sure Brett would be happy to explain it all to you."

Camille's gaze easily found Brett in the crowd. She'd spent most of the afternoon watching Cal as he put his heart and soul into anything they put in front of him.

But she'd accidentally taken more than a few peeks of the man putting his heart and soul into helping the kids around him.

For the first time since she and Clara arrived Brett's head came her way, his eyes pinning her in place.

Clara leaned a little closer. "I maybe shouldn't have asked you to hold Faith."

One of the other coaches stole Brett's attention and Camille let out the breath she'd been holding.

"Be careful." Clara lifted her brows. "That's how you end up with twins."

Camille turned her head toward Clara, her eyes staying on Brett until the last possible second. "What?"

"I've seen that look before." Clara reached out to swipe across Faith's mouth with the soft fabric of a receiving blanket. "They look at you like that and then it's only a matter of time."

Camille struggled to swallow. "Are you sure?"

"You're holding half the proof." Clara sighed as Ella started kicking her legs and fussing. She frowned down at the irritated baby in her arms. "Are you serious?" She shook out the lightweight blanket stacked on top of the diaper bag at her side before draping it across her shoulder and over the baby grabbing at the front of her shirt. "I hope for your sake that Brett only makes babies one at a time. It's impossible to keep two fed."

Faith started huffing, working up a little fit of her own.

"I never really thought about having any more kids." Camille stood from the green folding chair she'd been sitting in to watch the final day of football camp. She rocked Faith from side to side. "I didn't think I would ever want to."

"I understand." Clara peeked under the blanket as Ella continued to fuss. "It's kind of crazy how things can change."

Faith's upset gained a little more momentum that no amount of rocking seemed to calm.

"Your momma is busy, little lady." Camille bounced the six-month-old a little more. "You have to wait your turn."

"She might be better if you walk her around a little." Clara adjusted the blanket. "That one's nosy as hell so looking around will occupy her."

Camille smiled down at the blue-eyed little girl in her arms. "Are you nosy?" She turned toward the end of the field. "We'll be back."

The football field was just outside of town, situated between the high school and the feed mill. It was where Brett, Brody, Calvin, and Wyatt had spent most of their week, leaving early each morning and coming home just before dinner each night, completely wiped out from the day.

Like Clara promised, Faith calmed down as they moved, her Pace-blue eyes scanning everything around them as she blew raspberries into the breeze.

Camille came to the end of the metal bleachers that ran along the side of the field. She glanced back to see if Clara was ready for Faith yet, but it appeared Ella was taking her time.

"Looks like we need to keep going." She slowly walked up the side of the bleachers, moving toward where the concession stand sat. It was locked up now, but soon enough would be open to service the events that filled the space most of the fall.

It was odd to be moving around a place she hadn't been to or thought of in years. The last time she walked these grounds was in high school. Back when she had the whole world in front of her.

Before bad decisions and fate narrowed her options.

"I'm going to give you some advice you probably won't need." Camille tipped her head to peek down at Faith. "Don't ever let someone else tell you what to do." She smiled a little. "I don't think you'll have any problem with that, but just in case."

A car door closing caught her attention, dragging it to the lot behind the locker rooms reserved for the visiting team. There was no reason for anyone to be using it. The other lot was much closer and easier to reach, and there were plenty of spaces available since the camp was all that was going on.

Camille leaned, looking for the source of the sound.

An engine started, stopping her feet. She watched the space between the concession stand and the locker room. A flash of color passed between them as tires squealed against the blacktop.

She pulled Faith closer, taking a few steps back as the color of the car registered.

The lines of it seemed familiar.

Like something she'd seen before.

Her steps sped as she continued to back away.

But suddenly her retreat was stopped, halted when her back slammed into a wall.

Camille spun around, keeping her arms around as much of Faith's little body as she could manage.

But the spin was a little too fast, and her booted foot was not as easy to maneuver as she expected. Camille started to wobble, her brain racing as she fought to keep thinking.

Keep looking for ways out.

"Hey." Brett's hands went to her arms, holding tight as they steadied her. "I didn't mean to scare you."

All the air rushed from her lungs as she leaned toward him, holding Faith between them as her heart raced.

Brett smoothed down her hair. "I thought you heard me."

"It's okay." She blinked a few times, trying to straighten the blur in her vision. "I was just walking Faith around while Clara fed Ella."

"I saw that." His eyes moved over her face. "Everything okay?"

She bobbed her head in a nod. "Fine."

Everything was fine. Good.

Wonderful even.

Camille sucked in a breath, shoving down the urge to focus on the bad. To let it take back what she'd finally claimed. "Are the boys done?"

Brett's blue eyes barely narrowed. "They are." His head tilted to one side. "You sure you're okay?"

"Yup." Camille plastered on a smile. "Just a little embarrassed to realize I know nothing about football."

Brett watched her a second longer before easing to her side, keeping one arm draped across her shoulders. "I'm pretty sure you're going to end up knowing more than you want to know." He grinned at her. "Probably tonight before Cal passes out."

"He seemed like he was doing okay." She resisted the urge to peek back over her shoulder toward the lot where she'd seen the car. "But I'm not sure I would know the difference."

"He did better than okay." Brett led her up the side of the bleachers. "The coach for the team he will try out for next year came over a few times this week to watch him."

Camille's attention snapped toward Brett. "Really?"

"Really." Brett reached out to wiggle the tip of one finger against Faith's belly as she started to fuss. "He's got one hell of an arm. We just need to get his feet moving a little faster." Brett's smile softened. "I'm hopin' he got his momma's running legs."

Camille glanced down at the boot on her foot. "Hopefully not my current running legs."

Brett laughed, the sound lightening the weight in her chest. "I don't know. I bet you're still pretty quick."

"I'll wait a few weeks to find out." She bounced Faith for the last few steps, trying to keep the little girl from working up to a full-fledged fit.

"What's wrong?" Brody was at Clara's side, decked out in the same khaki shorts and polo Brett wore. The cowboy hat was missing from his head, replaced with a baseball cap embroidered with Moss Creek's team mascot. He reached for his daughter. "Did Uncle Brett scare you?"

"She's just hungry." Camille passed the little girl to her daddy. "I was trying to keep her occupied while Clara fed Ella."

"Mom!" Calvin raced across the field, a bottle of sports drink in one hand and Wyatt close at his side. "Did you see me?"

"I did." She caught his sweaty body in a hug. "Brett says you're doing really well."

Calvin smiled wide. "Wyatt's doing real good too." He slung one arm over Wyatt's shoulder. "He's going to play offense so we can be on the field together."

Brody leaned down to pass Faith to Clara, taking a loopy-looking Ella and cradling her against his chest. "We'll keep working on it." He reached out to pat Wyatt on the back. "You did a great job this week."

Wyatt beamed at Brody. "Thanks."

"Picture time." One of the other coaches hollered their way across the field.

Brett shot her a wink. "We'll be right back."

Camille pointed to Ella. "Want me to hold her?"

Brody grinned as he backed away. "Nah. They need to get used to seeing the Pace girls in these pictures."

"Hell." Clara groaned. "I'm going to be stuck at these things forever if he gets the girls to play."

"Football isn't your thing?" Camille eased down into her seat, watching as the boys and coaches lined up for the commemorative photo.

"Not even a little." Clara smiled as Brody lined Wyatt up in front of him. "But they love it, so I guess it'll have to be my thing."

"I didn't realize Cal wanted to play sports." It was one of the many things she'd been blind to. "Much less that he might be good at them."

"Sometimes you just have to tread water." Clara glanced her way. "Do whatever it takes to keep your head above water, you know what I mean?"

"I do." Camille's chest went tight as Brett took the spot right behind Cal, both hands coming to rest on her son's shoulders. "But sometimes it's hard to realize you're not still drowning."

Clara's expression softened. "You'll get there." Her eyes went back to where her husband stood with two of their children. "And you'll be surprised how fast it happens."

****

CAMILLE STEPPED THROUGH the front door of the main house, her feet immediately slowing to a stop.

"It's all right." Brett's hand rested against her back, not pushing, just a solid force reminding her she wasn't alone.

"I know." It had always been all right.

That wasn't the issue.

The issue wasn't the Paces. It never had been.

It was her.

Brett leaned into her ear. "I'm right here with you."

He meant to be reassuring, and to some extent he was.

But Brett was the whole reason she was here. The whole reason everything was changing.

In good ways and in ways that scared the shit out of her.

"There they are." Maryann stood at the doorway at the end of the hall, an apron around her waist. "Come on in."

She didn't rush their way like Camille expected, just offered a warm smile and a beckoning wave.

Cal was the first to go.

Which wasn't surprising. He was the first to know he had a place here.

The first to know he was one of them.

But he was also young enough that he didn't understand how much they had to lose.

Camille tried to follow him, but her feet refused to budge.

"You want to skip this?" Brett's question was soft enough no one would be able to hear. "I'll fake a heart attack and say you have to drive me to the ER."

She snorted out a little laugh. "Your mother would see right through it."

"Absolutely she would." His hand moved up, slowly rubbing a comforting path along her spine. "But she'd never admit it."

"I'm just..." The bad tried to creep in again, threatening to darken the good.

Smother it out.

Camille forced a smile. "I'm fine." She made her feet move, starting with the boot that protected her injured ankle.

Everyone else was there when they walked into the kitchen. Brett and Brody still wore their coaching uniforms and Wyatt and Cal were still sticky and sweaty. Mae sported one of the navy t-shirts she wore every day to The Wooden Spoon and Clara might have had a little spit up in her hair.

No one changed before showing up. They came as they were.

Camille's feet moved a little easier.

Maybe she didn't have to be fine to be here.

She could just come as she was.

A little uncertain.

A little afraid.

A little hesitant.

"I heard you did amazing this week." Maryann already had Calvin, her eyes completely focused on him as he rambled on about everything he'd learned. All he'd accomplished.

The pride on his face tightened Camille's throat and made it hard to breathe.

Because she'd missed something else about her son. But this time it was something good.

The little boy she brought to Red Cedar Ranch was just like she was now. Uncertain. Afraid. Hesitant.

But that little boy disappeared somewhere along the way. He'd been replaced by a child who felt safe. Confident.

Capable.

Loved.

And unfortunately, not much of that was because of her.

It was because of the people around her. The people around them.

Camille swallowed hard as she made her way to the counter where she sat down the tray of pasta salad she'd made earlier in the day. It was barely in place before two bodies slid in at each side.

"Hey." Mae reached for the foil covering the pasta. "What'd you make?"

"Pasta salad." Camille smiled a little as Mae scoffed.

"You know how much shit I get for not making you come in one day a week to make this?" Mae shook her head. "They won't shut up about it."

"I've heard it too." Nora leaned sideways against the counter. "Some of the guys who work on our crew tried to bribe me to have her make them some."

"Mae has the recipe." Camille wrote it down before she left her part-time job at The Wooden Spoon to take the position at The Inn. "It's not that hard."

"You would think." Mae frowned. "But they can tell the difference." She leaned closer to the tray. "You must put some sort of magic in there."

"It's celery salt." Camille glanced up to find Brett watching her the way he always did.

Like he was ready to swoop in and save her at a moment's notice.

"It's not just the celery salt." Mae grabbed a fork from the stack on the counter and stabbed it into the tray before shoving the bite into her mouth. "Maybe you stir it more than I do so the eggs break down a little better."

Camille lifted her shoulders. "Maybe?" She looked to Brett before turning back toward Mae. "I could probably come to The Wooden Spoon to make it one day a week."

"No fucking way." Mae shook her head. "You work too much as it is."

Camille rubbed her lips together. "It's not so bad anymore." Another peek Brett's way. "Brett's working at The Inn now."

Mae chewed through the rest of her pasta salad, a slow smile creeping onto her lips. "So you and Brett are going to run The Inn together?"

It was on the list of things she was still working to embrace.

To accept.

To believe.

One more item in the pile of good she was holding tight with everything she had.

Camille barely nodded.

"Normally I would say working with your husband is a terrible idea." Mae looked over Camille's shoulder to where Nora stood. "But that one makes it look like fun."

"It is fun." Nora crossed her arms. "I'm not sure Boone could handle the kitchen at The Wooden Spoon, though."

"Hey." The man in question snuck in at his wife's side, wrapping Mae in one of his arms. "I've waited tables before." He pressed a kiss to Mae's temple. "Didn't mess anything up either." Boone was clearly proud of his accomplishment, grinning from ear to ear as he moved to where his brothers were clustered together.

Mae waited until he was out of earshot before leaning in. "He messed all sorts of stuff up, but no one wanted to tell him because he was trying so hard." Her eyes went to where her husband was quietly conversing with his brothers. "And then he left all his tips for the girl who had to miss her shift to take care of her son."

Nora shook her head. "Those damn Pace men."

Mae nodded along. "Right?"

Camille understood what they were saying. Felt it all the way to her toes.

A sense of belonging she'd never had blossomed in her chest, warming her from the inside out.

She almost smiled as Brett's eyes found her again. "We never stood a chance."

CHAPTER TWENTY-TWO

BRETT STRUGGLED TO keep his eyes off where Camille stood with Nora and Mae.

Brody kept his voice low as he scanned the room. "Have they seen the car anywhere else?"

Brett dragged his attention from where Camille was chatting with his brothers' wives, a small smile twisting her lips. "Just the one time at the Stop-and-Go."

Grady stopped by the field earlier in the day to touch base about the mysterious woman who showed up just over a week ago. "But by the time he got turned around the car was gone."

It was a disappointing development, that was for sure. If only Grady had been able to stop the car and find out exactly who the woman was.

And what in the hell she wanted from Camille.

"I'm glad we got that camera in at The Inn." Brody sipped at the beer in his hand. "How's it working out?"

"Good." Brett made sure to tell all their guests about their new policy and so far everyone was understanding. Probably because it didn't really cause any issues for them. They could still get in whenever they wanted, they just had to wait for him to unlock the door remotely. "I sleep a hell of a lot better at night knowing all the doors are locked."

"I bet." Brody looked across the room, eyes landing on where his daughters were doing their damnedest to sweet talk Bill into giving them dessert before dinner.

There was a good chance they'd succeed too.

"I'll be back." Brody crossed the kitchen, headed straight for where Leah and Michaela sweetly smiled up at Bill.

"You think you'll have any?" Boone grinned as Brody tried to keep a straight face in front of his older twin daughters.

"Don't know." Brett always thought he wanted a big family. A loud house filled with chaos. "I'm happy just havin' her and Cal."

It was strange how quickly things had changed. How fast he felt settled. Content in a way he couldn't have imagined.

"Cal's one hell of a kid." Boone's eyes went to where Cal and Wyatt were sitting together at the table, eyes glassy, hair a mess. "He and Wyatt both."

"Says something about their mothers." Brooks leaned back against the wall, crossing his arms. "The fact that they raised such good boys in spite of what was going on around them."

Brett's eyes went back to Camille, just like they always did. "I think I want to build a house behind The Inn."

"Makes the most sense." Brooks tipped his head Brett's way. "Heard you offered your cabin to Clint and Elijah."

"No reason for it to go to waste." Brett swallowed down the last of the water he came in with. "And they're here more than anyone else is. Only makes sense they get the better living quarters." Clint and Elijah had only been

249

COWBOY SEEKING SOMEONE TO LOVE

working on the ranch for a couple years, but they were always up to take on any extra work that needed done.

Like sitting on a porch for hours at night to make sure Camille and Cal were safe.

"You get your stuff out yet?" Boone smirked his way. "Or are you still tryin' to sneak it in so she doesn't notice?"

"I'm sure she noticed." He'd brought in all his clothes and toiletries over the past week, hauling it into The Inn one bag at a time. "I'm not sure she's ready to admit it yet, though."

Camille had come a long way in the little bit of time they'd spent together, but she still struggled with certain things. "I'm trying not to overwhelm her."

"Been there." Boone lifted a brow. "Luckily yours probably responds better to bein' overwhelmed." He smiled a little. "You overwhelm Mae and she pulls a knife on you."

"If Camille was like that Junior probably would have ended up gettin' what he deserved a whole hell of a lot sooner." Brooks' frown was deep. "I might argue he still hasn't gotten all of it."

"I'd agree with that." Brett eased away from his brothers as their mother started uncovering the food. "Hopefully it's comin' to him eventually."

Focusing on what Junior deserved wouldn't get him anywhere. It's why he tried not to do it.

But damn it was hard.

"How you doin'?" He eased in close to Camille, doing his best to keep as much distance as he could stomach between them. Camille wasn't quite ready to lay out what they were to Cal, and that decision laid solely on her shoulders.

"Pretty good, actually." She smiled as Mae helped Calvin fill his plate. "But I do question your family's party reasoning."

"I told you." He risked another step closer. "We have a lot to celebrate." Brett tipped his head toward the little boys stacking their body weight in food onto their plates. "And they worked hard this week."

"From what I saw they weren't the only ones working hard." She peeked his way, a sly smile on her lips.

"Didn't figure you came to stare at the coaches."

"Not all of them." Her little smile held. "Just one." Camille's expression changed, getting more serious. "Thank you for everything."

"You don't have to thank me for that. Cal's one hell of a player. He earned his place."

Camille's eyes met his. "I wasn't talking about camp."

"Get your dinner." His mother came past, waving them toward the counter. "These boys are tired. They need to get to sleep."

Brett let Camille go first, sticking close as she worked her way down the line of food, scooping out a little of everything before going to sit in the chair next to Calvin.

"Looks like she's finally figuring out she's stuck with us." His father came up behind him, snagging an extra serving of Camille's pasta salad.

"I hope so." He'd spent the past week trying to figure out how to make the reality of her situation clear, but it was an impossible task. "I'm doing all I can."

"These things just take time, son." Bill rested one hand on Brett's shoulder as he moved behind him. "There's gonna be growing pains. Days where she's unsure." He tipped his head down, eyes serious as they held Brett's. "When a woman gives up everything she knows to step into your life you've got to give her room to grow." He lifted one brow. "That's the hardest part 'cause you want

251

to fix everything." Bill barely shook his head. "But you can't."

Brett glanced to where Camille and Cal sat.

It never occurred to him that she was living in a new world.

She was still in Moss Creek. Still surrounded by all the same people she'd always known.

But everything would be different from now on.

New.

"I'll keep that in mind."

Bill's eyes went to rest in the same spot as Brett's. "I would."

Brett finished filling his plate as his dad found his place at the head of the table, surrounded by the family he'd helped create by bringing a woman into his world and convincing her to stay.

Hopefully Brett could do the same.

****

CAMILLE SAT AT the edge of the pool, dangling her feet into the water as he swam from one side to the other. The water felt amazing after spending all day sweating in the hot sun, and the slow laps helped work out the tension that always seemed to be binding his shoulders.

On the last pass he did a flip, kicking off the wall and heading right for Camille's toes where they slowly moved beneath the surface.

She yelped a little as he grabbed the two toes who refused to be separated, tugging on them as he surfaced.

She managed a glare. "You almost made me drop my book."

"I'll buy you another one." He scooted between her thighs. "As many as you want."

"Well you would have to buy this one for Lucy Schroder." Her glare slipped under the weight of a smile.

"And she is pretty particular about what happens to the library books."

Brett leaned to one side, trying to get a better look at the cover of Camille's current read. "That doesn't look like the last few you read."

Most of her books featured a couple embracing or a mostly shirtless man sporting rock-hard abs, but this one seemed a little darker.

A little more intense.

"I thought I'd try something a little different." She turned it his way. "It's a psychological thriller."

"That's a big jump from romance." He'd picked up a couple of her books as he straightened up before bed, sneaking a few lines here and there. It didn't take many pages to see the appeal.

Especially for a woman like Camille.

She turned the cover inward, hazel eyes going down to rest on the book she was nearly halfway through. "It sounded interesting." She pressed her lips together, running them across each other. "I don't think I'll read books like this all the time, but maybe here and there."

"What's it about?" Brett rested his arms on the concrete at each side of her thighs, letting his thumbs brush across her skin.

Camille's lips twisted into a little smile. "A woman who moves across the country to get away from her abusive husband."

"How did you come across this book?"

"Lucy suggested it." Camille's lips pressed tight together for a second. "I think she ends up killing him in the end."

"So it has a happy ending then."

"I think that's why Lucy suggested it." Camille set the book behind her, far from the water dripping off his skin. "She's like a therapist and books are her prescription."

"That is about the best description of a librarian I've ever heard." He eased closer. "And I saw you giving Mariah a little of your stash."

Camille laughed. "That's what I'm calling it from now on." She wrapped her arms around his shoulders. "My stash."

"Have you read enough about the husband killer, or should I do a few more laps?"

"I think I'm good for the night." She traced a line down his shoulder, chasing a drop of water making a path back to the pool. "I'll save the rest for tomorrow."

"Tomorrow is Saturday." Brett pushed through the water, heading for the stairs.

"And?" Camille strapped the boot back onto her foot before slowly pushing up.

"SummerFest is this weekend." He grabbed his towel, using it to knock off most of the water still hanging on before wrapping it around his waist and slipping into his flip flops. "I thought we could take Cal down to check it out."

Camille followed as he went inside, the chilly blast of the air-conditioning sending goosebumps across his skin.

"What would you think of maybe talking to him while we're there?" She barely peeked his way as he came to a dead stop beside her.

"What do you want to talk to him about?"

Her eyes slowly lifted his way. She was quiet for a few long seconds. "Us."

Once again she'd surprised him. Taken leaps where he expected baby steps. "I'm ready to talk to Cal whenever you are, Sweetheart."

Camille started walking again, moving to the base of the stairs. "What will we tell him?"

Brett stayed at her side, keeping his voice low as they moved down the hall toward their room. "That's up to you too."

Camille knew Calvin better than anyone. She knew what the best way would be to handle this.

"What would you want to hear if it was you?" She unlocked her door and went in, sliding the book in her hand onto the dresser.

"The truth."

Camille turned to face him. "What's the truth?"

She might be fishing. Looking for an admission he'd been willing to offer for longer than he could remember.

And that was fine.

"That I'm here to take care of both of you." Brett moved closer to the woman he never expected could be his. "That I love him." He reached up to trace a line down the side of her face. "That I love you."

Her eyes barely widened as she inhaled softly.

"I know that's a lot to hear." He caught the end of the braid keeping her hair out of her face. "But it's the truth."

Her head barely tilted to one side, her eyes holding his.

Then she lunged at him, grabbing on tight as her body hit his.

He managed to catch her, wrapping both arms around her back as he tipped toward the bed, the force of her hit knocking him off balance.

They dropped together, falling onto the soft blanket he'd spent the past week sleeping under.

Camille's hands went to his hair. To his chest.

To the towel around his waist. She tugged at it, managing to get it loose before he rolled her body under his. The wet from his trunks immediately soaked into the thin fabric of her dress.

"Damn it." He fought the tie at the waist loose, chucking them and tossing the soaked shorts into the laundry basket across the room.

Camille immediately reached for him, her hand closing around his already straining dick. She was turning out to be anything but hesitant in the bedroom, and it was a blessing and a curse.

Another thing he was pretty sure he should thank Lucy Schroder for.

Brett managed to get her dress shoved up and panties pulled down before Camille's thighs wrapped around his hips, pulling him close.

He'd been thinking about taking her out to run when her ankle was healed, but if she built up any more strength in her legs, he'd probably end up finishing on her belly every time she locked them around him.

"Maybe that book was a good choice." Brett reached between their bodies, working his hand down until he found the spot he needed. "Because I'm thinkin' you might end up killin' me."

"You're not my husband." She fisted his dick a little tighter, making him groan against her skin.

"Not yet." He pulled down the cup of her bra, freeing a nipple he immediately caught in his mouth.

Camille arched under him as he worked her clit, sucking the nipple in his mouth in time with each pass of his thumb.

It was the only hope he had. Get her as far as he could and pray he could hold out on the final stretch.

It was the only plan he'd been able to come up with. No woman had done this to him before. It was as if his body had already given up.

Already waved the white flag, surrendering to the quiet woman laying waste to all his best intentions.

"Brett." She pulled him closer, ankles locking in place, pinning his hand between them.

"You've got to give me room to work, Sweetheart." He reached for the lidded bowl on the table at his side of the bed. "Otherwise we're both stuck."

Camille's eyes opened and she peeked down, her legs immediately relaxing just a little. "Sorry."

"Nothin' to be sorry for." He leaned in to brush his lips over hers. "I'm not ever gonna complain that the woman I love wants me."

He'd only meant to say it the once.

But it was like a seal had been broken.

Now it was all he wanted to say.

Not because he expected to hear it back.

It just felt good to finally let it out.

Speak the truth he'd been living with for so long.

He tore open the condom, using every bit of space Camille gave him to get it in place before resting his hands at each side of her head, hoping to steal a few seconds to find some focus.

"I'm going to marry you, Camille." Brett held her gaze, spilling out the truth she claimed to want. "I'm going to build you a house with the biggest fucking library it can hold." He leaned close, nosing along her neck as he slowly eased his body into hers. "I'll buy you any book you want." He ground out the last word as she tightened around him in a small pulse that nearly made him see stars and stole any self-preservation he still possessed.

All he could do was hold on, fight his way through the most perfect war he'd ever waged, praying he could hold the line just long enough.

He rocked into her, each move a perfect torture he would never get enough of.

Camille held him tight, arms and legs keeping him close as she moved to him, meeting each thrust, each piston of his hips as he drove himself into her.

It took everything he had to hold on, teeth clenched, eyes shut tight, hands gripping her hair. The second she arched against him he was gone, his climax chasing hers, racing after it.

Her breath was short in his ear, choppy and sharp as her legs dropped from his waist and her arms went limp, her whole body relaxing under his.

But it was short-lived.

A knock on her door sent Camille sitting straight up.

Brett rested one hand on her belly. "Relax, Sweetheart." He stood up from the bed, tossing the covers across her body before grabbing the towel from the floor and wrapping it around his waist as he walked to the door. He squinted out the peephole to find one of their guests standing on the other side.

He cracked it open just enough to look out with a smile. "Evenin'."

Based on the apologetic look on his face, the man on the other side clearly knew he was interrupting something. "Is there any way I could get another towel or two?"

"Of course." Brett kept his easy smile. "Give me just a second and I'll be right out."

He closed the door, dropping his towel as he snagged a pair of shorts from his bag before going to where Camille laid across the bed, covers clutched tight to her chest.

Her eyes stayed locked on his as he leaned down and pressed a kiss to her lips. "Go ahead and let me know when you're ready for me to get started on that house."

CHAPTER TWENTY-THREE

"HAS GRADY FOUND out anything about that chick that showed up at Maryann's?" Mariah stood at the stove, mashing up a log of sausage for the morning's biscuits and gravy breakfast.

"I don't think so." Camille kept her eyes on the computer screen in front of her. "It was probably nothing."

It had to be nothing. End of story.

The car at Cal's practice was nothing. It was fine.

Probably just someone there to pick their kid up and they parked in the wrong lot.

Everything was fine.

Good.

Mariah lifted a brow at her. "I guess anything's possible."

Camille pressed her lips together as she scanned the lines of options to add to the week's grocery order for The Inn.

"Do you need anything added to the list?" She scanned all the items added so far.

"You might want to check the snack drawer. I think it took a pretty hard hit this week." Mariah dropped a few scoops of flour on top of the cooked and crumbled sausage.

Camille went to the back of the island and pulled open the drawer she kept filled with granola bars, cracker stacks, and applesauce for Cal. She stared down into the mostly-empty drawer that served as one of the few spots in the building her son could call his own.

Mariah leaned her way. "Football makes him hungry."

The drawer was bare except for a granola bar and a single pouch of applesauce.

"Holy cow." Brett's voice startled her, sending her spinning his way.

His blue eyes were fixed on the depleted bin. "Cal burned through that, didn't he?"

She chewed her lip. It was clear her son had outgrown the drawer. "I guess I can buy double of everything."

"I think we're past the drawer being his only option for snacks." Brett leaned against the counter. "I think for now we need to get a little fridge and stick it in the closet around the corner."

It was a good idea. Maybe even a great one.

Brett straightened, rounding the counter to where the laptop she'd been using to place their grocery order still sat. He worked through the screens, adding an extra gallon of milk, string cheese, lunch meat, and a number of other items before giving the screen a single nod. "That should be a good start for him." His eyes rested on her. "And we can pick up a fridge tonight after SummerFest."

Camille glanced up at him. "Thank you."

Once again Brett fixed everything, stepping in like her knight in shining armor to handle something she couldn't quite seem to.

She fought to keep the smile on her face. "He'll be excited."

Brett tipped one finger under her chin. "It's not just for him." He pressed a kiss to her lips. "I like a nice snack myself."

"You *are* a snack."

Camille's eyes rolled Mariah's way.

Her friend was grinning wide. "Did I say that out loud?"

Brett laughed, the warm sound smothering out the bad trying to creep in at the edges of the first real happiness she'd had in years. "I'm going to take that as a compliment." He turned back to Camille, his expression making her heart skip a beat. "I'm gonna go take care of the pool then we can get ready to head out."

She tipped her head in a nod. "Okay."

Everything was okay. Always would be.

She'd gotten the bad done and over with.

There was no more space for it in her life.

Only good.

Camille watched as Brett went out the door to crouch down next to the edge of the pool.

"I bet we could sell tickets if you could get him to do that in his boots and jeans." Mariah shook her head. "Hell, we could probably sell tickets to watch him breathe in jeans and boots."

"I'd pay." Camille leaned back against the counter, crossing her arms as Brett got the net and started skimming the surface.

Mariah snorted. "You get it for free."

"And I'd still be willing to pay for it." She smiled a little, the clench in her chest easing more with each passing second. "What's that tell you?"

"It tells me that I should start cowboy shopping." Mariah went back to the stove, lifting the lid on her simmering gravy as the first set of steps came down the stairs.

"I tried to tell you that." Camille tore her eyes from Brett and went back to her grocery list, choosing a pick-up time that would offer plenty of room for enjoying SummerFest and picking up a fridge. "But you're being stubborn."

Mariah sighed. "Sometimes you can just only handle so much." She leaned back to check on the biscuits browning in the oven. "Right now I don't have it in me to take on anything else." Her expression was sad. "Even if it's good."

"It's hard for good and bad to coexist." Camille glanced toward where Brett worked outside.

It would have been impossible to let him into her life a year ago. She would have always been waiting for the other boot to drop.

Metaphorically.

She couldn't have enjoyed any of it. Everything would have been tainted by the bad.

That's why there was no room for it now.

"Ain't that the truth." Mariah's expression shifted in an instant as the first of their guests arrived for breakfast. In a flash she was all happiness and bright spirits. "Good morning. Did you sleep well?"

The rest of the morning was consumed with coffee and juice refills. Answering questions about the day's schedule and what places she recommended visiting outside the ranch.

By the time dishes were rinsed and racked in the two dishwashers it was time to move the laundry in the washer to the dryer. Camille left Mariah wiping down the counters and hustled up the stairs to do one of the hundreds of tasks on her list for the day.

Going to SummerFest meant she had to fit it all into a much smaller block of time, and even with Brett on hand it was still tough to get it all done on a regular day.

"How's it goin'?" Brett leaned in the open door right as she finished reloading the washer.

"Good." She chose the cycle and switched it on before turning to face him. "How's the pool?"

"Clean and ready for fun." He shot her a wink. "Just like me."

She couldn't help but smile. "I might like you better dirty."

It was out of her mouth before she realized how it sounded.

Brett's brows crept up. "Are you flirting with me?"

"Definitely not." She reached out to barely touch the fabric of his t-shirt. "You're just cleaner than you used to be."

"Sounds like you were doin' a lot of lookin' I didn't know about." Brett caught her hand, pulling it to his lips. "Sneaky woman."

"I'm not sneaky." Her smile held, widening all on its own. "You were everywhere I looked. There was no avoiding you."

"That was by design." He ran his lips along her skin.

"Maybe you're the sneaky one then."

He used his hold on her hand to pull her close, holding her tight as he spun them into the laundry room and out of sight. "I'm not above sneakin' to get close to you, Sweetheart."

There was only one reason they needed to sneak now.

And hopefully that could be rectified today.

Camille relaxed against his chest, breathing in the scent of his skin. "I don't want to sneak anymore."

"I like hearing that." He reached up to run one hand down her cheek. "But we need to give him time to adjust to this. New things are hard, even when they're good."

That was the truth.

Sometimes being good made it even harder.

"Mom?"

They had a second of warning. Just long enough for Brett to put enough space between them so it didn't look like quite as intimate of a moment as it really was.

Luckily Cal didn't seem to notice. He smiled brightly the second he saw her. "When are we leaving?"

Camille smoothed down the front of her t-shirt. "As soon as Brett's ready."

"I'm ready now." Brett lifted his brows Calvin's way. "Are you ready?"

Cal pressed his lips together as he gave them a slow nod.

It was an odd move that Brett didn't miss. "What's wrong, Buddy?"

"I was wondering if Wyatt could come with us."

Brett glanced her way. "That's up to your momma."

She wanted time alone with Cal to explain her relationship with Brett.

But telling him no because of that seemed selfish.

"Sure." They could tell him another time.

She could be patient, especially for her son.

Cal jumped in place as he spun away. "I'll go tell him."

Camille glanced Brett's way. "Sorry."

"Nothin' to be sorry for." He draped one arm across her shoulders, pulling her close to press a kiss to the side of her head as they walked toward the stairs. "We've got all the time in the world."

Time used to be something she simply ran down. Waited out as it passed, feeling trapped.

It was odd to think of it as something good she could enjoy.

Even look forward to.

Cal and Wyatt were already at the door when she and Brett got there, talking about everything they'd seen going up over the past few days as SummerFest was set up downtown.

"Can we ride the rides?" Cal stuck close as they went out the door.

His excitement was contagious.

"Sure." Camille hooked her purse across her chest as they walked, her cast making her gait a little lopsided.

"Can we have an elephant ear?"

"*You* can have an elephant ear." She grinned. "*I'm* having a funnel cake."

Cal glanced at Brett. "What's Brett going to have?"

"Brett is stealing some of your momma's funnel cake." Brett opened the passenger's door, holding it as he waited for Camille to get inside.

Cal and Wyatt jumped into the backseat, continuing their questions. "Can we have corn dogs?"

Camille turned to look at them between the seats. "Yes." She cut Calvin off before he could ask anything else. "You can eat anything you want."

Cal and Wyatt both grinned back at her as Brett settled into the driver's seat.

"Holy heck, woman." He reached between his legs, looking for the lever that would push back the seat in her base-model sedan. "How do you drive so close to the wheel?"

"Just fine considering I don't have legs a mile long." Camille scrunched her face up at him as she turned back toward the windshield.

"When will you be able to drive again?" Cal's seatbelt clicked into place behind her.

"I can drive now, it's just not real easy with the boot on." She glanced into the backseat as Brett slowly drove down the gravel lane. "And Brett was nice enough to offer to take us so I didn't have to worry about it."

Cal and Wyatt quickly fell into a conversation about the week they spent at football camp, chatting about the other kids and the coaches.

The ride was oddly relaxing, lulling her into a peaceful place she never thought she would find.

Her son was healthy and happy and loved.

She was healthy and happy and loved.

By a man willing to go to lengths she didn't expect to exist outside the pages of one of the books Lucy Schroder packed into her weekly library bag.

"Wow." Brett's brows shot up as he leaned forward, looking out at the crowd of cars and people packing the downtown area. "Looks like everyone decided to spend their Saturday the same way."

"That's okay." Camille saw plenty of familiar faces as they crept along the line of cars and trucks parked on the empty field just outside of Moss Creek. Brett found a spot right as someone vacated it, putting them relatively close to the rides and games and food overtaking the south end of town.

Brett parked, lining her car up in the small space. Cal and Wyatt were out almost immediately, standing at the back end of the car while she carefully got out and navigated the uneven ground.

"You okay?" Brett's hand barely came her way.

"I'm okay. Just making sure I don't break anything else." She lowered her voice. "Don't want you trying to carry me around this place."

"I'd do more than try." He gave her one of the winks he snuck her way whenever Cal was around before turning to the boys. "What first?"

"Rides." Both boys were on the same page, so they went to the ticket booth where Brett bought enough tickets that the boys could ride everything at least twice.

"That's a lot of tickets." Camille eyed the perforated strips.

"I'm guessing they'll pull this same thing on Brody and Clara tomorrow." He tore the tickets in half and passed her one stack. "We'll give them those as a peace offering."

She took the tickets and tucked them into her purse.

It was so strange to be in a family where people thought of things like that.

Helped each other out.

Her family was never like that. Even before her parents died she and her sisters weren't close.

When they were gone, so was any connection with her siblings. The last time she saw either of them was at their father's funeral.

And maybe the fault for that wasn't completely on them. It was a mistake she didn't plan to make again.

"Maybe sometime we can watch the big girls overnight so Brody and Clara can have a little break." Camille moved along beside Brett, trailing Wyatt and Calvin as they headed straight for a set of enclosed two-seaters that spun while racing along a hilly track.

"I think that sounds like a great idea." Brett's eyes slid her way. "Course we'll have to find somewhere to stack them up at night."

"That's true." She chewed her lower lip, trying to work up the nerve to add what she was thinking. "We could watch them at your place."

Brett shook his head. "My place isn't my place anymore, Sweetheart." He leaned into her ear, resting one hand on the small of her back. "My place is your place."

Camille's eyes snapped up to his face. "Who's in your cabin?"

"Clint and Elijah." Brett's eyes scanned the area around them. "No reason to have it sittin' empty." His hand slid up her back to press between her shoulder blades. "So if you want a place that's not The Inn to watch the girls then you'll have to let me build you that house I've been talkin' about." Brett backed away. He tipped his head toward where Calvin and Wyatt were loading onto the ride. "You keep an eye on them while I go get us that funnel cake."

Camille stared after him as he disappeared into the crowd.

She slowly turned to where Cal and Wyatt were loaded into a purple seat, metal bar pressed tight to their lap, laughing wildly as the ride started to move.

Her eyes stayed on them, following their path as everything spun faster.

And faster.

And faster.

Fast enough she lost track of where they were.

But not where she was.

That was easy to find.

Because she was going to let Brett Pace build her that house.

They would have parties of their own.

Cal would have more than a kitchen drawer.

More than a tiny bedroom.

He would have a home.

Camille moved closer as the ride slowed to a stop, edging in as the passengers started to file off and into the crowd. Unfortunately all the cowboy hats made it hard to find two little boys. She wove through the herd of bodies, looking for her son's dirty-blond head.

She reached the fencing surrounding the ride and there was still no sign of the boys.

"Hey there." One of the waitresses at The Wooden Spoon bumped in at her side. "How's it going?"

"Good." Camille gave her a quick smile. "Have you seen Calvin?"

Cecily shook her head. "No." She wiggled her brows. "But I did see Brett Pace." She leaned in. "Rumor has it you're seeing him."

"Yup." Camille caught sight of Wyatt as he pushed through the crowd heading her way. She immediately walked away from where Cecily was still talking, going straight toward where Wyatt was looking frantically from side to side. "I'm right here, honey." She waved one hand his way as she hobbled across the uneven ground.

Wyatt's head snapped her way and he ran toward her. "Calvin needs help."

Her stomach bottomed out. "What's wrong?"

Wyatt's eyes were wide and watery. "Some lady grabbed him."

CHAPTER TWENTY-FOUR

BRETT BALANCED THE plate of fried dough and cherry pie filling on one hand as he wove through the crowd, headed back to where Camille was watching the boys scramble their brains on the fastest spinning ride in the place.

"Fancy meetin' you here." Ben Chamberlain eyed the treat he was carrying. "Where'd you find that?"

Brett tipped his head toward the trailer selling all varieties of carbs. "Nelly's Cakes and Ears." He tucked the plate close as a group of teenagers came dangerously close to bumping into him. "This one's the cherry pie funnel cake."

"I'm gonna have to get me one of those." Ben did a quick scan of the people milling around them. "Everything going okay?"

"Seems like." Brett caught sight of Liza Cross a few yards away, her eyes fixed on the man across from him. "How about you? Things going okay for you?"

Ben barely lifted his shoulders. "I think they're goin' as good as they're ever gonna go."

The head ranch hand from Cross Creek Ranch was caught in a position Brett could have easily been in himself.

Stuck on a woman who couldn't figure out how to move beyond the past.

"Sorry to hear that." Brett glanced at where Liza still stood, chatting with a few of the women from town, her gaze lingering on Ben. "I wish I had advice for you."

"I'm not sure it would matter." Ben shook his head. "Sometimes it just is what it is."

Ben was as good of a man as it got. He stayed at Cross Creek when everyone else bailed, doing whatever it took to keep them above-water after the death of Liza's abusive husband.

Brett leaned away from a pack of women pushing strollers. "I still wish it was different."

And not just for Ben's sake.

His eyes went to where Liza was standing, but the spot was empty.

"Appreciate that." Ben slapped him on the shoulder. "Let me know if there's anything I can do for you."

"Same goes for you." Brett tipped his head Ben's way as the older man made his way toward Nelly's.

Brett turned carefully, avoiding the bodies constantly moving around him as he worked toward where he'd left Camille.

But it turned out Liza wasn't the only one whose spot was empty. He did a slow spin, scanning the heads around him, looking for any sign of the three that he came with.

They couldn't have gotten far. Especially in the crush of people making it almost impossible to get anywhere fast.

Brett worked toward the rails surrounding the ride, thinking that maybe the boys had enough fun they decided to line back up to ride it again.

He caught sight of one of the kids from football camp as he passed. "Carter, have you seen Calvin and Wyatt?"

The little boy grinned up at him. "Hey, Coach Pace."

"Hey." Brett kept his eyes moving as he repeated his question. "Have you seen Calvin and Wyatt?"

"No."

Brett gave the kid a pat on the shoulder. "Thanks."

Maybe they moved to another ride.

Brett reached into the pocket of his shorts as he walked, pulling out his phone and dialing Camille's number.

He kept moving as it rang, heading to where the next-closest ride sat at the back corner of the lot, lined up against the road that blocked in the space.

Between the crowd and the trailers set up to house the giant generators supplying the power that fed the rides and food trucks, it was impossible to see very far.

The last ring sounded, and a second later Camille's soft voice came through the line, barely audible above the crowd as she politely asked him to leave a message.

Brett disconnected the call and tucked the phone back into place as he kept moving. Sooner or later he would find them.

There were only so many places they could be.

The next ride over was a ship that swung from side to side, flying high enough to send more than a few riders screaming as it whipped through the air.

He tried to catch the faces lined across the boat, but it moved too fast, forcing him to wait until it slowed down, each swing climbing lower and lower as the ride worked toward a stop.

But there was still one rider hollering at the top of their lungs.

Brett went still as the sound registered.

It wasn't a rider yelling.

The sound was coming from behind one of the wide generator trailers parked along the edge of the narrow road.

And the sound of it dropped his heart to his feet.

It was a voice he'd only ever heard soft and sweet. Calm and kind.

But what he was hearing now was none of those things.

He couldn't make out the exact words, but the emotions behind them were clear.

Rage. Aggression.

Fear.

The plate in his hand hit the grass as he started to run, racing toward the sound of Camille's voice. The closer he got the more he could decipher.

And it only made him run faster.

"Let him go."

It was clear and loud, leaving no room for him to question what was happening.

Brett raced around the corner of the trailer blocking his view, clipping the edge with his shoulder as the air froze in his lungs.

Camille stood on the small shoulder of asphalt next to a familiar green sedan, both feet braced as she fought the dark-haired woman from the video his mother took. Cal stood between them, shoving at the woman holding his arm in a death grip as she tried to drag him toward the open back door of the car.

Brett barely made it two more steps before another body came rushing from between the trailers in a flash of blonde hair and curse-laden threats.

Headed straight for the dark-haired woman.

The collision was hard and fast, slamming the newest arrival and her victim into the car idling on the road. The vehicle rocked as they hit it, a mass of screeching, swearing, chaos.

Camille took full advantage, wrapping both arms around Cal and dragging him away from the scene as his would-be abductor wrestled the blonde who was quickly gaining the upper hand. Their tangled bodies rolled along the side of the car as it started to move, engine revving as the people inside tried to make their getaway.

Brett went straight for it, grabbing onto the open back door as he pounded the roof with his fist. "Stop this goddamned car."

The dark-haired woman managed to get one hand fisted into Liza Cross's hair, twisting it hard enough to pull a clump free as they rolled down the hood.

"You filthy heifer." Liza worked one arm around the woman's neck, cranking it tight as they continued to slide along the car, getting dangerously close to dropping off the front.

"Get that thing stopped." Ben Chamberlain came running their way, headed straight for the driver's door. He reached through the open window just as Liza dropped out of sight.

The car jerked to the left.

But it was too late.

The bounce was unmissable.

Brett slammed the door closed, getting it out of his way as he rushed toward the front of the sedan, stomach turning at the thought of what might be waiting for him.

The dark-haired woman was rolling away from Liza, gasping for air, one hand at the reddened skin of her neck.

Brett dropped to his knees beside Liza, reaching for her unmoving body. She sucked in a breath as his hands moved her matted hair from the sticky skin of her face.

"No." Ben dropped to the ground at her other side, immediately grabbing for her.

Brett shoved one hand to his friend's chest. "We can't move her."

"Like hell." Ben shoved back at Brett, hard enough to knock him to his ass, before carefully touching Liza's unmoving body.

But Liza wasn't the only woman who might be hurt.

Brett pushed up to his feet, spinning to where Camille used to be standing.

She was fucking gone again.

The sound of a transmission shifting dragged his attention to the car angled across the road.

A level of anger he'd never possessed sent him to the driver's door. He reached in through the open window to grab the man behind the wheel, pulling him out by the shirt he was wearing. "You son of a bitch."

Junior Shepard's father sputtered, arms waving, feet kicking as Brett wrestled his pudgy body out and into the open.

One of the Shepard men was finally going to get what he deserved.

"Leave him alone." Junior's mother was in the passenger's seat, screaming like she had any right to stop what was happening.

Brett dragged the older man free of the car before immediately slamming him back against the side with enough force to knock the wind from his lungs.

"My chest." Junior's father clutched his chest. "I'm having a heart attack."

"Good." Brett slammed him again.

All he saw was black, the icy creep of rage taking him to a place where nothing mattered but dishing out what was deserved.

He'd done it many times in his life. Earned the reputation he and his brothers still carried.

And it was time to do it again.

He had Junior's father pinned in place with one hand, the other pulled back and ready to strike.

"Nope." Grady Haynes grabbed him, yanking him away. "You got places to be besides a jail cell."

Junior's dad slumped down the side of the car, hands going to his knees as he sucked in air.

Grady spun Brett away, shoving him hard toward the line of trailers.

Brett tried to turn back. "That piece of shit tried to take Cal and hit Liza with his car."

"It's under control." Grady gripped the back of Brett's shirt as he kept pushing.

Brett craned his neck, trying to get a better look at where Liza laid on the ground. A group of medics already surrounded her, blocking out all of her but the bottoms of her feet. "Is she okay?"

"She's hurt." Grady didn't slow down. "But there's nothing you can do for her."

Brett skidded his feet, fighting his friend's shove as he twisted from side to side, scanning the space. "Where's Camille and Cal?"

"Where in the hell do you think I'm taking you?" Grady added his free hand to where he gripped the back of his shirt. "And you're makin' it hard as hell."

Brett turned to face the direction they were moving, catching a glimpse of Camille where she stood behind Wes Eldridge. He planted his feet, shoving hard against the ground as he fought to get to her faster.

Grady let him go with a sharp swear.

Camille's wide hazel eyes snapped his way. Her skin was pale. Her face and neck scratched in red, angry lines.

Brett grabbed her, pulling her close.

She pressed her face to his chest, body sagging as she let out a shuddering breath.

"It's okay." He cradled her head in his hands, pressing his face to the top of her head and breathing deep. "You did good."

"I tried to fight her."

"You did more than try, Sweetheart. You fought like hell." He lifted his head to look for Cal and Wyatt. Both boys sat at the open back end of one of the ambulances while a medic bandaged a scratch dug into Cal's arm. "He's safe because of you."

She shoved at him, leaning back to look around. "Where's Liza?"

He couldn't tell her the truth. Not yet. "She's with Ben."

"I took the boys and ran. I wasn't trying to get away, I just wanted to find someone to help." Camille's lower lip quivered. "Grady saw me and—"

"You did exactly what you should have done, Sweetheart." He pulled her close again. "We needed more help. You were right."

"I wasn't trying to run away." She said it more firmly this time.

"I know that." He ran one hand down her back, trying to soothe her any way he could. "Because of you Grady caught them all."

Camille's lips pressed together, eyes getting watery. "Why would they do that?"

"It seems like Junior didn't fall far from the tree." He wanted to look back, try to gain another look at Liza, but if he looked Camille would look.

"Who was that woman?" Camille tried to lean around him, her eyes going in the direction of the scene she didn't need to see.

"Grady will find out." He gently angled her toward where Cal and Wyatt were. "Let's go over here."

He kept her close as they walked, Officer Eldridge following at his side.

Brett deposited Camille next to Cal before leaning down to come eye-level with the little boy. "I'm proud of you, Buddy."

Cal seemed to be the least fazed by what happened. His cheeks were a little pink, but his eyes were clear and his spine was straight as he held a cold pack to the bicep already sporting the beginnings of a handprint-shaped bruise. "That lady told me she had a present for me."

Wes stepped closer, reaching into his front pocket to pull out a little notepad. "I'm gonna write this down, that okay?"

Cal tipped his head in a sharp nod. "She came up to us as soon as we got off the ride. Pretended to be real nice."

Wes's eyes lifted. "Did you know she was pretending right away?"

"Yeah." Cal glanced Camille's way before looking back up at the cop. "She reminded me of my Grandma Shepard. She pretends to be nice too, but she's not."

The only reaction to Cal's statement was a slight clench of Wes's jaw. "Did she tell you who she was?"

Cal shook his head. "Just said she was a friend of my dad's and that she had a present for me." He sat a little taller. "That's how I knew she was lying." His eyes narrowed. "My dad doesn't have friends. No one likes him."

"What happened next?" Wes continued to write across his pad.

"I told her I didn't want her present. Then she grabbed me by my arm." Calvin looked toward where Wyatt sat at his side. "That's when Wyatt ran away to get my mom."

Wes tipped his head Wyatt's way. "Good job."

"Thanks." Wyatt did look a little shocked by what happened, but he was still sitting straight, shoulders square, wearing a brave face.

"Then my mom ran up and started fighting the lady." Cal's eyes went to Camille. "She punched her right in the face."

Brett couldn't control the lift of his brows or the swell of pride in his chest.

Wes flipped the front of his notebook closed before tucking it back into his pocket. He crouched down in front of the boys. "You two did a real good job today." He reached out to shake each of their hands. "And you don't have to worry about that lady anymore."

"I know." Cal's tone didn't carry a hint of fear or uncertainty. His mouth lifted in a half smile as he looked at his mother, eyes resting a second before coming Brett's way.

"My mom and Brett will keep me safe."

CHAPTER TWENTY-FIVE

CAMILLE SHIFTED IN the uncomfortable chair, trying to ease the numbness beginning to set in.

"How fucking long is this going to take?" Mae shoved up from her own chair and walked to the opposite side of the small waiting room. "It's been forever."

"The doctor said it would be at least five hours." Clara peeked under the blanket thrown across the baby tucked against her chest. "We just have to be patient."

"I don't want to be patient." Mae walked back their way, working into the pace she used to pass the first two hours they spent at the hospital. "I want to see her."

"We all want to see her." Nora huffed out a breath as she slumped lower in her chair. "This is freaking stupid."

"What's stupid is that they let Junior on that goddamned *Meet a Convict* website." Mae turned to Nora. "What sort of psychopath wants to date a man convicted of attempted murder?"

"The same kind of psychopath who agrees to kidnap his kid for his parents." Camille's stomach turned. "At least they found each other. They all belong together."

Clara snorted. "They're going to be together for a long time." Her lips twisted into a smirk. "In prison."

"Maybe his girlfriend and his mom will end up at the same one and they can braid each other's hair." Nora crossed her arms. "And I thought my ex's mother was evil."

"At least I'm not the only one with bad taste in men." Camille managed a little smile.

"You're in the majority on that one." Clara pointed Mae's way. "She's the only one of us who hasn't made that mistake."

They all jerked to attention as the door to the room opened. The doctor they spoke with earlier strode in, still wearing his scrubs.

Mae was in front of him before he could take three full steps. "How is she?"

"She's working on waking up." He looked around the room. "There was a lot of damage."

Camille stood up, immediately followed by Clara and Nora. "But you were able to fix it, right?"

He hesitated.

Mae stepped closer. "You were able to fix it, right?"

"I did as much as I could." He held his ground as the women slowly moved in around him. "The rest is up to her."

Mae's eyes narrowed. "What does that mean?"

The surgeon glanced Mae's way before shifting away the tiniest bit. "It means her recovery will depend on how hard she's willing to work. The more she puts in at physical therapy, the more mobility she will regain."

"Oh." Mae relaxed a little. "That's fine then."

Camille let out a sigh of relief. If Liza's healing was in her own hands then everything would be fine. "When can we see her?"

"It will probably be in the next thirty minutes or so. Everyone wakes up differently so I can't give you an exact time." The surgeon went on to thank them for their patience before making a hasty exit.

"Okay." Mae nodded her head. "This is good. She will do all the therapy and everything will be fine." She rested one hand on her stomach. "I thought I was going to puke when he first said he did his best."

"I thought you were going to punch him." Nora grabbed her purse. "So I'm a little relieved that it was vomit and not violence putting that look on your face."

Mae tipped her head to one side. "It might have been a little of both."

"I'm going to the ladies' real quick." Nora went toward the still open door. "Anyone else need to go?"

They'd been in the room since the woman at the reception desk saw Clara breastfeeding. She immediately found them a private place so Clara could comfortably feed, and they could comfortably worry.

"Me." Clara leaned down to ease the sleeping baby in her arms into the vacant side of the double stroller parked in front of her.

"Me too." Mae picked up the three empty cups of coffee lined down the table next to the chair she'd occasionally sat in. "It was really nice of the receptionist to bring us coffee, but I'm feeling it now." She deposited the cups in the trash as the whole group filed out the door and into the larger main waiting area for the hospital.

A man sitting in one of the chairs suddenly stood, cowboy hat held in his hands, eyes focused on them.

Mae softly smiled. "You guys go ahead. I'll catch up with you." She walked toward where Ben Chamberlain stood, looking about as broken as she'd ever seen a man look.

Nora slowly walked the same direction. "I'll be there in a minute too." She joined Mae and Ben, immediately resting her hand on Ben's arm.

Clara watched as their friends spoke to Ben in hushed words. "Why are we so stubborn sometimes?" She quickly looked Camille's way. "Not us specifically, just women in general."

"Because sometimes we are so used to things being one way that we can't imagine they could be any other way." She'd been stuck in it herself. "It's hard when so much has been bad to let yourself think things might be good. It's almost scarier." She swallowed hard. "There's more to lose then."

It's where she was now. Facing how much she had to lose.

Before it was just Cal, which was bad enough.

Now she had Brett. A home. Family.

Friends.

And today she almost lost some of that.

But for the first time in her life she fought for it. Fought the bad.

Refused to just roll over and accept it for what it was.

Because the good was finally winning.

"We should go get started. By the time I get both these girls changed and pee, Liza will probably be back to giving everyone the middle finger."

Camille turned to Clara. "I didn't even think of that." She shook her head. "She's going to be so mad if she can't do that."

Clara smiled a little as they walked down the hall toward the bathroom. "That alone will get her through physical therapy."

Camille watched the twins while Clara used the bathroom, then she took her turn while Clara started changing diapers.

Nora and Mae came in right as they were finishing up.

Camille tossed her paper towel into the trash. "How is he?"

"A saint." Mae bumped one of the stall doors open. "Sometimes I want to smack her."

"To be fair, there were a few times I wanted to smack you." Camille leaned back against the counter.

Mae peeked out the still-open door. "Fair enough." She closed the metal panel and latched it into place. "I don't even know what her problem is."

Clara turned from where she was wrestling Ella into a new diaper on the changing station. "She hasn't told you?"

"Nope." Mae's answer carried out from the stall. "Won't even discuss him."

Nora came out of her stall and washed her hands. "Whatever it is, I'm pretty sure it's complicated as hell." She shut off the water.

"It's always complicated as hell." Clara switched out the twins, strapping Ella back into her seat before pulling Faith out. "She's not special."

"Yeah, but it's not usually *she killed her husband* complicated." Nora dried her hands before using the paper towel to pull the door open. "We ready?"

Clara dropped the second wet diaper into the trash before unlocking the wheels on the stroller and pushing it through the open door. "I hope she's doing okay." She chewed her lower lip. "Some people don't come out of anesthesia well."

They walked out to find a nurse peeking into their vacated room. She turned to face them. "I'm betting you're the family of Liza Cross."

They all paused before slowly nodding, their answer coming out in near unison.

"We are."

****

CAMILLE DROPPED DOWN to the sectional in the great room of The Inn, her upper body falling against the back as her head dropped to the cushions. "Holy hell that was a long day."

Brett eased down beside her. "How's Liza?"

She tipped her head his direction. "Pissed."

"That sounds about right." He reached out to smooth her hair behind one ear. "Did you girls get her situated?"

"Pretty much." Camille worked her shoe off her foot. "Nora and Mae are staying with her tonight to make sure she does okay."

"How are *you* doing?" He ran his fingers down her arm, needing to touch her.

Needing to see that she was okay.

Camille barely shook her head, eyes far away. "I don't know."

"It's a good thing you don't have to decide right away then." Part of him was worried this might set her back.

Might make her want to pull away from him.

Staying back while Camille went to the hospital with Clara, Nora, and Mae was one of the hardest things he'd ever done.

Her eyes finally came his way. "How's Cal doing?"

"I think he might be fine." Brett kicked his feet up on the upholstered ottoman. "We threw the ball around. Took a little swim. Ate some food and did some dishes."

Camille perked up a little at the mention of food. "What did you eat?"

"Are you gonna tell me you haven't eaten?" It was past three in the morning. She'd been up for almost twenty-four hours, and the last time he saw her eat was breakfast.

Brett dropped his feet to the floor and shoved up from the sofa. "Not even a snack from the vending machine?"

"I had a lot of coffee." Her head rocked to follow him as he walked toward the kitchen. "But that feels like it's wearing off."

"You're gonna eat some food and then you're getting your pretty little ass upstairs and into the bed." He opened the fridge, digging through the containers left over from dinner. "Mariah made spaghetti." He dropped a healthy portion out onto a plate before popping it into the microwave and setting it to cook while he slid the remainder back into place. "But we had quite a few guests head into town to spend their evening at SummerFest, so we've got a fair bit left over."

"I hope they had more fun than we did." Camille yawned, blinking her watering eyes. "I didn't even get a funnel cake."

"Technically you owned one." Brett reached into the microwave to stir around the pile of pasta before closing the door and setting it to cook for another minute. "Unfortunately it's on the grass somewhere."

Her lips pressed into a deep frown. "I can't believe what happened."

Brett shook his head. "I can't either." If someone told him Junior Shepard had enough swagger to con a woman from prison then he'd have called them a liar.

Laughed in their face.

"It sorta makes me feel better." Camille chewed her lower lip as she watched him over the back of the couch. "I might have stayed but I never tried to break the law for him."

"She didn't just try, Sweetheart." Brett pulled out the refillable water bottle Camille always used, adding a healthy dose of ice before filling it to the top with the filtering tank he kept on the counter for her to use since she refused to drink the bottles from the fridge. "She succeeded. She's sitting at county right now."

Grady called earlier in the evening to let him know that they booked a woman named Ronnie Ratliff on attempted kidnapping and assault.

286

"What about his parents?"

"They were both booked on attempted kidnapping and his father got an assault with a deadly weapon charge for running over Liza." Brett turned back to the microwave to give the spaghetti one more stir before setting its final cook cycle.

"Good." The relief in her voice was clear.

Or maybe that was exhaustion.

Either way made sense.

Brett collected a fork and a paper towel while the food finished cooking before stacking everything onto a tray and heading in to where Camille waited.

"You ready for—" He stopped, staring down at her. "Sweetheart?"

The only answer he got was a soft snore.

Camille was angled to one side, head tipped back, mouth agape.

She'd passed out in under two minutes.

So back to the kitchen he went. After wrapping a layer of clear plastic over her plate and sliding it into the fridge he grabbed her water, hooking it over his arm with the webbed loop attached to the top, before going to where Camille was sprawled across the couch.

She was going to wake up hungry as hell, but he'd deal with that in the morning.

Because right now he was going to take full advantage of the situation.

He eased both arms under her, working her away from the sofa and up against his chest, tucking her close as he made his way up the stairs with the woman who was everything he always knew she was.

Today proved it.

Camille was sweet and strong. Calm and quiet, but fierce and determined.

She wasn't the broken woman everyone expected her to be. Not by a long shot.

Brett unlocked their door, jostling her as little as possible in the process. He eased her onto the bed before shutting off the lights and turning on the television, switching it to her favorite show just in case she woke up. Then he stretched out beside her, closing his eyes as Bob Ross's soothing voice filled the silence of the room.

Camille shifted on the bed, rolling to her side and curling up against him, slinging one arm and one leg across his body like she did every night. He leaned to press a kiss to her head as she sucked in a deep breath that ended on a yawn.

He opened his eyes to find her looking up at him, she slowly blinked her heavy lids, a soft smile lifting her lips. "We should build a house so you can just leave me wherever I crash."

EPILOGUE

"AUNTIE CAMILLE, WE'RE home." Brett's voice carried in through the open double doors as a herd of footsteps thundered down the hardwood of the hall.

She had just enough time to get her open book onto the table beside the overstuffed chair before a set of running bodies launched her way, squealing as they hit the ottoman under her feet and wiggled into place at her sides. Michaela and Leah stared up at the wood-covered ceiling, wide smiles on their faces.

Brett came to stand in the open door. "I didn't realize how popular this room was going to be."

Camille shot him a grin. "Girls love their libraries."

"I noticed." He turned as Calvin and Wyatt slowly walked down the hall, sweaty and exhausted from a full day of practice. "Make sure you put your clothes in the laundry room."

"Kay."

Camille lifted her brows at Brett. "I think you wore them out."

"They are both giving it all they've got." His shoulders went a little straighter. "I think Cal might end up starting."

Both boys worked their asses off all winter and spring and it paid off. Each easily made the team, and now it looked like they would be in the starting lineup for the fall games.

"That's fantastic." Camille inched down the extra-wide overstuffed chair as the girls rolled to the center, taking over her vacated spot.

"I should warn you." Brett reached out to snag her as she walked his way. He pulled her close. "My mother called to let me know she found her cowbell."

Camille smiled up at him, wrapping both arms around his waist. "You can never have enough cowbell."

Cal might only have one grandmother, not even blood-related, but Maryann was more than enough. She loved him with a fierceness that Camille couldn't believe she ever managed to ignore.

"She's having shirts made too." Brett smoothed one hand down her back. "And hoodies for when it gets cold."

"Good." It was a word she used regularly.

Felt every day.

Often enough that the bad was no longer a threat.

And there was still bad. There always would be.

But it was nothing compared to the good.

"You think it's good now." Brett pulled her out into the hall of the home they built adjacent to the inn they ran together. "Wait until you hear how loud she is."

Camille stayed tucked into his side as they walked toward the kitchen. "I can imagine."

"You think you can." Brett's expression was serious. "She can whistle between her fingers."

"That doesn't surprise me." Camille dodged Cal as he walked with a bowl full of milk, headed to the chairs lined across the large island Nora designed to make hosting family parties a breeze. "What time is everyone coming over tomorrow?"

"One." Brett opened the fridge, pulling out a bottle of water for each boy and setting it next to their bowls of cereal and sliced banana. "He looked around the open area that took up most of the first floor of their house. "We've got a lot to do between now and then."

"That's okay." Camille lifted the lid on the slow cooker filled with pot roast. "We've got lots of extra hands."

She turned to where her son sat with his best friend. "You boys feel like helping us decorate for tomorrow?"

Wyatt nodded, a little milk dripping from his lower lip. "Sure."

Brett pointed their way. "Finish up your snack and then jump in the shower."

Cal tipped back his bowl, downing the last of the milk in it before rinsing it and lining it into the dishwasher. He rushed toward the front of the house, steps stopping near the front door. "Dad?"

Brett leaned to look down the hall. "Yeah, Buddy."

"Do you know where my bag is?"

"If it's not in here then you must have left it in the van." Brett glanced to Wyatt. "Did you bring yours in?"

Wyatt slowly shook his head.

"I'll go get them." Brett grabbed the keys, pointing one finger Cal's way. "You go take a shower."

Camille backed out of the way as Wyatt rinsed and racked his bowl before following Calvin up the stairs. She wiped down the counter where they ate, finishing up just as Brett came back in carrying both bags. He hooked the keys to the van that replaced her small sedan six months ago back in place.

"If we add any more kids to this family we're going to need a bus to tote them around."

"Can you imagine your mother pulling up to The Wooden Spoon with a bus-full of grandkids?" Camille couldn't help but grin at the thought.

"We probably shouldn't give her any ideas." Brett started up the steps with both boys' bags. "She'll be at the dealership first thing tomorrow morning."

Camille peeked her head into the library and found both girls stretched out in her chair, shoes off, each reading one of the books from the shelf she kept just for them. "Are you girls sleeping in here tonight?"

"Yes, please." Michaela was the first to answer. "Can Wyatt and Calvin sleep here too?"

"That's up to them." It was how their sleepovers usually went. All four kids piled up in the library on air mattresses on the floor.

Soon Ella and Faith would be big enough and that number would climb to six.

Michaela turned to her sister. "They will sleep here."

She wasn't wrong. Wyatt and Cal were the ultimate big brothers. They were patient and attentive to the two little girls who couldn't get enough of them.

And while Calvin technically wasn't a brother, he still worked hard to fill the part.

Which had her thinking.

Camille lifted her brows at the girls. "I'll be right back. Stay in the house."

They both nodded like they wouldn't consider escaping at the first chance they had.

Past experience determined that was a lie.

Camille made her way up the stairs to where Brett was in their room, shirt gone as he got ready to take a shower of his own.

He paused just outside the door to their bathroom. "Everything okay?"

She turned to peek down the hall as Wyatt came out and Calvin went in, rotating through rinsing off the sweat and dirt of the day. "I was thinking."

Brett went very still.

Like he knew what she was going to say next.

He probably did. He knew her better than anyone else ever had.

"About?"

She stepped deeper into the space, lowering her voice. "Time is going so fast."

It was something she still wasn't quite used to. Days stretched out for years before she came to Red Cedar Ranch.

Now they were gone in a flash.

And if she wasn't careful too many would pass. "If we want to have a baby we should probably think about doing it soon."

Brett lifted a brow. "Do we want to have a baby?"

It was a decision he'd left squarely in her court. Brett made it clear from the very beginning that she and Cal were enough for him.

More than.

And it wasn't that Brett and Cal weren't enough for her...

It just felt like something was missing.

Like someone was missing.

Camille barely nodded. "We do."

****

CAMILLE SHIFTED A little on her feet as Brett pushed the length of her blonde hair to one side so he could slide the zipper up the back of her dress into place. "Nervous?"

She spun his way, scoffing. "No."

He grinned at her. "Good."

"There's just a lot going on." She reached out to smooth down the front of his shirt as Leah and Michaela came through the open door to their bedroom, spinning in circles in their dresses.

Michaela dropped to their bed in a fluffy, pale green pile of satin and lace. "Can we have a snack?"

"Absolutely not." Brett checked the clock on the dresser. "We need to get downstairs. Everyone will be here soon."

Leah squealed a little as she turned to race down the hall toward the stairs with Michaela close behind.

Only four other people were in on their secret, outside of the minister waiting downstairs.

Calvin came out of his room, tucking his pale green plaid shirt into his jeans. Wyatt walked behind him in his matching shirt and jeans, carrying both their hats. "Is this right?"

Life was so busy and complicated with football and The Inn and the ongoing criminal case against Junior and his cohorts that Camille decided a full wedding was more than she could juggle.

But eloping like Mae and Boone wasn't something she wanted to do either.

So they settled on a surprise wedding, hidden under the guise of an end of summer party.

Brett paused, reaching out to straighten Calvin's collar. "You look good, Buddy."

Calvin grinned. "You too." His eyes went to where Camille stood. "Wow."

"That's what I said." Brett tipped his head toward the stairs. "We need to get ready. Everyone will be here any minute."

The boys headed down in front of them, affording him the opportunity to steal one last minute with the woman about to officially be his.

Camille was already smiling when he turned to her, catching her face in his hands. "You ready?"

Her smile widened. "Definitely."

He wanted a few more seconds to savor having her alone, but the sound of tires on gravel meant their time was up.

Brett snagged her hand in his. "Show time."

The kids were lined up at the door, peeking out the sidelight windows as they came down the stairs.

Camille held her dress up as she carefully followed behind him. "Who's here?"

Calvin turned to face them, grinning. "Everyone."

"All at once?" Camille went straight to one of the narrow windows, looking out. "How did that happen?"

"Sometimes things just work out." He reached for the doorknob as their family made their way toward the porch carrying the food they believed was for a simple celebration. "Everyone ready?"

The girls both bounced in place, giggling.

Calvin and Wyatt both nodded.

He turned to Camille to find her eyes were already on him. The smile she gave him nearly stopped his heard. "Definitely ready."

The second the door was open both girls rushed out in a flurry of fluff and flower petals as they ran out onto the porch, laughing like maniacs as they chucked handfuls from their baskets.

Cal and Wyatt were next, standing straight and a little stiff as they went down the steps and onto the small sidewalk.

"It's time." Brett reached for the bouquet of flowers sitting in a vase on the table just inside the door, sliding them free before passing them Camille's way.

She held them as tightly as she held his hand, her smile holding as they stepped out onto the porch together.

Starting the biggest surprise party his family had ever seen.

****

BONUS BITS ONE

Nora

NORA TWISTED THE giant paper napkin draped across her lap.

"Why's it so damn cold in here?" Brooks scowled from his seat in the corner of the small examination room. "Is it always this cold here?"

"Yes." She wiggled her toes, trying to ease the nerves biting at her skin.

"They know you're sitting there naked, right?" He crossed his arms. "Next time we're bringing you a blanket."

"I'm okay." She forced on a smile. "And I'm only half-naked."

It was a decent joke.

But neither of them laughed.

Mostly because nothing seemed funny right now.

There was a soft knock at the door. A second later it cracked open. "Ready?"

No. Not even a little. "Yes."

The woman's eyes went straight to the machine dominating the dimly lit room. "Have you ever had a vaginal ultrasound before, Mrs. Pace?"

"No." Nora clenched her hands together. "I've never had any ultrasound before."

The tech gave her a soft smile as she reached out to pat Nora's forearm. "We'll just take it one step at a time."

Brooks lifted out of his chair, just enough to drag it across the floor, the sound echoing through the quiet room as he moved as close to her side as he could get.

The tech lifted an intimidating-looking wand from a holder on the side of the machine. "This is what I'll be using to see what's going on." She pressed a button and the table Nora was on began to recline. The tech pulled out a set of stirrups, positioning them before settling onto a stool. "Do you need me to help you get your feet in place?"

Nora shook her head. "I'm okay."

She scooted down, resting her heels into the metal cups as she worked her butt toward the edge.

Brooks' hand came to hers, holding tight as the tech prepped the wand.

"Would you like to insert it, or would you like me to do it?"

Nora stared at the ceiling. "You can do it."

Brooks leaned closer, resting his head against hers as the tech moved the wand slowly, her eyes locked onto the screen as she took measurements and photos. The only sound in the room was the quiet click of each photo she took of what might have been.

Because deep down Nora knew the truth.

It was over. Ended before it really began.

Again.

The tech carefully removed the wand. "You can go ahead and get comfortable." She removed the cover on the wand and went to work cleaning it before loading it into a machine and pressing a button.

Nora scooted up the table, working into a sitting position as the tech washed her hands.

She went to the door, offering a soft smile. "The doctor will be in to go over the results with you in just a few minutes." Then she was gone.

"Maybe it's nothing." Brooks' hand slowly stroked across her back. "Maybe—"

"It's not nothing." She turned toward him. "You know that. You saw."

He'd been right at her side when she woke up, the wetness between her legs sending her into an immediate panic.

She thought they might make it this time.

Thought this could be it.

But it wasn't.

Again.

Nora shifted on the padded paper under her, the sticky cling a reminder she didn't need.

The next knock at the door counted down the final seconds before the truth she knew would be confirmed.

She'd lost another baby.

Number three on the days she was willing to count.

The doctor was kind but curt as he laid out what she already knew then left her to redress.

They left the office with an appointment to come back for a blood test in a few days to make sure her body completed the 'evacuation'.

It was a terrible word.

Then again, all words were terrible when they were used to explain a loss of something wanted so desperately.

Brooks held her hand the whole way home, but he didn't say a word.

There was nothing to say.

He helped her into the house, setting her up on the large sectional in the great room. After bringing her a giant bottle of water and the remote, he tucked her under the fluffy pile of her favorite blanket, pressed a long kiss to her forehead, and went upstairs to take a shower.

Giving her a moment to herself.

Nora stared at the blank television screen, listening as the shower switched on upstairs, unable to do anything but be numb.

Maybe this was what happened when you spent your whole life thinking you shouldn't have kids.

Your body ended up believing you.

A soft click sent her spinning toward the door.

Maryann stared back at her with wide eyes. "I thought you might be asleep." She backed out the still-open door. "I can come back later."

"No." Nora straightened. "It's okay." She tried to smile. "You can come in."

Maryann took a couple slow steps in, lifting the bag in her hand. "I brought some food in case you got hungry."

"Thank you." Nora twisted the soft fabric of the blanket as Maryann went to the kitchen and unloaded the bag, stacking the containers onto the counter.

"It's nothing fancy. Just some snacks you can grab easily." Maryann turned to the fridge.

"I lost the baby." She blurted it out, sniffing as her nose started to run. "Again."

The numbness holding her together suddenly disappeared, rushing out as the tears started to slide free.

Maryann was at her side in an instant, pulling her close and holding her tight. She rocked them gently, stroking down the back of Nora's head as everything tumbled out. The sadness. The pain.

The guilt.

And through it all Maryann held her, tight enough to keep her from breaking apart.

Tight enough to remind her she wasn't alone.

Would never be again.

Nora sucked in a shaky breath, trying to calm the upset still clawing at her insides. "This sucks."

"It does." Maryann stayed close, keeping one arm around her shoulders as they sat side-by-side on the couch.

"I thought this one might be it." Nora wiped at a tear as it crept from the corner of her eye.

She'd made it farther than the last two times.

Far enough she told Maryann.

"They're going to do some testing to see if they can figure out why this keeps happening." Apparently three was the magic number when it came to miscarriages.

"That will be good." Maryann smoothed down her hair. "Hopefully you can get some answers."

Nora swallowed at the lump in her throat. "What if I don't?"

Maryann's blue eyes stayed on her face, strong and steady. "Then we'll cross that bridge when we come to it."

Nora fought the urge to cry again, but these tears came from a very different place. A place she hadn't realized was empty until she came to Moss Creek.

Until she gained something she hadn't really had before.

A mom.

Someone to be there no matter what. To be strong when she felt weak.

To hold her while she cried.

Brooks could do all the same things. Did do all the same things.

But it was different.

Nora nodded. "Okay."

Maryann gave her a little smile. "How about you get comfortable, and I'll bring you a little something to eat?" She didn't wait for an answer.

Because right now Nora wasn't the only one suffering.

She saw it in Maryann's eyes. The same sadness. The same helplessness.

She was struggling too.

Maryann went to the kitchen and started flipping open the containers she brought, stacking a plate with cheese and crackers and nuts and salami.

She came back with the plate and set it down on the coffee table in front of Nora before turning to pack the rest in the fridge. When she was done Maryann grabbed the bag she came with and started for the door.

"Do you have someplace to be?"

Maryann paused. "Not for a few hours."

"Would you want to watch a movie?" Nora scooted to one side, lifting the blanket stretched across the cushion next to her. "I'll share my blanket."

Maryann pressed her lips together, blinking a few times before setting her bag on the table next to the door and turning Nora's way. "There is nothing I'd rather do."

BONUS BITS TWO

Ben

THE SMALL HOUSE at the center of Cross Creek Ranch sat silent.

Not a single light was on in the place.

Not in the windows.

Not on the porches.

Not in the yard.

If he didn't know better he'd think no one was home.

But he definitely knew better.

Ben slowly made his way to the front door, watching and listening for any sign of where the woman inside might be hiding.

And that was most certainly what was happening.

Liza was hiding.

He stopped at the door and gently rapped his knuckles against it, just like he'd done hundreds of times before.

Always hoping it might be the last.

This time was no different.

The air was still and silent as he waited, hoping to hear her voice.

But there was no answer. Normally he would make himself walk away. Try back later.

This time that wasn't an option.

He cracked the door open, just enough so he could see a sliver of the small living room that took up the front of the house. "Liza?"

Still no answer.

It was the reason he was here instead of sitting at the bar with a few of the other hands, trying to wash away the anger he couldn't seem to shake.

He'd gotten a call from Brooks Pace about an hour into a bottle of whisky. His wife Nora had been trying to reach Liza for an hour. Based on recent events, she was worried Liza might not be making the best decisions and landed herself in a spot she couldn't get out of.

Which was pretty par for the course.

Luckily one of the waitresses was clocking out right when he needed to leave and she was nice enough to drive him back since he was in no shape to find his own way home.

Ben pushed the door wider, listening for any sound of the woman who never seemed to stop wrecking his world.

"Liza." He said her name louder, the edges sharpened by a frustration he'd planned to bask in tonight, giving it free run until the morning came and he had to put it back in its place.

Right next to everything else Liza forced him to bank.

Ben turned to take one more look across the yard.

He might not be the best one to check on her right now. Not with where his head was.

A soft sound dragged his attention back into the house.

Bringing his boots with it.

His steps barely made any sound against the worn and scarred wood as he moved through the space that smelled like her. Soft and sweet.

Deep and dark.

Just like the woman.

He was almost to the stairs before the sound he'd heard registered.

It was water.

Trickling through pipes.

Ben moved a little faster, taking the stairs two at a time as he raced for the bedroom he'd spent a single night in.

Right before he'd made the biggest mistake of his life.

A mistake he might never stop paying for.

Because while the rest of the world saw Liza as an unbreakable force, he knew the truth.

Liza could be broken.

He knew.

He'd done it.

The door to her bathroom was closed, no sliver of light peeking up at him as he twisted the knob.

Locked.

Ben banged on it with the back of his fist. "Liza."

He tried to take a breath, but there wasn't room inside him for anything else.

Not even air.

He was full up.

Full of anger. Full of hate. Full of frustration.

Full of regret.

And now full of fear.

Something had to come out.

He slammed his fist into the wood again, this time hitting hard enough it rattled on the hinges. "Liza Cross, open this fucking door."

There wasn't anything in him willing to wait for an answer. He took a step back and kicked the center of only one of many things currently lined up between them, fueling the force with everything he'd been bottling up.

Everything he'd been holding back.

The latch failed but the hinges held and the door swung inward, slamming against the wall hard enough to knock the knob into the plaster.

He took two steps into the cool, dark air of the small room, grabbed the shower curtain and whipped it open.

Liza's body was curled inside the basin of the ageing clawfoot, eyes closed, skin pale, lips blue, her right arm draped over the side. Cold water poured from the shower head, pelting her unmoving form.

All the anger. All the hate. All the frustration. All the regret was gone in an instant, leaving a void that fear immediately took over.

He reached for her, scooping her up as the icy water rained down on him, adding to the chill racing across his hide.

Ben pulled her up and out of the tub, holding her limp body close as he angled her through the door and into the bedroom. The covers were already back so he laid her across the mattress, being careful not to bump her injured arm as he rested his hands on her skin.

She was so fucking cold.

He yanked the blankets up and around her, tucking them tight to her body as he scooted closer, pushing at the clumps of wet hair stuck to her face. "Liza."

She was breathing, but not much else, and every second that passed dug dread deeper into his gut.

Deeper into his soul.

He'd spent years thinking she would come around.

Realize the truth of what he said that day.

That she would finally understand he'd done it for her.

They all suddenly seemed like such a fucking waste.

All the time he could have had.

All he could have given her.

"Liza, please." His hands were on her face, pressing into her skin. "Please open your eyes." He dropped his forehead to hers. "Come on, Sweetheart. Wake up."

Her body had been through so much in the past few days, and she wasn't one to give herself any grace.

Not ever.

She pushed too hard.

Too far.

Always.

Thinking she had to prove something everyone already knew.

He shouldn't have left tonight. Shouldn't have put his needs above hers.

Again.

He reached under the blankets, praying she'd be warmer, but the skin under his palm was just as cool.

She wasn't warming up. Not fast enough.

Ben kicked off his boots and knocked the hat from his head before stripping off his shirt and jeans and sliding under the covers with her, pulling her close, one hand pressed to the side of her face as the minutes ticked by.

Suddenly she started to shake, body quaking, teeth chattering. Her lids lifted, but her eyes didn't seem to find focus.

"Liza." Ben turned her face toward his, thumb stroking her cheek as she seemed to finally see who was there with her.

Just like always.

In spite of what she thought.

What he'd made her believe.

Her blink was slow and heavy.

He pulled her closer, bringing more covers in around them as she continued to shiver.

Liza stared at him, the pink slowly coming back to her cheeks as her skin warmed against his.

The panic pushing him along slipped, making space for old anger to flare. "What in the hell were you doing?"

She never thought before she acted.

Never considered danger.

Never worried about getting hurt.

Or worse.

And a few days ago it could have been worse.

Much worse.

She came inches from that fucking car crushing more than her arm.

He could have lost her forever. Lost the chance to figure out how to make it all right.

And it pushed him over an edge he didn't know existed.

Sending him into a freefall he didn't know how to stop.

Liza's expression was blank as her eyes held his. "Leave me alone."

The request was raspy and rough.

And denied.

"No."

He'd left her alone once. Walked away when she needed him most.

Left her to the wolves thinking they were sheep.

Her chin trembled, but her expression remained flat. "Go."

He'd given her time.

He'd given her space.

Now he was clean out of both.

The fall he was caught in stopped, slamming him into the one place he should have claimed as his own long ago.

Ben shook his head, holding Liza's gaze as tight as he held her as he offered up the first of many promises he intended to make and keep.

"I'm not goin' anywhere."

Made in the USA
Monee, IL
29 April 2023

32682811R00184